Bolan's adver
snarl like a demented animal

The warrior drew a twinge of satisfaction from the bloody face that turned to glower at him. Humiliation spurred the hulk into a headlong charge, long arms outstretched, hands aimed at Bolan's throat.

With ten feet separating them, Bolan took a breath and launched himself directly into the enemy's path. There was numbing pain as boots collided with his abdomen, and then the hulk himself was airborne, howling in dismay until the jolt of impact slammed his jaws together.

Closing on his opponent's blind side, the Executioner let the groggy titan struggle to his knees. It gave the soldier better access to his target as he drove a boot heel home into the rising giant's kidney.

Bolan put enough force into a final kick that would have killed an ordinary man, his heel impacting on the point where vertebrae and skull were joined. The giant gasped and toppled forward on his face. Dead? Unconscious? Bolan didn't give a damn. *He* was alive and standing.

MACK BOLAN

The Executioner

DON PENDLETON's EXECUTIONER

MACK BOLAN

Assault on Rome

A GOLD EAGLE BOOK FROM

WORLDWIDE

TORONTO • NEW YORK • LONDON • PARIS
AMSTERDAM • STOCKHOLM • HAMBURG
ATHENS • MILAN • TOKYO • SYDNEY

First edition July 1987

ISBN 0-373-61103-X

Special thanks and acknowledgment to
Mike Newton for his contribution to this work.

Printed in Canada

"While stands the Coliseum, Rome shall stand;
When falls the Coliseum, Rome shall fall;
And when Rome falls—the world."

—Lord Byron

"While I stand, savages will not destroy four thousand
years of history to gratify their own inhuman needs.
If it requires a bloodbath to preserve the legacy of
man, of civilization, so be it."

—Mack Bolan

THE
MACK BOLAN
LEGEND

Nothing less than a war could have fashioned the destiny of the man called Mack Bolan. Bolan earned the Executioner title in the jungle hell of Vietnam.

But this soldier also wore another name—Sergeant Mercy. He was so tagged because of the compassion he showed to wounded comrades-in-arms and Vietnamese civilians.

Mack Bolan's second tour of duty ended prematurely when he was given emergency leave to return home and bury his family, victims of the Mob. Then he declared a one-man war against the Mafia.

He confronted the Families head-on from coast to coast, and soon a hope of victory began to appear. But Bolan had broken society's every rule. That same society started gunning for this elusive warrior—to no avail.

So Bolan was offered amnesty to work within the system against terrorism. This time, as an employee of Uncle Sam, Bolan became Colonel John Phoenix. With a command center at Stony Man Farm in Virginia, he and his new allies—Able Team and Phoenix Force—waged relentless war on a new adversary: the KGB.

But when his one true love, April Rose, died at the hands of the Soviet terror machine, Bolan severed all ties with Establishment authority.

Now, after a lengthy lone-wolf struggle and much soul-searching, the Executioner has agreed to enter an ''arm's-length'' alliance with his government once more, reserving the right to pursue personal missions in his Everlasting War.

PROLOGUE

The runner dared not pause for breath, although his lungs were burning, starved for oxygen as he raced through the musty catacombs. Behind him, death was closing rapidly, intent on running him to earth before he could escape.

As if escape were possible.

The runner could not allow despair to sap the final ounce of hope and strength that still survived. But increasingly the tunnels had begun to look alike. God knew they smelled the same, stagnant and with the reek of death about them. It was appropriate, of course, considering his situation, but the runner needed no reminders of his desperate state. He had already seen enough of death to last a lifetime and beyond.

They might be close enough to hear him now, and it was fear that finally forced him to a walk, then stopped him altogether as he pressed against a sloping wall that stank of mildew. Although desperate for air, the runner forced himself to hold his breath, to ignore the pounding of his heartbeat, which was as loud as cannon fire inside his skull. He listened.

Nothing.

For an instant he had stiffened at the sound of pebbles suddenly disturbed, but then he recognized the scuttling sound of rats and let himself relax a little. He could cope with rats, the other vermin of the tunnels, just as long as his pursuers did not overtake him. If they caught him, there would be no questions, no interrogation. Retribution would be swift and final, carried out with all the contempt reserved for traitors.

He could no longer be a part of what was happening, the evil that was growing here, beneath the streets of Rome. With understanding came responsibility, and youthful revolutionary zeal could not withstand the brutal shock of cold reality. He had been foolish from the outset, had allowed himself to be manipulated, used, but that was over now. Whatever might become of him, the runner had a duty to himself and to the city. He must help to root the evil out, expose it to the cleansing light of day, and see it shrivel, die.

The labyrinth was new to him, unfamiliar, although he had been shown a single means of exit from the maze. In time he might have gained more knowledge, known the layout better.... With understanding came the need to act, a grim determination to proceed and only hindsight told the runner that he should have waited for another day or two, made certain of the avenues of escape from the tomb.

He had been forced to kill a comrade, and the act of murder had already sealed his fate, but they would be primarily concerned with silencing him. The very fact of his escape attempt would mark him as a traitor, and punishment for traitors was inevitable, inescapable. If he was fortunate, they would be swift. If they took the time to play with him, protract his suffering...

The runner stopped himself before these defeatist thoughts could freeze his legs beneath him and destroy his will to fight. The pistol in his belt was extra weight, but he could still defend himself if it came down to that, and he would sell his life dearly if his former comrades overtook him in the tunnels.

If...

There was a chance that he could find the exit, make his way into the streets above and tell his story to police before they caught him. If he could reach protective custody, there was a chance, however slim, that he would survive. It was not hopeless yet. Not yet.

He took another moment in the darkness to regain his bearings, fairly certain now that he had not been running in circles for the past half hour. If he was correct, if all his senses had not been disoriented by the sunless days of living underground, then he was drawing closer to his destination, homing on the exit that would take him back to daylight and escape.

If he was wrong he was as good as dead.

Too late to start all over, and it would be suicide to retrace his steps in any case. He was sure they were after him by now, no matter what his lead, and any backtrack would decrease the odds of his survival, risking head-on confrontation with the enemy in claustrophobic tunnels where the smell of death was pervasive.

Better to continue running, to put his hopes in speed and distance, in the firm belief that he had missed no branching tunnels, was not lost inside the endless maze.

Dead men watched him from the walls with sightless eyes, and now the runner knew that he was close. The shriveled saints were marking his escape route, showing him the way, but he would have to thank them later, when his need was not so pressing.

The exit *must* be close by now. He visualized the ladder, metal rungs rusty with the dampness of the underground, ascending to the street where citizens and tourists went about their business, blithely unaware of lurking death beneath their feet. They would be shocked when he appeared among them, terrified when he revealed the secrets he had learned. But if the momentary terror saved their lives, then it was all worthwhile.

The runner cursed himself, his youth and the exuberance that had seduced him into mortal danger. If his example could prevent the havoc that was coming, if by word of mouth or through the agonies of death he could preserve the ancient city he loved, it might be worth the cost. It might...

The scuffling sound behind him was not rats, unless the vermin had grown ponderously large and taken to wearing boots. The runner caught his breath before a ragged sob could worm its way between his teeth. He ran as if his life, his very soul depended on the outcome of the race. And they were closing on him when he spied the ladder, barely visible, some thirty yards ahead.

The weary dash became a breathless sprint, the ladder and salvation drawing closer even as he realized that there was something wrong. That shadow, there, seemed large... awkward. Was his vision failing in his extremity? Could shadows move?

The gunman rose to stand erect, the pistol with the oblong silencer extended toward the runner's face. A stranger, someone he had never seen before, but there were countless hunters in the maze, and it was not the man behind the gun who mattered, anyway. The bullet mattered, and it could not miss him at point-blank range.

The runner halted, staggering with lost momentum, his back against the wall. No matter if he crowded the bones of martyrs; he would be with them shortly, one among the dead of centuries, at home with the decay and silent darkness of the tunnels. In his belt, the automatic pistol was a useless weight. He knew that he could never draw and fire in time to save himself. It was a wasted gesture, but it was all he had.

The gunner saw it coming, taking time to smile and shake his head before he fired. The silenced automatic coughed once, twice. The runner registered his mortal wounds with almost clinical detachment, waiting for the pain and thankful for the anesthetic properties of physical exhaustion. Impact drove him back into the wasted arms of long-dead men, and he welcomed their embrace. It would be peaceful here.

Slipping through the grip of fleshless hands, he waited for the final darkness to arrive and carry him away.

1

The tall man walked in the moonlight, savoring his solitude. Around him, marble tombstones marched like stubby soldiers over gently rolling hillsides. From the east, a gentle night wind teased his hair and carried salt aromas from the Tyrrhenian Sea. Westward, Naples was a dappling of colored lights that tinged the sky without imparting warmth.

At peace with his surroundings and the restful dead, Mack Bolan seemed to wander aimlessly among the stones. He might have been a solitary mourner, paying respects to some departed loved one, or a victim of insomnia, pursuing sleep in the company of those who never wake. In fact, his sojourn at the cemetery dealt primarily with life, but death was all around him, and the soldier recognized its touch against his cheek.

As always, he had come prepared to deal in death if it should be required. He wore a lightweight raincoat, and beneath it, in a special leather harness, hung an Ingram MAC-10 submachine gun, primed and ready to explode at Bolan's touch. If more firepower was required, the sleek Beretta 93-R hung below his other arm, and extra magazines for both 9 mm weapons filled the pockets of his overcoat.

He was prepared, and hoped that it would not come down to killing. He was prepared to play it straight, the suitcase that was filled with cash secure in the shadow of a tombstone twenty paces to his left. If no one on the opposition team got hinky, if they did not overplay their hand, then all concerned could walk away intact. And he would hunt them down another day.

For now, the safety of a single hostage was his first priority. Recovering the prisoner was paramount; it overshadowed Bolan's urge to visit retribution on the enemy and wipe them out on sight. But once the hostage was secure...

The object of contention was a U.S. military attaché assigned to Rome, one Arthur Bishop. He had been kidnapped six weeks earlier, his driver and an innocent pedestrian chopped down by automatic-weapons fire in daylight on the Via Nomentana. After searching fruitlessly for a month, authorities in Rome had virtually given up the chase, and the Americans were powerless to act outside their jurisdiction.

Theoretically, at least.

The CIA had scoured its clandestine sources, seeking any germ of information on the missing man's location, the identity of his abductors. Failing to locate the hostage, Company agents were more successful with their secondary mission. They identified the terrorists involved in the abduction, double-checked the rough ID and passed their information back along the chain of command.

Had they been privy to the ripples of amazement in official Washington, the objects of attention would have certainly been pleased. It was, as an assistant to the CIA director told his closest aides, like stumbling across a ghost. You couldn't quite believe your eyes at first, but there was no more room for doubt once it had grabbed you by the balls.

And there was no mistake. The "ghosts" were very much alive, as evidenced by their communication with authorities, demanding ransom for their hostage. Someone, somehow, had breathed new life into the moldering remains of the Red Justice Column.

More extreme than rival factions of the Red Brigade, the RJC had come up against Mack Bolan once before, much to their sorrow. He had thought the group was finished; Washington had celebrated its extinction as a major victory in the covert war on terrorism. They had all been wrong.

The RJC was back, it seemed, and with a vengeance. In selecting Arthur Bishop as their mark, the "strategists" had not only thrown down the gauntlet before America, but they had also demonstrated access to superior intelligence. For Bishop was no ordinary attaché; he was the CIA's established chief in charge of all clandestine operations throughout the Mediterranean district.

Which did not make him indispensable, by any means. The Company was ready to absorb its loss, if need be, and a suitable replacement was already waiting in the wings in case the drop fell through. Like every other person in the Company, Arthur Bishop was ultimately expendable. The brass would buy him back, if that was possible. If not, they would extract a fitting measure of revenge and go about their business undismayed.

The call came from Hal Brognola, Bolan's ally at the Justice Department and current link with the Oval Office. Bolan had demolished his official bridges with the government following the assault on Stony Man, but he remained in touch with Hal, Leo Turrin and certain other members of the Phoenix team. After reluctant agreement he was available at need, for certain "special" missions, which the Executioner selected on the basis of his own criteria, no strings attached.

And there had been no question of remaining neutral at Brognola's mention of the RJC. Alive and functioning, Red Justice constituted grave unfinished business for the Executioner. If he could rescue Arthur Bishop, fine. Once Bishop was secure, or if the deal blew up in Bolan's face, he meant to root the bastards out and see them dead before he caught the next flight home.

He owed it to the past and present victims of the RJC, to all the innocents who might become its victims in the future.

He owed it to himself.

A job unfinished left the soldier vulnerable, and it mattered little if the RJC had been revived by former members, the survivors of his first campaign, or if the name had simply been appropriated by some up-and-coming gutter trash with revolutionary aspirations. Either way, Red Justice had survived a close encounter with the Executioner, and Bolan would not rest until he put it right.

Until he put the bastards down for good.

The soldier checked his watch again by moonlight. Fifteen minutes left before the scheduled midnight drop, and still his enemies had not appeared. If they were working on a double cross, the terrorists should have placed advance men in the cemetery, armed and ready to surround the middleman, to relieve him of the ransom money on arrival. Bolan's aimless wandering among the headstones had confirmed that he was alone so far, unless they had a sniper watching him through telescopic sights. The thought raised the short hairs on the back of Bolan's neck, but he dismissed it swiftly. The members of the RJC were terrorists, not soldiers; their violence of the past, as in the Bishop case, had been performed at point-blank range, or through the handy anonymity of timed explosives.

Bolan knew he would see them coming. And if they planned to take him down, their move would come when they were close enough to have the cash within reach, to make the kill a certainty.

He drifted back in the direction of the suitcase, wondering idly how Bishop's captors had decided on the price. A million dollars for the ransom of a man who was, ostensibly, a middle-ranking diplomat might seem excessive by the standards of the day. In Rome the average politician's ransom would amount to little more than half that figure, and the soldier wondered if his enemies were counting on the fabled Yankee affluence, or if they knew the covert role Bishop played for the CIA.

Such information was available, of course, but rank-and-file terrorists seldom had the intellect or funds required to gather hard, first-rate intelligence. They normally selected targets in the public eye for maximum publicity, and scaled their ransom in accordance with the captive's reputation. It was out of character for such a group to choose a secret operative the first time out, and even more unusual for them to hit their target so precisely.

Their precision worried Bolan, with its implications of a functioning, mature, intelligence-collecting apparatus. If the RJC had managed to acquire official ears in Rome—and it was possible, he knew—then this time it would be a different kind of war entirely. If someone from the U.S. consulate was being indiscreet . . .

The soldier stopped himself before his own imagination could betray him. For the moment he was playing out the role of a delivery boy, his sole concern for the safe return of Arthur Bishop from captivity. Beyond that, any information he could gather on the RJC would be a bonus, gravy on the side, and he would seize on any slim advantage the enemy might offer. Any clue at all that might betray the whereabouts of a command post, individuals associated with "the cause."

A flash of headlights at the cemetery gates immediately darkened as the driver pulled inside. Bolan watched the black Fiat sedan as it pursued a winding path between the headstones, drawing closer by the moment.

The soldier slid one hand inside the pocket of his raincoat, reaching through the open slit to find the Ingram's pistol grip. He flicked off the safety and curled his finger loosely through the trigger guard, relying on the leather harness to support the weapon and absorb a measure of its recoil if he had to swing it up and into action on short notice.

Bolan counted four men in the car: the driver, someone riding shotgun, two in back. There could be others crouched on the floor or in the trunk, but he would have to face that danger if and when it came.

Bolan stooped to lift the suitcase, never taking his eyes off the approaching Fiat. He held the bag aloft as headlights briefly flashed, illuminating man and bag, the headstones at his back, confirming that he had obeyed orders and come alone to the midnight rendezvous. When the driver was satisfied, he killed the engine.

Three car doors opened simultaneously, and the gunners exited as if they had rehearsed the move. In back, the fourth man had a harder time, and Bolan noted that his hands were bound, his mouth taped shut and a piece of heavy cloth had been wound around his head several times, covering his eyes.

The hostage.

The shotgun rider had been chosen as their spokesman, though he clearly was uncomfortable with English.

"You have brought the money?"

Bolan raised the bag again, his concentration equally divided now between the gunners and the Fiat's license plate. The car had probably been stolen, but at least it was a starting place.

"Right here."

The mouthpiece flinched, as if the close proximity to so much wealth unnerved him, made him edgy. That was good, if it encouraged him to make mistakes, but it was bad if he or any of the other goons got trigger-happy in their nervousness.

"I count."

He had the bastard hooked, and it was time to reel him in.

"I need a word with Mr. Bishop first."

The shooters traded surreptitious glances, and the driver shrugged, as if the subject were a matter of complete indifference. Behind him, terrorist number three untied the captive's blindfold, jerked it roughly from his face and left him blinking in the darkness. Bishop raised his hands awkwardly to rub his burning eyes. A palm between his shoulder blades propelled him forward, past his other captors and into no-man's-land, where he fell heavily to the ground.

"I count the money now."

"Your show."

He tossed the suitcase underhand, so that it landed near the shotgunner's feet. The man took a mincing little two-step backward, but recovered swiftly, scowling at the suitcase, then at Bolan.

"Wait," he ordered with as much authority as he could muster.

Bolan didn't answer. He was checking Arthur Bishop over, noting mottled bruising on his forehead and along his jaw, the flaky crust of blood where ropes had chafed his wrists for weeks without relief. The captive's mouth was taped, preventing speech, but he was watching Bolan closely now, the dark eyes intent upon conveying some silent message. Bishop cocked his head in the direction of the shotgun rider, who was kneeling in front of the suitcase, lifting back its lid to scrutinize the cash inside. The lid obscured the guy's hands from view, and in a heartbeat Bolan understood the captive's message, knew the gunners had him marked to die.

"Get down!"

He aimed the words at Bishop, but the rising Ingram had a different target, nosing through the open flap of Bolan's raincoat, level with the shotgunner's face. The hidden hands were sliding up and into view, an automatic pistol clenched between them, and Bolan caught the peripherals of gunners two and three who were erupting into action, clawing at their holstered hardware.

The Ingram stuttered, parabellum shockers ripping through the open suitcase lid and finding flesh beyond. Bolan's human target never had a chance to fire his weapon. The impact blew him backward, and the guy thrashed briefly in his death throes.

Already sweeping on and tracking, Bolan hesitated as the hostage crossed his line of fire. Another second, either way, and Bolan might have cut him down, but now the military attaché was clear and running toward the sidelines as the soldier found his secondary target crouching by the driver's side of the Fiat.

The wheelman had his side arm out, and he was tracking into target acquisition when a stream of parabellums cut him off at the knees. He toppled, screaming, into Bolan's line of fire. A second burst exploded in his face, and his life was snuffed out before he had the chance to use his weapon.

Hardguy number three was bobbing and weaving, rising up to peg a shot at Bolan here and there. The rounds were wild, a fading whine in the darkness, but he might improve with time if Bolan gave him half a chance. Instead, he held down the Ingram's trigger and blew out the Fiat's windows, creating an unholy racket that was guaranteed to spook a novice gunner into taking foolish chances. Knowing the guy could break either right or left, provided that he broke at all, the soldier held his ground and waited.

When it came, the gunner's move was sudden, filled with desperate energy. In other circumstances, matched against another gun, it might have passed for skill, but desperation gave the novice no edge at all against the Executioner. A smashing figure eight of parabellums lifted the terrorist completely off his feet and spun him half around before collision with a gravestone stopped him cold. Bolan did not need to stand and watch the man's life run out of ragged wounds. His business now concerned the living—and escape.

The Ingram stuttergun was warm against his flank as Bolan turned to look for Arthur Bishop. He found him stretched out on the grassy carpet of a grave, facedown. At first he thought the hostage might have sought cover as a precautionary measure, but he spied the spreading stain beneath the man's shoulder blade, the hole where one stray round had drilled in close beside the spine to penetrate a lung.

He knelt beside the prostrate figure, turned him over gently, cradling the head in tender hands. Bishop's eyes were open, pleading, weak hands reaching for the tape that sealed his lips. Bolan pulled the makeshift gag away, his fingers moist as Bishop coughed a crimson bubble from his ruptured lung. It took a moment for the dying man to clear his throat and find his voice again.

"Red Justice..." he began.

"We've got them covered," Bolan told him, wishing it was true.

"The tunnels...watch...no warning—"

Sudden, ragged coughing overwhelmed him, bloody spittle coming up in waves that drained his life away. When he went limp in Bolan's arms, the soldier didn't need to check his pulse or search for other vital signs. The single stray shot had silenced him forever, cutting off the warning he had seemed so desperate to impart.

Or had it been a stray?

If they had planned to snuff the courier on sight, the RJC never intended to release their hostage in the first place. Bishop might, unwittingly, have stumbled onto certain secrets the terrorists could not afford to share. His execution might have been an arranged conclusion to the midnight drop, or Bolan's final adversary might have panicked when he saw the pigeon poised to fly.

Whichever, Bishop was unable to provide any information now. Bolan turned to his victims, riffling their pockets, probing into wallets, removing the contents of the Fiat's glove compartment. Nothing. The terrorists were professional enough to leave their personal ID at home, and it would take a fingerprint comparison to learn their names, addresses, all the other information crucial to construction of identity.

Any thoughts of dealing with the terrorists, negotiating any sort of peace, had vanished with the death of Arthur Bishop. Peaceful coexistence with a cannibal was tantamount to suicide. The soldier knew that from grim experience, and Bishop's friends at the CIA would be reminded of the fact before the day was out.

You dealt with savages from strength, or not at all. The ostrich option, seeking refuge in a kind of blissful ignorance, might buy a period of false tranquillity, but in the end the problem still remained unsolved. A savage did not understand negotiations; he was fundamentally unable to accept the notion of a compromise. With savages, the victory was all or nothing, each and every time. They understood defeat, but only of the most decisive, lethal sort. A savage left alive upon the field of battle would return to cut your throat some night, while you were sleeping in the bosom of your family, deluded by impressions of a lasting victory.

There was no lasting victory against the savages, as long as one of them was left alive, and Bolan's everlasting war was testimony to the sheer resilience of his enemies. As often as they rose from smoking ashes, wounded but alive, the Executioner was pledged to strike them down again. As it had been in Vietnam, in Pittsfield and Chicago and New York, in Tuscany. As it would be, this time, in Rome.

2

Rome was beautiful at sunrise, but the Executioner had no eye for the scenery. As he followed the Tiber's western bank and wove through the early-morning traffic, Bolan's mind was fully occupied with the mission at hand and his target: the Red Justice Column.

To begin with, the name was a joke. Red Justice, as first organized, was a sorry collection of felons, ex-convicts and thugs from the streets, thrown together in a group as "freedom fighters" who were interested solely in the loot that might be gathered from their various extortion schemes. The RJC had no more revolutionary fervor than the Mafia, but leaders of the Column had observed the Red Brigades, the Baader-Meinhof gang and others; they had learned the terminology, the postures that would validate their "war of liberation" in the headlines. In reality, the leaders saw a way to profit from the rising tide of terrorism sweeping Western Europe, and they had been quick to climb aboard the gravy train.

A favored practice in the early days was child abduction. With accumulated years of criminal experience behind them, members of the RJC were well aware that frightened parents—and especially frighten *wealthy* parents—would do anything, pay any price, to see their offspring safely home. The usual targets were industrialists, businessmen of every sort and lower-ranking members of the government. Schooled by centuries of paying homage to the Mafia and the Camorra, victims knew that there was no reliable recourse to the authorities. Police were more than likely on the take, or else intimidated by the very criminals whom they were sworn to put away. If a policeman could be found who would arrest the perpetrators, if a judge and jury should defy the odds by bringing in convictions, retribution would be swift and terrible against the prosecution witnesses, the victims of the crime, their families.

It was a way of life.

But members of the RJC had overstepped their bounds with the abduction of Louise DiAlto and her daughter. Deceived, perhaps, by their own empty propaganda, certain members of the Column had decided it was time to tackle every revolutionary's enemy: the great United States. Louise DiAlto was the wife of Colonel Mike DiAlto, aide to the chief of staff for logistics and administration in NATO's Southern Command. A ransom was demanded for the safe return of wife and daughter. There was nothing new or strange about the crime, but it evoked a new and different response from the American authorities.

Instead of paying off in cash, the NATO high command had flashed an SOS to Washington, where it was registered with Hal Brognola and the staff at Stony Man. Instead of ransom money for its treasury, Red Justice had received a hellfire visit from the Executioner. With help from Colonel DiAlto, Bolan had retrieved the precious hostages and scourged the RJC with cleansing fire.

He had been forced to kill a woman in the process, and the soldier thought about Emilia Salerno as he drove along the riverside. No lady, that. Emilia had been a heartless bitch with murder in her soul, and there had been no hesitation, no regrets, when he dropped the hammer on her, ringing down the curtain on a wasted life.

The Tuscany campaign had been a classic search-and-savage mission, but the Executioner had learned some valuable lessons in the course of his pursuit. For openers, he learned that no extremist group, no matter how bizarre or insincere, escaped the notice of the KGB. Dzerzhinsky Square had placed an agent with the RJC, one Victor Karpov, to facilitate the flow of cash and arms, to suggest potential targets with an eye toward the embarrassment of Western powers. Karpov had gone home to Moscow in a body bag, but there were countless others waiting in the wings to take his place, and Bolan dared not overlook the possibility of Soviet involvement with the new, resurgent RJC.

Another cruel surprise, although it should have come as no surprise at all, had been the Column's link to traitors both in the Italian government and in the NATO high command. Illicit cash could turn a soldier's head, or buy a senator if it came down to that, and Bolan's private war had taught him well enough the grim potential for corruption in his fellow man. He recognized the fact of treason, of duplicity and greed, but in the flesh it never ceased to sicken him. A savage acted out of instinct, carnal hunger, and would feed upon the innocent until he was destroyed, but traitors made a conscious choice to turn upon their own and see them die or be enslaved, all in the pursuit of private gain.

The savages and traitors often ran together, and Bolan had a single antidote for both. He sought them out, traced them to their lair, exterminated them with cleansing fire. It was an endless task, as others rose to take their place in droves, but while his life and strength remained, the Executioner would take them as they came.

This time around, Red Justice might be an entirely different proposition, but he doubted it. The resurrected Column had already turned to kidnapping for ransom, and the bungled ambush in the Naples cemetery showed him that the brains behind the operation were attuned to maximizing profits while ignoring all the standard rules of revolutionary gamesmanship. With most extremist groups, delivery of ransom would assure the safe release of hostages because, if nothing else, the group might wish to try its hand at kidnapping another time, with other targets. Terrorists who earned a reputation for accepting ransom and eliminating hostages were short on credibility, to say the least; without a realistic prospect of success, potential victims would rely upon police and SWAT teams rather than negotiating price.

The "new" Red Justice Column had already played its hand and come up losers. Because of Arthur Bishop's murder, any future ransom bids would have to come complete with powerful assurances of safe delivery. It might already be too late to save the Column's so-called reputation, but the Executioner was not prepared to let his adversaries waste away or leave them to be picked off piecemeal by security police. Annihilation was his goal, and it could only be achieved by getting closer to the RJC. If possible, he would attempt to get inside the Column, smash it from within and make damned certain that the ghost would never rise again.

Bolan had worked out the details of a cover with an assist from Hal Brognola, back in Wonderland. He would be traveling as Mike Belasko, mercenary, gunrunner, contract assassin with a constant need for ready cash. Belasko was the sort who looked at the size of cash denominations only and never got around to ideology. The Executioner had known a hundred such men, a few of whom were still alive, and Bolan had no doubt that he could pass inspection. With the RJC's connections fresh in mind, he had prepared a backup system, with Brognola on hand in Washington to verify Bolan's cover if and when the call came through to Justice. The Italian security police and the carabinieri had been briefed on Mike Belasko's record via Interpol, and were presumably on notice of his presence in the area. Completely ignorant of Bolan's mission, they would render no assistance in the crunch, and would in fact compound his danger.

Bolan turned west at the Palace of Justice, following traffic along Via Tacito to reach the hotel where Belasko had booked reservations. The desk clerk examined his passport with casual disinterest, accepted his money and offered to ring for the porter—an offer Bolan declined. He was traveling light, but the larger of his two bags contained certain extras provided by Brognola: the Ingram MAC-10 with its silencer, ammo, grenades. There was more in the trunk of the Peugeot sedan: seven pounds of plastique, detonators and timers. The car was a rental, with papers made out to Belasko, and Bolan felt a good deal safer with the goop outside. If anything should happen to the car or the explosives, he could do without. The other weapons might be crucial to survival, and he kept them close beside him as he climbed the stairs to reach his third-floor suite.

Bolan locked the door behind him, spent a moment checking out the three connected rooms, before he settled down to business. Mike Belasko was not wanted by authorities in Rome, but his supposed record made him naturally the object of suspicion. The security police, especially, might take an interest in his Roman holiday, and Bolan spent the next three-quarters of an hour shaking down his suite, alert to any sign of listening devices. In the last analysis, it mattered very little if the suite was bugged or not, since Bolan meant to carry out his business elsewhere. But Belasko would have checked, and Bolan had to live the part before a casual—or not so casual—observer would be fooled by his performance.

He left the telephone alone; there was no way to check for taps in any case, and he did not intend to use the phone for anything more sensitive than ordering room service. Bolan's business lay outside the hotel, and there were hours yet before he could be about that business, hours yet before darkness offered him the shelter he would need.

He took a shower, then ate a leisurely lunch downstairs and found an English-language paper in the lounge. The death of Arthur Bishop was reported on page one, with photos of his wife in tears; the man himself in better days;

the cemetery killing ground where he had fallen with three others, still unnamed. The story closed with a recap of recent terrorist acts, but made no mention of the RJC. The authorities were playing it close to the vest, and that was fine with Bolan. If the Column suffered no immediate embarrassment in public, members might not feel the urge to answer with an aimless, mindless act of carnage.

Maybe.

After finishing the paper, Bolan walked the three long blocks from his hotel to Castel Sant' Angelo, and north from there to Saint Peter's Square. The arching colonnades on either side had been designed to welcome all the pilgrims of the world, but Bolan felt no welcome here. He could admire the architecture for its timeless majesty, but he could find no peace of mind or soul. The stain of terrorism reached even here, into Vatican City, where savages once had attempted to murder the Pope. Before a crowd of thousands they had opened fire, and only providence—or pure dumb luck—had saved the man who was a symbol of forgiveness, peace and understanding to the world.

As he followed the tourists with their cameras and guidebooks, the lovers strolling hand in hand, the children darting in and out around him, Bolan took a momentary respite from his everlasting war. He visited the cool, dark grottoes beneath St. Peter's Basilica, and the Vatican Necropolis, with its double row of papal tombs below ground level. Bolan marveled at the world that lay below the Vatican, a world where life and death had mingled into something simultaneously grim and starkly beautiful.

Returning once again to the sunlight, Bolan visited the Sistine Chapel, lingering before Michelangelo's rendering of the Last Judgment. On his left, the chosen were welcomed on high by the angels of light, while to his right, the damned had been forever frozen in a headlong tumble toward the raging fires of hell. Overhead, the master's vision of creation was a bit more cheerful, but the final scene, of Noah's drunkenness, reminded every pilgrim of humanity's capacity for failure on the very brink of final victory. The message carried no surprise for Mack Bolan, but it was depressing all the same. He sought the open air and wandered through the papal gardens until closing time.

The city had begun to change as Bolan retraced his steps toward the hotel. Another hour of fading daylight still remained, but the nocturnal denizens of Rome were starting to emerge in all their finery, the night shift coming out to play. It was the signal he had waited for since his arrival. The time was ripe for him to make his move.

Somewhere in Rome, the leaders of the RJC were going about their lives, recovering from the snafu in Naples, plotting strategy and waiting for a chance to strike. They could not permit the loss of Arthur Bishop's ransom, that much was clear. They would have to retaliate. The nature of their chosen action still remained to be discovered, but from grim experience, the soldier knew that violence would only escalate until the savages were laid to rest. While they survived, there could be no security in Rome, no peace.

It was the Executioner's appointed task to see peace restored, however temporarily. But he knew there would be more carnage before the job was done. He hoped the innocents might be permitted to escape intact; if not, it would be that much worse for any savages who fell into his hands. The streets of the Eternal City might run red before his work was done, and Bolan's blood might join the rest, a sacrifice to everlasting war against the cannibals.

He was prepared for death, though he had never consciously pursued it. When it came, the soldier would be ready to accept his fate and face the final judgment of the universe. No follower of any recognized religion, Bolan still believed in good and evil, right and wrong. He viewed the abstract concepts in a concrete manner: evil must be punished, finally eradicated if it was within man's power; good might never be rewarded, in the sense of manna falling from the heavens, but the concept still involved a sense of duty that could never be effectively denied.

A soldier stood against the tide of evil or surrendered to it, gave his soul away. Mack Bolan's world was black and white in that regard; there was no room for any shades of gray. He had already sacrificed too much, spilled too much blood, to compromise with his opponents this late in the game.

It would be all or nothing when he met the leaders of the rejuvenated RJC. But he would have to meet them first, and that would take finesse, a modicum of ingenuity mixed in with pure, raw nerve.

Red Justice wasn't in the telephone directory. The killers had no published address, and they offered no employment applications to prospective members. Bolan knew that he would have to seek them out among the dens and warrens where they lived and worked their evil on a daily basis.

He was ready for the hunt, and there was no time like the present to begin.

3

Via Veneto is Rome's equivalent of Hollywood and Vine. By day, the avenue's boutiques, cafés and luxury hotels are thronged with tourists seeking contact with the beautiful people: celebrities and models, movie stars on holiday, designers hustling their latest fashions. After nightfall the action is a bit more frenzied; the sophisticates and sinners mingle freely, trading favors on the avenue when wealthy businessmen are finished for the day. A man or woman can find virtually anything on Via Veneto by night, and Bolan took his business there as a beginning point for the assault on Rome.

The cafés do a thriving dinner trade on Via Veneto until midnight, but the soldier wasn't hungry. He bypassed restaurants—some open on the night, some tucked away behind plush velvet drapes—and homed in on the bars, the discotheques, where Roman nightlife throbbed with a vitality all its own.

Unlike committed terrorists, the mercenary members of the Red Justice liked the good life, with its flash and sweet aroma of material success. Unless the men he sought had gone to ground after Arthur Bishop's murder, Bolan knew he would find some traces of them in the gaudy world of Rome by night, if he devoted time and energy enough to their pursuit. If they had left no trace on Via Veneto, there were some other districts he might try, but for the moment it was the place to start.

Leaving the Peugeot at his hotel, he took the underground as far as Piazza Barberini, emerging onto Via San Nicola della Torentino and strolling north and westward past the offices of a dozen major airlines. A person could book a flight to anywhere on Earth from Via Veneto, but Bolan hoped that he would have to look no farther for his prey. Time was of the essence now, and he could not afford to let his adversaries organize another action while he walked the streets in search of leads. Bolan had to find a handle on the problem soon, before it blew up in his face.

The first two discotheques he tried were full of flashy youngsters, swirling aimlessly to heavy-metal rock and roll. The music deafened him, and he was stricken by a sickly smell of desperation underneath the cover scents of smoke and rich perfume. The faces etched with empty plastic smiles reminded him of junkies on the street, each desperate for a different kind of fix to drive away the loneliness. Some casual encounter for the night, a fevered pressing of the flesh, and with a little luck, tomorrow might not look so bleak, so sterile.

These were not the places that he wanted, and he kept moving, leaving the desperate to themselves. The Column's younger members might seek out a discotheque in search of drugs or easy sex, but they would not be there to recruit a gunner. No, he needed someplace dark and relatively quiet, where the serious pursuits were drinking and the consummation of illicit bargains. If he searched industriously he would find the right place, but he was worried about the time he might be wasting in the interim.

The next bar was obviously a gay establishment, and Bolan passed it by without a second glance. The prostitutes were out in force, both male and female, trolling up and down the avenue in all their finery. He was approached a dozen times as he walked the block between Via Firenzi and Via Leonida Bissolati, turning the offers away with a gruffness that fit the Belasko persona. Role camouflage de-

manded a commitment to the play, and Bolan's character
had come to Rome on business. He was looking for a sponsor, someone who would put his gun to work, and he was
not especially particular about the targets that were chosen.

Mike Belasko would go anywhere, do anything, if he was
paid enough up front. He had not come to Rome to waste
his time, his cash, on hookers and their games. Committed
to the role he must project for all the world, Belasko-Bolan
passed the women of the night, rebuffed them rudely, even
threateningly, when they grew insistent. He had business
elsewhere, and he would not be delayed.

Rome's proximity to Eastern Europe, Africa, the Middle
East, made the Eternal City an eternal marketplace for secret agents, terrorists and mercenary soldiers on the make.
Despite the efforts of security police and other agencies, it
was impossible to close the door on covert warriors from
around the world. They came to Italy as tourists, got some
sun, completed their transactions and were gone again, to
fight their wars on other battlefields. A few, the terrorists,
had come to stay, and they were waging bloody war inside
Rome itself, against the innocent, the helpless. It was Bolan's task to single out the worst among them, bury them
before they had a chance to compound their atrocities and
spill more innocent blood.

He turned the corner onto Via Leonida Bissolati, heading south, and found the bar he sought within a half block
of the darkened El Al offices. The stark facade, in contrast
to the gaudy light displays of other bars and discos on the
block, encouraged Bolan to believe that patrons at La Av-
enida cherished privacy, the chance to sip their drinks and
carry out their business free from interruptions by the tourist class. It might not meet his needs, but it was somewhere
to begin.

The air was murky with cigar smoke, conversation audible despite the muted competition of a jukebox playing
something from the sixties. Bolan didn't recognize the tune

by name, but it called to mind the images of bygone days, when burning cities marked the landscapes of America and Vietnam alike. He shrugged the moment off and made his way between the Spartan ranks of tables, headed for the bar.

He ordered rum straight up and drank the first one down before the barkeep had a chance to turn away and deal with other patrons. While he waited for a refill, Bolan propped his elbows on the polished bar and drew the night man closer with a confidential nod.

"I'm lookin' for action," Bolan told him simply, keeping it in English. It was risky, but it was the only way to go on unfamiliar turf.

The barkeep tried to smile, but the expression was arrested in the middle of a crooked grimace, frozen by a scar that ran across one cheek and along his jaw, to disappear inside the open collar of his shirt.

"You want a woman, maybe?"

Bolan shook his head emphatically and jerked a thumb in the direction of the door.

"I didn't have to come in here for that," he growled. "They're cloggin' up the sidewalk for a friggin' mile." Bolan dropped his voice a notch, making the bartender strain to hear him. "I need work."

Scarface spread his hands and rolled his piglike eyes. "Not hiring now," he said as he frowned.

The thousand-lire note appeared in Bolan's hand as if by magic, slid across the bar and disappeared again inside the barkeep's massive paw.

"I reckon someone's hirin', though. I figure you might be inclined to tell whoever asks that Mike Belasko is in town and lookin' for a suitable position."

Bolan's money found a safe berth in a pocket of the barkeep's apron.

"Signor Belasko," Scarface echoed. "Suitable position."

"That's the ticket, bud. I'm booked at La Toscana through the weekend."

"La Toscana," Scarface echoed. "Is on Via Tacito."

"By George, I think he's got it. Set us up another tall one for the road, eh, bud?"

He took the glass of rum and overpaid, not waiting for his change before he spied an empty table near the door and headed for it, glancing neither right nor left. He had already marked the other faces in the bar, and felt the eyes upon him as he crossed the smoky room. A few were hostile, others curious, the majority disinterested. Clearly an American, he could not be employed by the security police. If he was CIA, he had no jurisdiction here but could be seeking information on a wide variety of subjects, with a fat expense account, perhaps, to prime the pump. If he was private, then he might be looking for a job, as he had told the barkeep, or he might be laying out some operation of his own, in need of able hands to back him up. In any case, the hungry and the hunted kept their eyes on Bolan, but discreetly; those with business of their own in progress let him pass without a second glance, but kept their voices low while he was close enough to overhear.

He had been seated only for a moment when the woman left her place along the bar and made her way between the other tables toward his own. She was slim and sultry, in a dress that might have been sprayed on, cut high and low to emphasize her assets. Bolan didn't need a second glance to realize that she was wearing nothing underneath. The darkness flattered her; she would have had a harder look in unforgiving daylight, but the soldier didn't care. He had already noticed her companion at the bar: Italian, with curly hair that overflowed his collar, and a leather jacket worn a size too large, which might conceal a multitude of sins.

"May I sit down?"

She settled in the empty chair without awaiting his reply. A sullen waitress veered in their direction, and the woman ordered wine.

"You are American." It didn't come out sounding like a question.

"So?"

"I like Americans."

"My lucky day."

"Could be."

"I hate to burst your bubble, sweetheart, but I'm here on business."

"So am I," she answered, smiling mischievously.

"Different strokes," he told her gruffly. "I'm not in the mood."

"For love? Or money?"

"What, the workin' girls are paying for it now?"

Her smile went stiff around the edges, but she saved it in a heartbeat, and he gave her points for working under pressure.

"I have a friend who would be interested in meeting you." She nodded toward the bar, and Bolan met the dark man's eyes. The stranger raised his wineglass in a silent toast.

"Well, that's a switch. Tell your friend no thanks. I'm straight."

She didn't even try to save the smile. "You are looking for a job. My friend is interested in talking business, but if you would rather sit and tell your little jokes..."

She rose as if to leave, and Bolan caught her by the hand.

"Hey, take it easy, sweetness. If your boyfriend's buyin', send him over. We can talk."

The woman disengaged her hand and sashayed back to her companion at the bar. They huddled for a moment, then the stranger got a bottle from the barkeep, and made his way to Bolan's table while his female spotter held her station at the bar.

"Signor Belasko?"

"In the flesh." He nodded toward the woman, who was busy warming up another stranger at the bar. "I like your callin' card."

If his remark had touched a nerve, it didn't show. "I am Enzio Petrucchi. May I join you?"

"Hell, why not? I'm gettin' used to unexpected company."

The stranger settled into a chair across from Bolan. In the process, Bolan got confirmation that the guy was carrying, an automatic pistol that was worn beneath the stranger's left arm in a shoulder harness. Bolan would be ready for any sudden move, and drawing a weapon out of shoulder rigging could be awkward with the hard edge of a table jammed against your throat.

"I understand that you are looking for employment."

"That depends."

"On what?"

"The pay, for openers. And after that, the job."

"You are a mercenary?"

"I've been called a whole lot worse."

"We may assume you have experience?"

"Three tours in Nam for Uncle Sam. On the private side, I know my way around Angola, Nicaragua, here and there."

Petrucchi's eyes lit up.

"You are a soldier of the liberation?"

Bolan laughed out loud, enjoying the confusion on Petrucchi's face.

"I am a soldier of the bankroll, buddy. Bleedin' for a cause is just the same as any other kind of bleedin', and in case you haven't heard, it isn't healthy. I get paid to make the other bastards bleed."

"Your politics are independent, then?"

"My politics are nonexistent. Ditto my religion. Get the picture? I am a professional at what I do, and seminars don't enter into it."

"I understand."

There was the slightest hint of disapproval in Petrucchi's tone. Bolan had no idea yet of the Italian's affiliations, and he might be wasting time in sterile conversation with some barroom revolutionary who was full of hot air. It was time to turn the tables and acquire some solid information.

"You ask a lot of questions," Bolan growled. "Now it's my turn. Have you got work for me, or are we jerkin' off here?"

"I, that is, my comrades have a need for men who take life seriously."

"It's the only way I take life. What kind of comrades are we talkin' here?"

Petrucchi hesitated for a moment, clearly wondering how much he dared reveal on short acquaintance with the man who called himself Belasko. When he resumed, his tone was cautious.

"I represent a group of men and women who are struggling for change in this society. The power structure has resisted our suggestions, laughed at our demands."

Bolan shook his head in sympathy. "Those friggin' power structures have a tendency to do that. It's a cryin' shame."

"We find it necessary to declare ourselves in, shall we say, more forceful terms? Examples must be made, if we are to be taken seriously."

"So, you're makin' a list and checkin' it twice. What's the pitch?"

"The . . . pitch?"

"The deal, for Chrissake. What's your offer?"

"I am not empowered to negotiate the final terms," Petrucchi told him sheepishly. "If you will come with me to meet our leader . . ."

"*Your* leader, bud. He isn't leadin' me around the block until I see the color of his money and we strike a deal that suits me."

"That is understood, of course."

"So bring him down here and we'll talk."

"I am afraid that is impossible."

"Oh, yeah? Your boy the bashful type, or what?"

A trace of angry color tinged Petrucchi's cheeks, but he controlled himself.

"Security police are interested in his movements. They have agents everywhere." As if to emphasize the point, he glanced around at the adjacent tables, scowling at their fellow patrons and reminding Bolan of a character from second-rate melodrama.

"So, we're talkin' hazard pay for openers," he growled. "It's gonna cost your boy top dollar if he wants to do a decent job."

"The cost should be no problem."

"Well, that's what I like to hear. What is this outfit anyway? I mighta heard of you before."

Before Petrucchi had a chance to frame his answer, half a dozen carabinieri entered the saloon in single file. They were incongruous in caps and uniforms with polished buttons, their Beretta automatic pistols worn in cross-draw military holsters with the flaps buttoned down. It was an awkward way to go with side arms, adding crucial seconds to the pull, and Bolan wondered how so few of them were murdered in the line of duty.

The policemen formed a line along the bar, displacing customers and glaring out across the smoky room at anyone who dared to meet their gaze. One of them—apparently the leader, if his attitude and the braiding on his uniform were indications—attempted to engage the bartender in conversation, snapping questions at him while the big man with the scar just shrugged and kept his eyes downcast. Across from Bolan, Enzio Petrucchi was intently studying his wineglass, face averted from the officers as if he feared he might be recognized.

But the carabinieri were not looking for Petrucchi. One of them had glanced at Bolan, done a sluggish double take, elbowed his companion and whispered urgently to him.

There were four eyes on him now, and Bolan played it casual as the second uniform hauled out a notebook and thumbed through the pages. He found what he wanted in a matter of seconds. He read it over, stared at Bolan for another moment, then proceeded down the line for a hasty consultation with his leader.

Bolan knew precisely what was happening. The officer had made him for Belasko, or believed he had. The bulletins were out, and while the fabricated mercenary was not wanted in Rome, that might not stop an overzealous officer from making an arrest on mere suspicion. Once in custody, once he had lost control, there was no telling where the deadly farce might end.

Aside from clashing with the RJC and Red Brigades at different times, the Executioner had also passed through Italy and Sicily on one of his campaigns against the Mafia. His face had changed since then, of course, as had his fingerprints, but there were other ways of making positive ID. Once he was in custody, his captors would have all the time in the world to make their case. As soon as Bolan was identified, as soon as word leaked out, the hard-core mafiosi from every province in the land would hungrily descend on Rome, to wreak vengeance on the man who had humiliated them. Once he was identified, the Executioner would not survive a day in jail.... And so, he could not let himself be taken prisoner.

Now the ranking officer was leading his subordinates toward Bolan's table. One of the rougher-looking patrons muttered something as they passed, and Bolan saw the members of the security force hesitate, each trembling with anger, and with something else. They were on hostile ground and they knew it, literally surrounded by the enemy, but there was pride involved, and Bolan knew that they would have to see their mission through. There could be no turning back without being tainted by cowardice and shame.

The solitary drinker offered no more comments, the security officers spent another moment glaring at him. They finally moved on to form an open ring around the table occupied by Bolan and Petrucchi, who looked decidedly uncomfortable.

"Signor Belasko?"

"Mmm? Who wants to know?"

The officer was edgy, self-importance arguing with his survival instincts, forcing him to keep his temper for the moment.

"We are the carabinieri. I must see your passport."

Bolan frowned. "I may have left it back at the hotel." He patted down the pockets of his jacket, then fished inside, fingers grazing the Beretta, veering off to nowhere. He could not afford a bust, but he was not about to kill these men in uniform to save himself.

"No... here it is."

He brought both feet up, underneath the table, kicking off with all his strength. There was a fleeting glimpse of Enzio Petrucchi going over backward with the table in his lap and an expression of amazement on his face, before the soldier scrambled to his feet and lunged at the officer in charge. His right was boring in on target as he made the move, and in the heartbeat that remained, there wasn't time for the astounded officer to raise his hands.

4

Bolan's fist impacted on the carabiniere's cheek and laid him out across the table just behind him, scattering the startled patrons seated there and shattering their glassware as the shaky furniture gave way beneath the man's weight. No time to see if there was any fight left in the officer; his backup squad was already in motion, tightening the ring and closing rapidly to save their leader from further indignities.

The soldier caught another glimpse of Petrucchi, scuttling backward in search of cover, as he feinted to his left, then spun hard right to meet the closest of his challengers head-on. A truncheon whistled past his ear, impacting on his shoulder with a flare of pain that nearly paralyzed his arm, but sheer momentum carried Bolan through the move. His knee slashed upward into his assailant's groin, and the fight went out of number two as Bolan stepped away to let the man fall to the floor.

The other four were on him in a rush, and Bolan took the only course available: he charged. Head down, eyes shielded by his one good arm, the soldier met his adversaries with a driving strength that came from desperation.

The impact toppled one of Bolan's human targets, and his heel came down upon the fallen carabiniere's fingers. Ignoring the panting screams that rose from his prone adversary, the soldier grappled fiercely with two other lawmen, who were trying to wrestle him to the floor. That left one man unaccounted for, but as he twisted to escape a clumsy double hammerlock, Bolan saw what had become of number six.

The surly patron who had offered insult to the uniforms a moment earlier was weighing in on Bolan's side, with no apparent motive other than a hatred of police. Peripherally, Bolan saw the hulking figure rise and lock the slender lawman in a bear hug, lifting him completely off his feet, retreating with his startled captive through the milling crowd of customers. Whatever might befall the officer, he was eliminated as a problem for the Executioner, which still left two distinctively active problems dragging him downward.

The soldier kicked out backward, raked a blue-clad shin and was rewarded with a yelp of pain. The carabiniere relaxed his grip on Bolan's right arm, instinctively responding to his own discomfort. That was the edge that Bolan needed. Pivoting, relying on the second officer to keep him balanced, Bolan put his weight behind a rolling judo toss that caught the starboard man off balance and dumped him on his backside in the middle of the floor. He rolled away, was scrambling nimbly to his feet when someone on the sidelines threw a vicious punch from nowhere, driving the disoriented lawman to his knees. A boot exploded in his face, and he was out of it before the angry crowd descended on him, kicking, stomping on his rag-doll form.

The shouting patrons obviously had been waiting for a chance to settle ancient scores with the police, and any lawmen would suffice as targets of their rage. The soldier could not help them now; it would be all that he could do to help himself.

The single carabiniere clinging to his arm had noted the assault upon his comrades by the assorted patrons of the bar. He hesitated for perhaps a heartbeat, reassessing options, and the lag provided Bolan with the necessary opening, an opportunity to make his move. He turned into the officer's embrace, his free hand reaching low and fast to catch the other's scrotum, twisting with an upward motion, bringing his assailant up on tiptoes. His other arm was free at once—the officer was intent on rescuing his genitals—and Bolan brought the elbow up beneath his adversary's chin with stunning force. The lawman's eyes rolled back and he was finished, toppling away from Bolan like a straw man.

Somehow, the officer in charge of the patrol had struggled to his feet, and he was ripping at the cross-draw holster that he wore, intent on hauling out his automatic. Bolan knew that he could beat his opposition to the draw, but that was no alternative at all. He was braced to run for cover when Petrucchi's girlfriend stepped in close behind the officer and swung a long-necked wine bottle against his skull.

The effect was literally explosive, *vin rosé* and shattered glass erupting from the bottle's wicker basket like a halo, blood and wine together streaming down the carabiniere's face as he collapsed to the floor. The other patrons set upon him instantly, and Bolan caught a fleeting glimpse of Scarface bulling through the crowd, a captured truncheon in his fist.

Before the Executioner could move to intervene, Petrucchi had him by the elbow, hauling him away from the arena.

"This way! Quickly!" he demanded, tugging Bolan fiercely toward an exit in the rear. Outside, the rising bleat of sirens told him reinforcements were arriving. There was no more time to lose.

The woman was with them, somehow, as they cleared the exit and emerged into a narrow, reeking alleyway. The passage stank of garbage and urine, but at least the air was free of smoke, and they would not be lingering in any case. Petrucchi led the way and Bolan followed quickly, with the woman running at his side. She laced her fingers through his and kept pace easily, without apparent strain. He was amazed to find her laughing as they ran.

Petrucchi flagged a cab on Via Barberini, and they rode in silence for perhaps a quarter of a mile, until they halted in the middle of a block on Via Ludovisi. A parking lot had been improvised near the Casino of Aurora, and Petrucchi tipped the young attendant, waiting while his Fiat four-door was retrieved. The small sedan had seen better days, but it was mobile, and the Executioner slid in beside Petrucchi. The woman sat behind him. Remembering her treatment of the ranking carabiniere, Bolan half turned in his seat, ensuring that she could not take him by surprise.

Petrucchi drove the Fiat like a madman, weaving in and out through traffic with a reckless disregard that seemed to be a common trait of Roman drivers. Bolan braced himself against the dashboard, noting landmarks as they passed. It could prove useful if he had to retrace their route alone. South along Via del Corso to the Piazza Venezia, with its monument to Victor Emmanuel II. On through the heart of Rome and veering off southwest to cross the Tiber at Ponte Garibaldi, and then southward once again on the Viale Trastevere, winding in and out through smaller, darker streets until they parked outside a small hotel on Via Dandolo.

Petrucchi disembarked and Bolan followed. Their companion, silent all throughout the crosstown drive, slid in behind the wheel and dropped the Fiat into gear. Before they reached the hotel lobby she was gone, the taillights winking out around a corner three blocks down.

"I call her if we need the car," Petrucchi said, and led the way inside.

The lobby smelled of age and benign neglect. From where he stood, the Executioner surmised that someone—the proprietor, presumably—was striving for an image of antiquity. Instead, the lobby just looked old, with fraying carpets, faded murals on the walls and easy chairs that didn't take it quite so easy anymore.

Petrucchi nodded to the wizened desk clerk, who repaid the gesture by appearing to ignore them absolutely. A creaking elevator took them up three stories and disgorged them in a corridor that mirrored the condition of the lobby. There were tarnished numbers bolted to the doors, and Enzio led Bolan to his left along the hallway, stopping in front of number thirty-seven. Bolan memorized the coded knock and waited, checking out the corridor and rooms to either side, alert to any sign of ambush. He was alone on hostile ground, and he could not afford to let his guard down for an instant.

The door was opened by a slick Sicilian thug who wore his hair greased back above a pockmarked forehead. Other scars gave his face a kind of lunar look that added to the menace in his eyes. The sentry shot a question at Petrucchi, listened to his windy explanation and reluctantly stepped back to let them enter.

Bolan had a chance to register the other faces in the room before a knife blade pressed against his jugular and the Sicilian ordered him to raise his hands. The frisk was smooth, professional, and Enzio stood openmouthed as the big Beretta was pulled out from under Bolan's arm.

"You had a weapon! Why did you not use it on the carabinieri?"

Bolan gave the younger man a sour glance. "Same reason that you didn't use that cannon you've been packin', boy. You waste a cop, you'd better be prepared to take the heat, because it never goes away."

Petrucchi was still chewing that one over when another man moved up beside him, smiling thinly at the Executioner.

"Your answer is correct," he said in cultured English. "If any of the carabinieri had been killed, the city would be in a turmoil even now. It happens that they all are safe, if badly bruised. Your wisdom has prevented great embarrassment, Signor..."

"Belasko." From the recitation of events at the saloon, he had no doubt the man must know his name already. There had been another pair of eyes—or several—in the bar, perhaps unknown to Enzio himself, and the report had run before them as they drove across town.

"Belasko, *sì*. And I am Carlo Frenzi. Welcome."

"I could use a drink," he said, although in fact he had consumed more than enough already. The excitement of the barroom brawl and their escape had burned up any traces of intoxication, and Belasko would be thirsty now that he had found himself on safer ground.

"If I may offer you some wine?"

"I won't say no."

His host led Bolan to the dining table, where three other men sat watching him in silence. Bolan took the chair that Frenzi indicated, and a jug of wine was passed around.

"Your weapon will be held until you leave. Security, *signor*."

"No problem."

"Enzio informs me that you are in search of work."

It was a subtle lie, of course; Petrucchi hadn't had the time for any explanations. But if Frenzi had another pair of eyes and ears inside the bar, so much the better. It would save the Executioner some time, cut through a few of the preliminaries.

"That depends."

"On price?"

"Primarily."

"So, you are not concerned with ideology?"

"As it affects the payoff, sure. Beyond that, you can keep your politics and your religion to yourself."

"We understand each other," Frenzi said with seeming satisfaction. "I have need of men who are discreet, professional. Our cause has need of soldiers like yourself."

"Which cause is that?"

"The cause of revolution."

"They're a dime a dozen."

Bolan felt a stirring in the others seated at the table, realized that they must understand some English. If Mike Belasko's attitude offended them, so much the better; Frenzi plainly valued independence...to a point. If Bolan took the bite, then he would be expected to conform and follow orders, but his thoughts were racing now, and threatening to run away with him. He didn't even know if he was dealing with the savages he sought.

"Our revolution is a bit more costly," Carlo told him, "both in lire and in lives. Our soldiers are expected to perform, but they are not expected to be paupers."

"I'm still listenin'."

"A man of your experience commands the wage of a professional, and there are certain, eh, how do you say it in America? Fringe benefits?"

"That's how we say it. And I love fringe benefits."

"Regrettably, it may be necessary to examine your credentials."

Bolan sneered. "I didn't bring a copy of my résumé."

"Perhaps a recent sponsor? One of your associates?"

Bolan paused to mull it over, making Frenzi wait.

"I did some work for Rikki Roybal."

"The Hyena. Killed in Turkey."

"Julio Ramirez?"

"Also dead. In Switzerland, they say."

"Well, it's a long shot, but you might try Tommy Morganslicht. He didn't care much for the way I hit it off with sister, Tanya, though, you get my drift? I mean, I'm all for families lovin' one another, but there's gotta be a limit somewhere."

"Dead. Both dead."

"That right?" He feigned surprise, although the Executioner's campaign against the vicious Zwilling Horde had led directly to their deaths. In fact, he was responsible for the extermination of the others he had named, as well. "Too bad about the lady, huh? But what the hell, that's life."

"Which leaves us with the problem of your references."

"I dunno what to tell ya, friend. Unless you wanna hire yourself a medium and put a call through to the other side, I guess you'll have to check me out through channels."

"That can be arranged," his host replied, "but it will take some time. You may remain with us, in comfort, while the necessary information is obtained."

"Hold up a second, there. You've got me playin' house, and I don't even know who's pickin' up the tab."

"We are Red Justice," Frenzi told him simply, and he felt the short hairs rising on his neck, the first rush of adrenaline. "Welcome to the revolution."

"Hey, I heard about you guys a while ago. Word was, you bit the big one."

Frenzi's smile was tight, emotionless. "Reports of our demise are . . . shall we say . . . exaggerated?"

Bolan smiled and sipped his *vin rosé*, examining the faces ranged around him at the dining table. No young revolutionaries these; the scars and waxen flesh all added up to years in prison, and he knew instinctively that there had been no basic change in ideology with the rejuvenation of the RJC. The leader's crack about "fringe benefits" had been enough to tip the Executioner that he was dealing with a group of terrorists-for-profit, guns for hire who weren't ashamed to free-lance if the price was right.

As it had been with Arthur Bishop, sure.

As it had been with the DiAlto family, first time around.

The cast of characters had changed, with Bolan's blitz and sheer attrition whittling the column down, new scum arising in the vacuum, filling in for fallen savages wherever vacancies occurred. He should have seen it coming, with a group more dedicated to the looting than the liberation of society. The scam was simply too damned sweet to fade away.

Which meant that he would have to pull out all the stops this time around. It would not be enough to simply cut the viper's head off, nor to hack the body up in pieces. He would have to finally incinerate the serpent, head and tail and all, before he was convinced that it would not regenerate itself, with a brand-new, rotten lease on life.

Arthur Bishop had been sacrificed to Bolan's failure. He would live with that blood on his hands, and it would strengthen his determination to prevent the next atrocity. And if the resolution of his mission should require a further sacrifice, the Executioner stood ready, with his own life on the line. As it had always been in Bolan's private, everlasting war, so it would be again, in Rome.

"As long as we're all revolutionary brothers here, what say I get my piece back?"

Frenzi thought about it for a moment, finally nodded to the slick Sicilian. Bolan reholstered the Beretta, feeling better for the weapon's weight against his ribs. If it came down to shooting now, before he met the rest of them and learned their plans, at least he had a chance. With any luck, before the storm broke, he might have an opportunity to fetch the other hardware from his room, retrieve the cakes of C-4 and the detonators from his car.

Bolan knew he might be needing all of it before his job was finished. And none of it might help him in the least if Frenzi and the others tumbled to his cover prematurely. Bolan's fate was in Brognola's hands if Frenzi chose to check him out through channels; he could only hope that Hal was on the job, that no befuddled second-stringer took the vital call and blew it. Either way, that end of it was out of Bolan's hands, and there was nothing left for him to do but play it by ear, reacting to the situations that arose. The soldier drained his wineglass, pushed it back across the table, waving off the proffered refill.

"We are crowded here," his host remarked offhandedly, as if the thought had just occurred to him. "Let us retire to some more spacious lodgings. Gentlemen?"

The others rose, and Bolan followed suit.

"Where to?" he asked, and hoped it sounded casual.

Across the dining table, Frenzi's smile was noncommittal.

"You are one of us now. You must share our sanctuary. We are going underground."

The dying words of Arthur Bishop rang in Bolan's ears. *The tunnels.* Bolan's scalp was crawling as he followed Enzio Petrucchi out into the corridor. It was too easy, right, and Frenzi was no fool. The "sanctuary" might as easily be Bolan's prison while they checked him out, and if he failed the test, it might become his tomb.

The tunnels.

Bolan didn't know precisely what was coming, but he sensed that Frenzi's comment was intended to be taken literally. They were going underground for real, and Bolan had no way of knowing when—or if—he would be coming out again.

5

"You may know something of the catacombs from history or literature."

Carlo Frenzi smiled at Bolan as they rode the elevator down. He had assumed the attitude of a professor, lecturing his class of one. The other Red Justice terrorists, who surrounded Bolan, had heard it all before.

"The catacombs are Christian cemeteries, nothing more or less. The one peculiarity is their location, which was dictated by the lack of available space in early Rome. The cemeteries are arranged in galleries, set one above another, like the floors of this hotel, but underground. The topmost are the oldest levels, as the newer galleries were excavated later, underneath the first."

He paused, as if expecting some remark from Bolan, but the soldier merely waited for the lecture to continue.

"There are many tales of Christians hiding in the catacombs, away from persecution by the Roman legions... but, alas, such tales are simply fiction. The authorities knew all about the catacombs, of course, and they were closed at the beginning of the purges. Still, the martyrs knew a trick or two, as you shall see."

The elevator shuddered to a halt at basement level, and they disembarked into a musty vault of stone and concrete. From appearances, the basement had been spared a cleaning for at least a decade; by comparison, the seedy hotel's lobby was a fashion layout. Ropes and veils of spiderwebs

were everywhere, in addition to abundant proof that rats
had made themselves at home. A stack of dusty crates that
could have been left over from the Second World War filled
half the basement; rusty tools hung above a workbench that
was warped from long disuse.

"This way."

He followed Frenzi toward the workbench, with its massive ornate cupboards standing off to one side, draped in
cobwebs. Bolan thought he had prepared himself for anything, but he was taken by surprise as Frenzi opened the
cupboards to reveal the gaping entrance of a tunnel.

"Follow me."

The terrorist commander fished a flashlight from the
pocket of his overcoat and shone it into the darkness beyond the entryway. Bolan had a glimpse of rough-hewn
walls and ceiling, dusty floor, the tunnel curving out of sight
some twenty feet beyond the entrance. Frenzi led the way
and Bolan followed closely, with the others on his heels. He
felt the short hairs bristle on his neck as someone swung the
secret doorway shut, entombing them within the musty
shaft.

"The martyrs had no opportunity to hide themselves inside the catacombs, as I have said, but they were not without resources."

Frenzi played his flash around the walls, the floor, the
ceiling, as he lectured. Bolan watched a rat the size of a chi-
huahua scuttle out of Frenzi's path; it scurried by him,
chattering in protest, and the others sidestepped hastily to
let it pass. Frantic squeaking ahead of them indicated that
bats or other rodents resented the intrusion into their pre-
viously private domain.

"Throughout the first and second centuries A.D., the
Christians were a hunted people, living by their wits as much
as by their faith. They excavated tunnels that could serve
them both as hiding places and as secret means of transpor-
tation when the streets above were taken over by patrols.

Some of their tunnels lead directly to the çatacombs on Via Appia Antica—the Old Appian Way—but others form a honeycomb beneath the city, undermining every part of Rome. And they are all connected.''

Frenzi reached the corner, sent his flashlight's beam ahead of them to test the darkness. The tunnel seemed to stretch forever, hungrily devouring the feeble light. A bat detached itself from somewhere overhead, performed an awkward somersault for the assembled audience, then vanished into shadow.

"With the acceptance and expansion of the Church by Rome during the next two centuries, the tunnels were abandoned and forgotten. Christians were no longer the oppressed minority. They had achieved respectability, converting emperors, attaining wealth undreamed of by their fathers. There was no more need to hide. Remembrance of the tunnels and the catacombs was wiped away for good by the barbarians—two hundred years of rape and pillage climaxed with the virtual destruction of society.''

It might have been a trick of the acoustics, but Bolan thought he could discern a note of admiration, envy, in the tour guide's voice as he described the fall of ancient Rome. All things considered, he was not surprised that Frenzi should identify with the barbarians in Roman history; his revolutionary clique was their historical equivalent, assaulting innocents with a profit motive, savaging society, impelled by lust and greed.

"A thousand years and more would pass before the catacombs were rediscovered, first in the Via Salaria, later here and there throughout the city. Excavation started in the fourteenth century, but even then the tunnels were forgotten. The historians and scientists were interested in graves and martyrs, but the secrets of the early Christians were forgotten. Miles of tunnels, excavated from the living rock, were overlooked by archaeologists who opened up the catacombs.''

They reached a branching of the tunnel—east and west, as near as Bolan could determine, though his sense of direction was rapidly deserting him. Frenzi didn't hesitate or even break his stride; he chose the right-hand tunnel, and the others followed.

"A year ago, while we were working on a tunnel of our own beneath a house on Via Ostriana, one of our men accidentally found an ancient passageway. In fact, he fell headfirst into the tunnel, broke his neck and never knew what he had given us. But we are grateful to his memory."

"The perfect hiding place?"

"And so much more. Within these tunnels, we can travel as we will around the city, undetected by the pigs of the security police. Each time they seek to pin us down, we wriggle through their fingers, leave them looking foolish like the poor, dumb animals they are. It is impossible for them to hold us now."

Frenzi's tone left something else unspoken, but the soldier didn't push it. He was watching for a distinguishing feature, a landmark, anything that might be useful if he had to make a swift retreat, retrace his steps to gain daylight. A hundred yards beyond the forking of the tunnel, after it had branched twice more with other shafts extending randomly to either side, he gave up. It was hopeless.

Just ahead, the tunnel widened almost imperceptibly, and Bolan felt a sudden draft of cooler, fresher air. The faintest hint of street sounds reached his ears.

"A *lucernarium*," his guide declared. "The shafts were randomly installed around the catacombs for light and ventilation. During daylight hours, they provide illumination of a sort."

Bolan kept the ventilation shaft in mind, but he knew that it would offer precious little in the way of light, no matter what the hour of the day. The vastness of the tunnels would absorb those shafts of light the way a blotter soaks up ink, and not one beam would be visible around the nearest cor-

ner. As far as ventilation was concerned, the draft did
nothing to relieve the dank pervasive mustiness that was a
feature of the underground.

The ceiling here was higher, and the walls on either side
were lined with marble slabs, inscribed with names and
cryptic symbols. Bolan realized at once that they were
marching through the center of an ancient graveyard, which
had been hollowed out beneath the surface of the earth.

"Not all the catacombs have been despoiled by tourists," Frenzi told him, smiling back across his shoulder in
the dim reflection of the flash. "They flock to St. Callistus,
St. Sebastian, Domitilla and the rest, but countless others
have remained intact."

He indicated tombs to either side with an expansive gesture.

"Meet the Benicelli clan, *signor*." He dawdled past the
tombs, his flashlight picking out the symbols etched in
marble, others pressed in terra-cotta. "Here, the anchor
stands for hope, presumably of satisfaction in the afterlife.
The dolphin represents the savior. Jonah and the whale are
symbols of the coming resurrection. There, the dove with
the olive branch depicts man reconciled with God."

There was no mockery in Frenzi's tone, although he
clearly felt no reverence for the religious symbols, either. It
was not uncommon for a terrorist to have a well-developed
sense of history, and Bolan wondered just how far his guide
had already progressed from simple greed toward twisted
ideology. Red Justice, the soldier knew, had begun as urban pirates, preying on the wealthy, but there was a possibility that its association with the Soviets or other radicals
had subtly changed the thinking of its leaders. Some, like
Frenzi, might have started taking all the propaganda seriously, thinking of themselves as liberation warriors, struggling against the "fascist" state.

But ideology would only make the RJC more dangerous,
creating instability where greed had once been a motive.

Mercenary criminals were smart enough to break and run when all the odds were stacked against them; revolutionary zealots might be more inclined to stand and die, to take the city's population with them when the heat came down.

They reached a narrow flight of steps that had been chiseled out of rock, and Bolan followed Frenzi's flashlight downward, past a second gallery of graves, a third, until the guide resumed his horizontal progress. Generations of the Benicellis lay around him and above, encased in marble, stone and terra-cotta, waiting patiently for Judgment Day. If Bolan had his way, the members of Red Justice would not have long to wait.

If he had anything to say about it, Carlo Frenzi's private judgment day was just around the corner. And closing fast.

They covered another hundred yards, then Frenzi's pace slowed as the tunnel made a looping curve around some natural obstruction that had stymied ancient architects. Abruptly, Bolan's guide stopped cold, his left hand raised in warning as his right hand extended with the flash, his thumb upon the switch and tapping out a coded signal. Another flashlight answered from the darkness up ahead, winking like a beacon.

"We go."

And Frenzi led the way, the flashlight angled upward to illuminate his face. When he was duly recognized, the hidden sentry barked an order to his backup, and the tunnel came alive with lights, revealing men and crates of hardware in a chamber roughly twice the size of Bolan's suite at La Toscana. Once again, he noted niches in the walls, but these were smaller than the others, occupied by standing urns. Some were empty.

"Welcome to the columbarium," his guide proclaimed. "Reserved for pagans and the poorer Christians who could not afford more ostentatious funerals. We have discovered several such facilities, and they are perfect for our needs."

"It makes a nifty ammo dump, I'll give you that."

From where he stood, the Executioner had noted crates of arms and ammunition, others marked with universal warning signs reserved for high explosives. Bolan didn't even want to think about the aftermath of accidental detonation so far underground, with human flesh in close proximity.

"An ammo dump, and more. We stand beneath the sanctuary of St. Cecilia in Trastevere. In the morning, several thousand tourists will begin their daily pilgrimage above our heads. An interesting prospect, is it not? This way."

He followed Frenzi down the length of the chamber, past gunners with resentment and suspicion in their eyes, until they reached a section of the tunnel where the walls on either side were lined with narrow, open doors. Frenzi ducked inside the nearest open arch and gestured for the Executioner to follow him. The architect had been a smaller man than average, and Bolan had to duck his head on entering the musty cubicle.

"Your quarters, for the moment," Frenzi told him, smiling thinly. "Here you will be safe from the police and any other outside interference."

Bolan watched a hand-size spider scuttle for the safety of a crevice in the wall, reflecting that it would be easy to remain awake, alert, inside these quarters.

"What did all those martyrs do for toilets?"

"Farther down the gallery, *signor*. Consider Enzio your guide while you are with us. He will be happy to escort you and be sure that you are comfortable, *sì*?"

Petrucchi muttered something noncommittal from the doorway, plainly none too thrilled with his assignment as Belasko's shadow. Frenzi would be more concerned about the stranger as a potential threat than as a guest, but Bolan was relieved that he had not been saddled with a more courageous keeper. Enzio had shown his colors in the barroom brawl, preferring to retreat instead of using either fists or sidearm. When the time came, Bolan had no doubt that he could deal with Enzio before the weasel had a chance to sound a general alarm.

When it was time.

For now, it would be Bolan's task to play the role of Frenzi's houseguest . . . but he saw no need to feign contentment with his lodgings.

"When's the last time anybody thought of sweepin' up around here?" he asked.

"Our energies are channeled toward the liberation struggle," Frenzi told him stiffly, in his best officious tone.

"You oughta liberate a vacuum cleaner next time out, and throw some bug spray in there while you're at it. Jesus, this place looks like Dracula slept here."

"Consider the accommodations temporary," Frenzi answered. "When your story is confirmed, you will of course be free to come and go as you may wish."

Bolan took the risk, although he knew the answer in advance. "And if it isn't?"

Frenzi's smile was genuine this time. "Then we shall have another martyr for the catacombs," he said.

And Frenzi left him, slipping through the doorway, leaving Enzio Petrucchi at his station just outside. The cubicle was fitted with a folding cot, a table and a camp chair—all the comforts of a cut-rate prison cell. Outside, the gunners were conversing softly in Italian, and he wondered if he should try to communicate with any of them, other than Petrucchi. But he didn't think the Belasko profile included being able to speak Italian, though Bolan himself had more than a working knowledge of the language. No matter; when the time arrived, he would be speaking to them in the only language savages could ever really understand, and they would hear him loud and clear.

Uncomfortable in the camp chair, Bolan racked his mind for any long-forgotten facts about the catacombs that Frenzi's discourse had omitted. There were images of Christians huddled in the darkness, clutching candles, muttering their incantations from illicit prayer books, waiting for the legions to surround them, drag them out to face the terrors of the Coliseum. Nothing useful to his present situation. Nothing but a nagging apprehension, verging on a certainty, that there was something he should recognize, some danger she should be aware of, even now.

The columbarium's location told him they had traveled some six hundred yards from the hotel on Via Dandolo. The Tiber was another hundred yards due west...but which direction *was* due west? Deprived of landmarks, robbed of sun and moon and stars, the soldier was reduced to guessing, and he knew that it would not be good enough in an emergency. He could retrace his steps until the nearest branching of the tunnel, and perhaps a short way farther. But he could easily get lost within a hundred yards, surrounded by the darkness and a private army pledged to his extermination.

The placement of the Column's staging area might be significant for yet another reason. If the charges hidden there were detonated, what would happen overhead, in St. Cecilia's sanctuary? Was there enough goop in Frenzi's dump to breach the pavement—what, three floors above? And if the charges had been planted closer, in the topmost gallery, as part of a deliberate strategy?

Alarm bells started clanging in the back of Bolan's mind, and now he had the missing piece, the peril that had eluded him earlier. The catacombs and tunnels might not be merely a staging area and covert transit system for the RJC. In fact, the underground might prove to be the battleground itself, a launching pad for acts of random terrorism that could bring the city to its knees.

Bolan wondered whether Frenzi had already planned that far ahead, and he knew he had the answer even as the question struggled to be born. The Column's leader was a man of foresight, even if his profit motive had been warped and watered down by two-bit revolutionary dogma. Frenzi would have seen the underground's potential from the outset, and his mention of the other caches, other staging grounds, alerted Bolan to the fact that soldiers of the RJC were stationed throughout Rome, beneath the streets, prepared to move upon command.

It was a chilling thought, but one that he would have to cope with if he was to counteract the threat. He would require some means of gathering the savages, of luring them off their stations, into one collective killing ground, before he made his move. If any of them slipped away with targets scheduled and a standing order to attack, he would have failed before he started, and the savages would be victorious.

But he was being premature, the soldier realized. It still remained for Frenzi to decide on his legitimacy, like a modern Nero voting life or death for gladiators in the Coliseum. If Brognola's cover held, he should be fine, for now. If it collapsed...

Then it would matter little if he found a way to outfox the soldiers of the RJC. He would be dead before he had the opportunity to move against them. Frenzi would make sure of that.

But either way it went down, the Executioner would keep one solemn promise to himself. His death would be expensive for the Column, and for Frenzi in particular. The reigning honcho of the RJC would not survive his clash with Bolan, not if it required the soldier's final ounce of strength, his dying breath to put a bullet through the bastard's brain. And he would take as many of the others with him as he could, damned right.

6

Carlo Frenzi moved along the sidewalk with assurance and determination in his stride. His face and name were known to the security police, but they would not be looking for him here, at the Palazzo di San Callistro. If they hunted him tonight—this morning, actually—it would be in the discotheques of Via Veneto, or a bar such as the one in which Enzio Petrucchi had encountered Mike Belasko. They would search for him there in vain, for he had business elsewhere, and he could not be detained just now by pleasures of the flesh.

The traffic had begun to thin as dawn approached, though it would never cease entirely. Taxis wove complicated patterns in and out among the private vehicles, while *vigili*—traffic officers—patrolled on Vespa scooters and in tiny, boxlike Fiats. As traffic neared the center of the city, many streets gave access only to cabs, pedestrians, the odd official vehicle. Woe to any tourist who encroached through ignorance upon restricted territory.

For all the pollution, noise, litter and exhaust, the bustling streets of Rome, the Rome of stars and sunlight, were vital, alive with the continuous activity that makes a city great. Its treasures and its famous architecture might be ancient, but the Rome that Frenzi recognized was fresh with each new sunrise. It might never change, but neither did it stay the same from one day to the next.

The world below the city streets was an entirely different proposition. Safer, in its way, but close and claustrophobic, heady with the smell of death too long confined. The underground provided sanctuary for his troops, their weaponry, but the perpetual reminder of their own mortality was telling on his men, beginning to erode their confidence. Red Justice was composed primarily of men who robbed and killed for profit, taking pleasure where they found it, as the ready cash allowed. But they would find no pleasure underground. Postponement of immediate desire had never been the strong point of his troops, and Carlo Frenzi had begun to wonder if they would respond to his commands when it was time.

The promise of fantastic riches was enough to hold his men briefly, but the promise must become reality, and soon, if any number of them were expected to remain with the cause. The Bishop ransom was a case in point: it was a decent plan that had disintegrated in an instant, costing three good men, the bad publicity attendant on a murdered hostage ... and the ransom money. Frenzi still had no idea precisely what had happened at the drop. Apparently his men had overreached themselves and come up short on skill or hardware. Either way, it was a blow against Red Justice, a disgrace that they would have to overcome. The murder of the hostage after the ransom had been delivered had hurt the credibility of the Column.

The death of Arthur Bishop did not shatter Frenzi's confidence. It was a costly error, one for which his next design would have to compensate. But there were ways of making up the ground that had been lost. The city might require a stern example, as a token of good faith, and Frenzi was the man who could provide it, on demand. When all concerned had been persuaded of his personal sincerity, negotiations could proceed. And if a few more lives were lost in the process, it would not be Frenzi's choice. The blood would lie where it belonged, on other hands.

In time, when he had taught them all a lesson to remember, Frenzi would emerge as someone to be reckoned with in both dimensions of the city. Underground, his word was law already, instantly obeyed by every soldier under his command—for the time being. And topside, once his own humiliation was forgotten and the humbling of the mighty government was the only topic of conversation, Frenzi's star would have risen to the zenith. His name would be revered alongside that of Guiliano, Garibaldi and the rest. The common people would be quick to recognize their savior as he waged relentless war against the state.

Already, he was chief among the so-called "terrorists" of Italy. The Red Brigades had withered to a shadow of their former strength, ranks decimated by arrests resulting from an incident involving an American general a few years before. The old Brigades were still a force to reckon with in Rome and its environs, but increasingly, the field of revolutionary action cried aloud for younger, fresher blood. If some of it was spilled before the payoff, Frenzi was prepared to write the losses off as a predictable result of urban warfare. Even a commander such as himself, with courage and intelligence to spare, could not expect to fight a war without accepting casualties.

It would be worth the risk, worth almost any price, to see his latest plan in operation. If it functioned smoothly—and he did not see how it could fail—the scheme would easily surpass the greatest efforts of the Red Brigades, the Mafia. His ingenuity would leave the competition speechless, sick with envy; they would call on him with hats in hand, to beg for his indulgence and to study at his feet.

It never once occurred to Carlo Frenzi that his ego might be coloring his perception, building up unrealistic expectations. Confident in his ability to win a stunning victory against the state, he entertained no thought of failure. If his plot should fail, then he would die, together with the men who followed him. But Frenzi found it difficult to grasp the concept of defeat. The death of Arthur Bishop was an aberration, one of the inevitable setbacks any field commander must expect in warfare. Had not Garibaldi suffered setbacks of his own, before he conquered Sicily and Naples? Had not the United States endured bitter losses, time and time again, before the antislavery forces had emerged victorious in civil war? An officer who never lost was never tested, never tried in terms of his endurance and ability to stand the heat. Already tested, Carlo Frenzi knew himself to be a winner, and he planned accordingly.

It would soon be time to test his master plan, to trot it out for all the world to see, and they would marvel at his genius. He would not, could not fail. He had anticipated every danger, running down the pitfalls in his mind, preparing his defenses with the cunning of a master strategist. His name might still be new to the authorities, to other freedom fighters who had been around for years, but there was a maturity about his thinking, in his preparations, that belied his age and seeming inexperience.

A child of rural peasant stock, the field commander of the RJC had grown up lean and strong. His father had been murdered by the mafiosi, claimed by an obscure vendetta, when the boy was twelve years old. The family's sole surviving male, he had been marked for death himself before he fled to Naples, living hand-to-mouth and sleeping on the streets, advancing swiftly into petty crime. He had become adept at swindles, picking pockets, burglarizing homes and shops. As the junior member of a street gang, he had battled with his brothers to protect a piece of scabrous territory in the slums. At eighteen, he had killed the leader of a rival gang—an accidental slaying, to be sure, but the authorities ignored such fine points in dispensing warrants of arrest.

The young man fled to Rome one step ahead of the police. His reputation had preceded him, and he was known within the circles of the Roman underworld as a man of respect, well suited to serious work. Petty hustlers steered clear, jobs were offered, and Frenzi was honored with overtures from the Camorra, which he politely declined. He had seen how the soldiers—the mafiosi and the camorristi—worked for peanuts while the bosses fattened on the sweat of their underlings. If Frenzi was to labor, he would labor for himself, deciding which jobs merited attention, which were worth the risks involved. If there were profits to be made, he meant to earn them for himself, employing backup muscle when and where it might be necessary, holding out the lion's share as recompense for all the planning that a leader was compelled to do.

He might have realized that the Camorra—like the Mafia, with which it shared so much in common—would not casually accept rejection from an independent hoodlum on the streets. Reprisals were inevitable, but his youthful arrogance had blinded Frenzi to the subtlety of his opponents. He was braced for an assault, attempts upon his life, perhaps... but there were other, less flamboyant ways of dealing with an upstart in the Roman underworld. When one of Frenzi's part-time flunkies had approached him with the perfect job, he had not suspected treachery. It was a residential burglary, with furs and jewelry included in the haul, and it had been too good to pass up. In fact, it had been too good all around, and the police were waiting for him as he slithered through a downstairs window, burdened with the loot that would have made him relatively wealthy. Snared outside the house and empty-handed, Frenzi's partner had agreed to testify and thereby save himself. The squealer's sentence was reduced to probation; Frenzi drew a term of seven years in prison.

Loss of liberty is often educational, and Frenzi viewed the prison as a secondary school of sorts; the inmates were both faculty and student body. As a young, attractive man, he drew the undesired attention of assorted prison wolves, the homosexuals who prey on newer convicts, seeking to accumulate a "harem" for themselves. At first he turned away their crude advances with a sort of rigid courtesy; when they persisted, issued threats, the object of their lust responded swiftly, violently. One man was dead, another blinded for life before they got the message. Carlo Frenzi was secure, and he got down to business.

"Business," in a penitentiary, consists of doing time and making contacts. Doing time is relatively easy, once the inmate sets his mind to living in a cage, with no immediate prospect of liberty. Time passes; days of the week soon become confused and indistinguishable from one another. If a prisoner maintains perspective, keeps his wits about him, he survives. When self-control is lost, the mind and body swiftly follow, wasted in pursuit of such distinctly hazardous diversions as prison may provide.

As for the contacts, some are useful to an inmate while in prison, others when—and if—he is released. The former may provide a convict with the little luxuries that make life inside more bearable: tobacco, alcohol, illicit drugs, the conjugal liaisons with a woman that will never be revealed on any visitor's agenda. Outside contacts are by far the more important of the two, providing that an inmate has no thought of going straight upon release. A working criminal can never have too many friends, too many tight connections in the world outside the prison walls. No matter what his line of trade, the outlaw will eventually require support: attorneys, bondsmen, hideouts, weapons merchants, doctors who neglect to fill out certain mandatory documents in case of bullet wounds. No other place on earth provides the working criminal with such a wealth of contacts as the modern maximum-security facility.

The prison is a college in its own right, schooling novices in all the finer points of crime. Professors in the gray academy may seem deficient in credentials, having obviously failed to honor the eleventh commandment: Thou shalt not get caught. But each man serving time—each lifer, espe-

cially—has years of criminal experience and countless jobs
behind him by the time he takes a fall. The very fact of capture and imprisonment is valuable in itself; the young learn
best by sound example, and a proved failure is the best example of all. Mistakes are memorized by cons in prison, all
the better to be shunned in future. From the groundwork of
a failure sprouts tomorrow's victory.

Of the seven years to which he had been sentenced, Frenzi
served a fraction more than five. The other time had been
remitted due to good behavior, with a year removed as the
result of Frenzi's voluntary intervention in a hostage situation. He had saved the warden's chief assistant from a psy-
cho run amok, sustaining superficial stab wounds in the
process. Some of those among the prison population had
been prone to question Frenzi's action, but the obvious reward had silenced their muttered criticism, and had set the
worst among them searching for an opportunity to be of
service, even risk his life in the pursuit of an accelerated exit
to the streets.

Emerging from captivity, the future revolutionary had yet
to develop a coherent vision of political involvement. He
was well connected in the Roman underworld—though his
discovery of the catacombs, the *real* underworld, was years
away—and Frenzi again turned to crime in order to score a
profit—by any means available. There was a score to settle,
with the *camorristi* who had set him up and landed him in
prison, and the debt was paid by Frenzi personally, in the
best tradition of vendetta. There was no one to suspect his
role in the assassinations of three ranking mobsters and a
top lieutenant of the carabinieri, no one to connect the former model prisoner with crimes of such unprecedented violence.

One lesson Frenzi had learned in prison was anticipation. He learned to read the coming trends in crime as some
men read the headlines, picking out tomorrow's scores while

others—the police included—struggled to keep pace with
what had gone before.

The late 1970s had been years of turmoil, with talk of
revolution that was obviously going nowhere much beyond
the usual student demonstrations, riots and the odd explosion, usually aimed at the Americans. As dedicated bands
of revolutionary terrorists began to organize in Rome, as
they were in Berlin and Paris, London and Madrid, the
watchful eye of Carlo Frenzi had noted the potential for a
handy profit in the changing trend of violent crime.

If Frenzi had been educated in the works of Marx, he
might readily have agreed that organized religion was the
people's opiate, designed to occupy their minds while bel-
lies growled with hunger. Almost certainly, however, he
would have displayed an equal scorn for politics of any
kind. A cynic to the bone, before and after his experience
behind the walls, he knew that politicians were predomi-
nantly thieves or fools, and neither class was mutually exclusive. Wild-eyed revolutionaries wasted too much energy
sniping at police and bombing banks in the name of the
cause, when they could just as easily have looted millions
from the vault and saved their ammunition for a roaring
getaway.

It had occurred to Frenzi that the revolutionary ranks
must necessarily include a complement of mercenaries,
gunning for a profit, and a brief reconnaissance had proved
him out. In fact, a group of purely mercenary terrorists had
already organized themselves for action, entering the kidnap racket in a minor way, expanding as the ransoms drib-
bled in. They had called themselves Red Justice, and while
their activities had little obvious relationship to any "Red"
philosophy—and no relationship at all to justice—it was
name enough. He had attempted to enlist, and he had been
awaiting call-up orders when the bubble burst.

The problem as he saw it, was a case of blind ambition
running far ahead of physical capacity. Somewhere within

the Column's hierarchy, someone had approved the kidnap of a military leader's wife and daughter. There had been risk enough in settling on Americans, a risk compounded by the failure of the RJC to heed persistent warnings out of Washington. A president with nerve enough to call the bluff of terrorists was sitting in the Oval Office now, and unbeknownst to members of Red Justice, he had set in motion the machinery for a restricted, covert war against his nation's enemies. It was the luck of Frenzi's predecessors that they fell into the category of a field test, human targets for the new, accelerated antiterrorist campaign.

Or so he believed, at any rate. It mattered not to Frenzi that survivors spoke in terms of combat with a single man. Destruction of the RJC had not been so complete that he could salvage nothing from the ashes. It had been ridiculously easy, come to think of it; how many greedy guns were anxious to forget the recent, painful lesson and enlist beneath the bloodied banner for another fling at gold and glory? The abduction of another U.S. hostage had been calculated to deliver Frenzi's message that the Column was alive and well, in spite of all the thunderbolts from Washington. If he had underestimated his adversary's capacity for vengeance, he would not be guilty of the same mistake again. Next time they moved against him, he would have covered all the angles in advance.

Perhaps with help from Mike Belasko.

He found a pay phone, dropped the coins and dialed a number from memory. At such an hour, Frenzi could be fairly certain that his contact was at home; he could be certain, also, of a temper tantrum when he roused the older man from sleep, but he was paying for results, and he would have them on his own terms. Now.

He waited through four rings, amused to paint a mental portrait of his contact, as he struggled up from sleep, entangled in his blankets, cursing now and groping blindly for the telephone receiver.

"*Sì?*"

"Good morning, Lupo."

"Uh? Good morning? Do you know what time it is?"

Then the code name registered with sleepy brain cells, cutting off the tirade. Frenzi's contact cleared his throat, an audible attempt to keep his wits about him now. "What do you want?"

"I need to have a name checked through your files, without delay."

"A name? A *name*? You wake me up at such an hour for a *name*?"

When Frenzi spoke again, his voice was like the cracking of a whip. "Do not forget yourself, my friend. Remember your position, and the price of failure."

"Yes." But grudgingly. "What is the name?"

"Belasko. First name Mike, or Michael. An American."

"What is he wanted for?"

"If I knew that, you would be useless to me, Lupo."

"Ah."

The man's tone told Frenzi that he might well have preferred to be considered useless. As a ranking officer in the security police, his duty was eradication of all terrorists, including the Red Justice Column. As a greedy man with lavish appetites, he had seen fit to sell his soul, and now that soul belonged to Carlo Frenzi, unconditionally. If the lazy bastard failed him, Frenzi had enough on file to guarantee him a substantial prison sentence... and a former lawman was as good as dead in prison. Lupo knew all that, had known it from the start, and Frenzi tolerated his irascibility, but only to a point.

"I need this information soon."

"How soon?"

"No later than this afternoon... say, one o'clock."

"I'll do my best."

"I know that, Lupo."

Frenzi cradled the receiver, perfectly secure in the knowledge that he would know Mike Belasko's history before the day was out. A man of such accomplishments would be no stranger to the police, the military, even Interpol. There was a file on Mike Belasko somewhere, and with Lupo's help, with a request from the security police to speed things up, the secrets of that file would be revealed to Frenzi.

And if his dossier stood up, Belasko might be useful to the cause. A man of his experience, his ruthlessness, would be an asset to the RJC. If he did not check out, for any reason... well, disposal of a charlatan would be the least of Frenzi's problems. There was room enough for one more body in the catacombs and tunnels. Another martyr laid to rest beneath the streets of Rome.

He hoped Belasko was legitimate, for they could use him now, of all times, with the Column's greatest coup mere days away. Regardless of the stranger's record, though, there was a test that he must pass before he could be finally accepted as a soldier of the cause. A test that lesser men might easily refuse.

If Mike Belasko took the challenge, Frenzi would be able to evaluate the man's performance under pressure. If he failed, evaluation of his skill would be superfluous. The dead were useless to a revolutionary movement.

Whichever way it went, if Frenzi's houseguest failed to pass the inspection of his record, or if he should bungle the initiation test, he would no longer be a problem.

He would simply be a corpse.

7

The cheap cigar reminded Hal Brognola of the brand he had
been forced to buy when he was going through law school
and when he had been a junior agent with the Bureau,
working offices from Jacksonville to Portland, paying his
dues. He didn't smoke anymore, thanks to some subtle
nagging from his wife, but more importantly to the realiza-
tion that he was damaging his health. A few frown lines
worked their way into his forehead at this last thought. Hell,
a man like Hal could be in perfect health, yet in this line of
work a single bullet could drop you in your tracks. Hal stifled a sudden urge to laugh out loud, thinking he'd be a
healthy corpse, then.

Those early days hadn't been exactly good, but increasingly Brognola thought that he would trade his present life
to have them back. His pay had been a damned sight lower
then, but, on the other hand, it had cost a damned sight less
to live. The kids were still to come, and even with the hours
he had been putting in, there had been time enough to spend
with Helen, dreaming, making love or simply walking hand
in hand. A simpler time—and better for it—lost, except in
memories.

Brognola knew that he was growing maudlin, and he
shook the moment off before the old, familiar ache could
reach too deep inside. He dropped the sodden cigar into his
ashtray and scooped up a handful of manila folders from his
desk to fan away the rancid smoke. Goddamn nostalgia,

anyway. Why did the sweetest memories have so much pain attached?

He set the folders down again and spent a moment drumming anxious fingers on the topmost cover. It was labeled Confidential, but he had the contents memorized, emblazoned on the inside of his eyelids. He could rattle off the contents, page by page, without referring to the copy in the folder resting underneath his hand. He knew it all by heart, and it was useless to him now.

The subject of the confidential file was an obscure Italian terrorist group, the Red Justice Column. The one-time subject of a Bolan blitz had been presumed extinct. But now the gang was back in business with a vengeance, chalking up a bungled snatch with four lives lost. Only God knew what else lay in store, what wild atrocities were in the works already.

In comparison with other European terrorists, Red Justice was strictly a bush-league operation. To Brognola's knowledge, it did not possess the strong financial backing of the IRA, nor could its strategists prepare a raid with the meticulous precision of the Baader-Meinhof gang. In terms of casualties, Red Justice couldn't hold a candle to the ETA in Spain, nor could its reputation match the fading Red Brigades for sheer ferocity. From the beginning, members of the RJC were recognized as bandits, plain and simple, seeking to disguise their crimes with revolutionary trappings. Strictly small-time.

Until now.

A part of Hal's uneasiness could be accounted for by the survival of the group itself. Bolan had eradicated every trace of the RJC terror merchants when he had pursued them during his Colonel John Phoenix incarnation. Destruction of the gang had been confirmed, together with elimination of its KGB control. If there were any survivors, they had failed to surface publicly...at least until the snatch on Arthur Bishop and the bungled ransom drop.

Brognola did not blame Bolan for Bishop's death.
Plainly, members of the RJC had planned a double cross,
intending to secure the cash and keep the hostage, while
larger sums were raised to purchase Bishop's freedom.
Someone had been nervous at the drop, had tried to ice the
courier, and Bolan had responded with an instinct born of
long experience. Survival was the soldier's top priority, and
Arthur Bishop's death had been a tragic, unavoidable result of RJC duplicity. Case closed.

Except that three dead goons in Naples did not pull the
plug on what was shaping up to be another reign of terror.
It would take a great deal more to put Red Justice out of
business permanently, wipe the stain away forever, and the
Executioner was working on that "something more" right
now. His life was on the line as long as he remained in Italy,
and there could be no rest for Hal Brognola while his closest friend was isolated in the hellgrounds.

Theirs was a unique relationship, by any standard. Hal
could not have readily defined their situation if his life depended on it, but it scarcely mattered. The connection was,
and would remain, top secret, known to fewer than a dozen
other living persons. One of those was sitting in the Oval
Office, waiting for an update on the Roman situation; the
remainder were involved with other battles of their own in
the continuing assault on worldwide terrorism. None would
ever share his knowledge with the outside world.

Brognola and the Executioner had met while Bolan was
a hunted fugitive, and something had sparked between
them, made them allies of the soul before they ever stood
together on the firing line. Brognola had risked his life and
his career to back the soldier's one-man war against a cancer eating at the vitals of America, and when that war
against the Mafia was climaxed by a victory of sorts, he had
persuaded Bolan to accept a secret pardon, join the everlasting covert war against another kind of savage. Born
again as Colonel John Phoenix, Bolan bore the cleansing

fire against his country's enemies, at home and in the killing fields of distant lands, until the treachery of trusted allies cost him everything, propelled him into outer darkness to resume his status as a renegade.

The loss of Bolan, in conjunction with the other losses suffered in a night of fire and blood, had very nearly doomed the Phoenix program. It survived, depending the the men of Able Team and Phoenix Force to give it striking power, a reconstituted team at Stony Man to keep the home fires burning and the machinery running smoothly. But Brognola ever felt the absence of his closest friend and comrade. Cautious feelers were extended by the White House, and summarily rejected by the man in black. It had required a crisis in Brognola's private life, the abduction of his wife and children by the Mafia and lackeys in the CIA, to put the soldier back on speaking terms with Washington....

Again, offers were extended, and apparently ignored. The soldier needed time in which to think, to compose the terms on which he would consider working for the government part-time. The offer of another pardon seemed to make no difference; neither was he interested in returning to the Phoenix base at Stony Man. Accustomed to his independence, to surviving by his wits, the Executioner was not enlisting as a full-time member of the team. Instead, Brognola was provided with a list of numbers where the warrior could be reached, but only in the direst need. While Bolan finally agreed to make himself selectively available, he would not accept every mission that was offered. The Executioner had enough enemies of his own and would choose assignments carefully, rejecting any efforts to manipulate his war, co-opt the personal crusade that had begun so long ago in Pittsfield. When he took on a mission, as in the case of Arthur Bishop and the RJC, he would rely upon the government for background information only; otherwise, he would be standing, fighting, on his own.

The White House had been dubious, disturbed and righteously annoyed, but there had been no thought of turning down the soldier's counteroffer. Bolan was an asset to the team on any terms, and if his independence made him something of a wild card, it would also guarantee deniability in case he bought the farm while acting on official business.

The rejuvenated RJC had been a mission Bolan couldn't pass. It was unfinished business. The Executioner could no more turn away while resurrected enemies continued to wreak their inhuman havoc than he could voluntarily stop breathing. The snafu with Arthur Bishop would increase his grim determination; Bolan would not feel responsible for Bishop's death, but he would recognize the need to find his killers and terminate them before they could disrupt the lives of other innocents.

If Bolan did not succeed in Italy, if he died, Brognola knew that part of him would wither up and die...but he would live to fight with renewed vigor, and keep on fighting while his strength remained. In Bolan's memory, and in the knowledge that their cause was right. Each of them had a solemn duty to fulfill, and if either one should falter in pursuance of that duty, he would lose a great deal more than life.

A man who could not face himself was worse than dead. A man deprived of honor, burdened with the guilty knowledge of a duty unfulfilled, was marking time, merely waiting for the Reaper to collect his bones and carry them away.

The purring of the telephone beside him startled Hal out of his reverie. He answered on the second ring, anticipation knotting inside his stomach like a nervous bride's first meal. His secretary's smooth, familiar voice did nothing to assuage the tension creeping up his spine and settling like leaden weights behind his eyes.

"Long distance, sir. From Rome. Security police. Inspector Bertolucci."

"Put him on."

"Yes, sir."

The line went hollow for an instant, ringing with the tell-tale murmur of an overseas connection. Hunched across his desk, his knuckles whitened where he gripped the telephone, Brognola waited for the caller to identify himself.

"Allo?"

"Hello?"

"Signor Brognola?"

"Speaking."

"Ah. Inspector General Riccardo Bertolucci, with Italian Security Police."

"Good morning, sir."

"Good afternoon."

"Of course. What can I do for you?"

He knew the answer going in, of course, but there was the charade, amenities to be observed.

"We have received a bulletin concerning an American, one Mike Belasko, issued by your department of Justice. I am seeking further information on this man, and I have been referred to you, *signor*."

"I'll tell you anything I can, if you'll hold on a moment."

"Certainly."

Brognola spent the time attempting to relax, allowing Bertolucci to believe that he was searching for Belasko's file. In fact, there was no file per se; Belasko's background was a pure invention, and the "facts" were safely stored inside Brognola's memory, available for instant recall. It would not do, of course, for him to have the "file" too readily available. Belasko was presumably a suspect of the watch and wait variety; there would be hotter items on his desk, and Bertolucci would be conscious of the fact if Hal appeared too knowledgeable, too eager to please.

"Here we are," he said at last. "Belasko, Michael John. Born 3-8-49. Three tours with the U.S. Army, Special

Forces, two of those in Vietnam. Received a general discharge following an altercation with superiors, no formal charges filed. Military decorations include the Silver Star, Bronze Star, three Purple Hearts. Rated expert, heavy weapons, demolition. Fifty-six registered kills in the course of his two combat tours. No fixed address since military discharge. Civilian employment unknown; suspected mercenary, smuggler of arms and other contraband. Reported active in Angola, Biafra, Guatemala, Nicaragua, as a gun for hire. Apolitical, available to highest bidder. Rap sheet follows."

There was silence on the line as Hal picked up a stack of interoffice memos, riffled through them for the benefit of sound effects before continuing his recitation off the cuff.

"Arrested in New York on charges of felonious assault, 11-16-80. Charges dropped for lack of evidence. Detained Chicago, 7-13-81, in reference to explosives. Released without charges after questioning. Arrested in Miami, 9-11-83, for driving with an altered operator's license. Fined $150 and released. No subsequent arrests or interviews on file, but he is one of several suspects in the execution slaying of an anti-Castro exile spokesman in Miami, August, 1982. Suspected as a possible supplier of the weapons used to rob an armored transport van, Schenectady, New York, September, 1984. Suspected of complicity in the assassination of a Contra leader in Honduras, January, 1985. Suspected . . . Well, I think you get the picture."

"Yes, indeed. Signor Belasko is a busy man."

"We call it armed and dangerous. Between the two of us, I liked him for a bank job down in Houston, six or seven months ago. Two sheriffs deputies and a pedestrian killed instantly by automatic-weapons fire. One of the tellers took a week to die."

"A desperate individual."

"You called that right. May I assume from the inquiry that you've got our boy on tap?"

A heartbeat's hesitation on the other end informed Brognola that Inspector General Bertolucci wasn't used to thinking quickly on his feet.

"Ah, no, unfortunately not. But as I said, we have received a rather sketchy bulletin...how do you say it in America?"

"A BOL. That's 'be on lookout.' "

"*Sì*. Precisely. But without a better feeling for the man himself..."

"I understand, and I appreciate your call. If everyone was half as conscientious, we might have Belasko in the bag by now."

"Of course, I will be back in touch if he is found within our jurisdiction."

"We'd appreciate it...and Inspector? Thanks again for calling."

"It was nothing. Ciao."

The line went dead, and Hal Brognola slowly cradled the receiver. "Ciao yourself, you bastard."

He was not deceived by Bertolucci's casual tone, the facile explanation for his call. A routine bulletin from Justice, circulated through the offices of Interpol, would not elicit transatlantic calls unless the subject had been sighted and was under scrutiny. Belasko—that is, Bolan—must have surfaced somewhere and attracted the attention of security police. He had not been arrested—Bertolucci would have mentioned that, no doubt—but he was recognized, and he was being watched. If the security police decided to arrest him, even for routine interrogation...

Suddenly Brognola was assaulted by another chilling prospect. In its former incarnation, members of the Red Justice had displayed a talent for corrupting civil servants. An Italian senator was bought and paid for, as were officers of NATO and NOCS. Inspector General Bertolucci might as easily be on the payroll now, reporting back to someone in the RJC on Bolan's bona fides.

That meant contact, almost certainly. Unless the RJC was interested in Mike Belasko, they would not waste time and energy in running down his background. It was easier to shine him on or put a bullet through his brain and dump him in an alley. Background checks suggested possible acceptance as a soldier of the cause, and that put Bolan where he had to be if there was any hope at all of ringing down the curtain on his savage human targets.

Contact, infiltration, meant that Bolan was encroaching on the area of highest risk potential. Because he was a stranger and a foreigner, the members of the RJC would be alert to any deviation from his cover, any slightest indication that Belasko was, in fact, a ringer. If his masquerade should be discovered by the enemy, then Bolan would be killed. It was that simple, and that final.

Brognola knew the soldier's skill when it came down to camouflage, impersonations of the enemy. On other battlefields, the Executioner had infiltrated families of the Mafia and groups of terrorists, annihilating from within. On rare occasions where his battle mask had failed him, Bolan's ingenuity and courage had been adequate to see him safely through the hellgrounds.

Each time he played the deadly game, the odds against survival lengthened, whittling the soldier's slim advantage of surprise until sheer guts and steely will remained. How many times could Bolan play the death hand, come up winners in a game where all the cards were stacked against him from the start?

Brognola didn't like to think about it, especially since the grim, inevitable end of Bolan's war provoked intensive pangs of guilt within himself. No matter that the soldier's arrangement with the White House left him free to pick and choose his own assignments, free from outside pressure or control. And never mind the fact that Bolan had already opted for the dead-end life-style months before he met Brognola for the first time, in Miami. In his heart, Hal knew that Bolan's sense of duty—to his country, to his private war—had predetermined his reaction to that final offer from the White House. Bolan could no more have turned the offer down than he could shed his sense of duty, turn his back on everything that he had fought for all these bloody years.

The warrior's friendship with Brognola played a role in his decision to enlist, albeit on a part-time basis, for another tour of duty on the fringes of the Phoenix program. Though Bolan was remote from Stony Man in body, his heart was somewhere in the Blue Ridge Mountains of Virginia, and a part of him was always with Brognola, too.

And there was guilt involved, oh yes.

Not a day went by without Brognola's questioning his own relationship with the Executioner. To what extent had he distracted Bolan from his primary mission, serving as the Judas goat and leading Bolan into greater jeopardy on behalf of strangers?

Never mind. There were no strangers for the Executioner where helpless victims were concerned. The guy had proved that much a thousand times and more. There were no strangers, either, when it came to targeting the savages who preyed upon those helpless victims. They were Bolan's mortal enemies from birth, regardless of their names or nationalities, in spite of ethnic backgrounds or political philosophies. A Nazi or a Communist, a savage white or black or red was all the same to Bolan. All fair game.

And if the Executioner had never met Brognola, never met the President, he still would have hunted the savages wherever they were found. Because he saw it as his duty, to the victimized members of his family and to the countless other victims who had crossed his path from San Francisco to Saigon, from Mazatlán to Moscow.

In some forgotten age, Mack Bolan might have been a knight in shining armor, saving damsels in distress and stalking dragons through medieval forests. But, as luck would have it, Bolan's everlasting war was here and now, against modern savages who would subvert a civilized society, initiate a new Dark Age in the 1980s. He was a professional survivor, living on the edge and waging war relentlessly against his age-old enemies. Brognola couldn't have distracted or diverted Bolan if he had tried.

Somehow, the knowledge didn't make Hal feel a great deal better.

Somewhere in the bustling Roman underworld, his closest friend was risking everything to root the dragon out and slaughter it before the monster had a chance to set the world on fire. If he succeeded, there would always be another dragon and another challenge waiting for him just around the corner. If he failed...

Then it was death, and Hal would live with that, as he had lived with other tragedies before. And he would keep on fighting, until the bastards got him, too.

And with his dying breath, the Fed would pray that there was someone out there, somewhere, who would grasp the fallen torch before it guttered into darkness.

8

A rustling sound woke Bolan from his nodding slumber and he stirred, surprised to find that he had slept. Against the far wall of the cubicle, perhaps ten feet away, a mangy sewer rat was staring at him with defiance in its beady eyes. The gray nose wrinkled as it caught Bolan's scent, transmitting an alarm to the synapses of the rodent's brain. It recognized a threat, but it was trapped, prepared to battle for its life against the hulking enemy.

He knew the feeling, sure, and Bolan didn't have the energy or interest for a game of cat and mouse. He stamped one foot and made as if to rise, the camp chair creaking with his weight. The rat saw daylight, or its sham equivalent, and bolted through the open doorway of its tiny cell.

Outside, a boot slammed forcefully against the ground; the grinding crack of heel on bone eclipsed a strangled squeal. Italian curses reached Mack Bolan's ears before Petrucchi thrust his head around the corner, glowering.

"There is no end to these filthy rats," he complained. "We kill at least a hundred of them every day, and there are always more."

"I sympathize."

The soldier's watchdog looked confused, but did not pursue the subject. He was stretching sleepily, and Bolan knew he could take out the skinny gunner any time he wanted to. Approaching from his blind side, one hand cupped beneath his chin, the other braced against the cranium, then a single, violent twist to separate the vertebrae and snap the spinal column where it joined the gunner's skull.

As if he were capable of mind reading, Petrucchi edged away from Bolan as the soldier left his cubicle. There was a certain wariness behind the little gunner's eyes; perhaps he had begun to question his own wisdom in selecting Mike Belasko. For an instant, Bolan thought that Carlo Frenzi might already have returned with the information he'd gleaned from the security check, but if the word had come back negative, the terrorists would not have let him sleep. A glance along the gallery revealed no sign of Frenzi, and he finally concluded that Petrucchi's nervousness was something personal, within the man himself.

There might be problems down the road with that one, but the Executioner had other things on his mind. Petrucchi was the least of all his worries; on a scale of one to ten, the little gunner didn't even rate.

Survival was the top priority. Disruption of the RJC was secondary, but the two were inextricably entwined. He was committed to the mission now, already deep inside the viper's lair, and there was no way he could disengage without committing virtual suicide. No matter what the ultimate report from Frenzi on his background check, the Executioner would have to take advantage of his placement, using every trick and tool at his disposal to annihilate his enemies.

Before he could wage war inside the viper's nest, however, Bolan would require a more detailed reconnaissance. And there was no time like the present.

"How about the ten-cent tour?"

"Eh?"

"A look around? How 'bout it?"

Enzio was dubious, but something in the man's face told Bolan that he found it risky to refuse. He had been placed in charge of Mike Belasko, after all, with orders from the top to keep him satisfied until the time arrived to welcome him aboard or drop him down the nearest empty shaft. However it turned out, Petrucchi, for the moment, was a soldier under orders. If Belasko was accepted, Enzio might well be punished for refusing such an innocent request.

"Too much to see right now," he offered, plainly hoping that Belasko would postpone his tour to another time.

"Let's hit the highlights, then."

Defeated, and plainly disappointed, Bolan's watchdog nodded in a kind of weary resignation.

"This way."

Bolan trailed him farther along the gallery, past cubicles that opened off to either side. Approximately half of them were occupied, and Bolan made a rapid head count, coming up with something less than forty guns on site. If there were other staging areas beneath the streets of Rome, as Frenzi had suggested, and if each was similarly staffed, then Bolan was up against a private army. No chaotic handful of demented terrorists or mercenary bandits this time out; the RJC had grown, and from the looks of things, its members had acquired some discipline along the way.

At one point, Bolan and Petrucchi passed a team of gunners stripping automatic weapons, cleaning each part meticulously, wiping down the pieces with oily rags as they were reassembled. Bolan saw the usual complement of M-16s and AK-47s, but the two M-60s took him by surprise. The ammo belts were coiled beside them, waiting for a double check by hand before they were returned to OD crates for storage. And the troops could raise some hell with those on a crowded street in Rome.

It would be Bolan's task to see that no one got the chance.

They walked another fifty feet along the gallery and found that other denim warriors were engaged in shaping plastic charges, molding them by hand and weighing each upon a butcher's scale. The finished charges were, in turn, delivered to a long-faced individual who had the task of seating timers in the plastic blocks, adjusting detonators and

double-checking wires. Assembling the charges in advance
was risky. An accident could set them off and bring the ancient stone cascading down around their ears. Again, the
soldier wondered whether accidental detonation underground would cause much damage on the street, three
stories overhead. He started tallying the finished charges,
then dropped the count at forty, deciding that it wasn't
worth the risk.

Petrucchi seemed attuned to Bolan's mood, or maybe the
explosives made him nervous. Either way, the man was relieved when Bolan left the demolition crew, proceeding on
along the gallery. The tunnel curved away from them some
thirty feet ahead, but in the distance, Bolan could already
hear rough voices shouting in Italian, cheering on some
contest that was hidden from his eyes. Petrucchi cast a
sidelong glance at Bolan, smiling for the first time since they
met, and the reversal of his dour mood set off alarm bells in
the soldier's mind. He followed Enzio along the tunnel,
braced for anything, but still he was surprised by what
awaited them around the corner.

Another columbarium had been converted into something of an arena for athletic contests, and perhaps two
dozen gunners ranged around the tiny stadium's perimeter
as they approached. Bolan automatically revised his head
count, growing even more concerned with the odds, but he
was soon distracted by the objects of his attention in the
center of the ring.

Two burly warriors clad in shorts and T-shirts were engaged in a display of martial arts, each circling the other
with a caution born of painful past experience. There
seemed to be no rules of combat, no particular technique
involved. As Bolan watched, the taller of the two combatants launched a kick at his opponent's face. Prepared for the
aggressive move, his adversary lunged beneath the kick and
drove a sharp karate chop into the tall man's groin. Bolan
winced sympathetically as the aggressor folded up and top-

pled to the stony floor, teeth clenched, eyes bulging, like a victim of an electric shock. The smaller man danced backward, shadowboxing through a graceful exercise that set his muscles rippling underneath the T-shirt that he wore.

Petrucchi glanced at Bolan, curiosity imprinted on his face, as if he sought Belasko's personal assessment of the match.

"Not bad," the Executioner allowed.

Petrucchi grinned, a weasel's smirk.

"You practice the martial arts, *signor*?"

He realized precisely what was coming next, but Bolan saw no easy way to disengage.

"I hold my own."

Petrucchi's smile was threatening to rip his face in two now, as he spoke to the other troops in rapid-fire Italian. Muttered comments passed around the ring of faces, then one of the commandos took a long stride forward, toward the center of the makeshift ring.

The bastard was a giant, at least six foot seven, broad across the chest and shoulders, with a rough-hewn face that bore the scars of countless contests. Wiry hair had been cut short against the skull, denying a handhold to his enemies in combat, and his massive hands were working hungrily as he took Bolan's measure from across the ring.

"Armand is . . . how you say . . . our champion," Petrucchi said, beaming. "No man has ever beaten him."

"I can believe it."

"You would care to try?"

It was the last thing Bolan wanted, but refusal would reveal a strain of cowardice in Mike Belasko, and the Executioner could not afford that misinformation to be imparted to his enemies. If he backed down now, he would be sacrificing any credibility he might already have achieved.

"Why not?"

Petrucchi whispered urgently to the giant for a moment, and an ugly snicker worked its way around the ring of mercenary terrorists. Bolan didn't need it broadcast over a PA system to know what Enzio was saying to the hulk, and Bolan made up his mind on the spot that he would punch out Petrucchi the first time he had the opportunity without endangering his mission.

Bolan slipped off his jacket and spent another moment removing the shoulder rigging. Finished, he deliberately bypassed Enzio's extended hand, entrusting coat and weapon to a total stranger rather than his chosen escort. There was time to register the insult in Petrucchi's eyes, a heartbeat to draw satisfaction from the weasel's anger, then a pair of massive arms was locked around his chest and he was airborne, hurtling through space.

He touched down on one shoulder, rolling, fighting to ignore the sudden, wrenching pain of impact. Breathless, dizzy, Bolan scrambled to his feet and faced his adversary, circling to his right and backward as the human hulk advanced. The guy was smiling at him, and his buddies on the sidelines were already urging him on, jeering at Bolan derisively. The Executioner ignored them, trusting them to stay out of the fight—at least for now—and get their kicks from ogling the show.

He let his adversary close the distance, feinting to his left and stepping close inside the giant's guard. The snap kick should have finished it, his heel impacting on the big guy's nose—except that Bolan's snap kick never landed. Steely fingers caught his ankle in midair and lifted, twisting, jerking Bolan off his feet and swinging him around like a slab of meat suspended from a butcher's hook.

This time, he was prepared for the release, the hurtling flight, and Bolan broke his fall with outstretched hands, ignoring the abrasion of his palms on rough, unfinished stone. He scrambled to his feet again, unable to suppress a grimace at the sudden twinge of pain that emanated from his hip. A few more brutal moves like that, and he could kiss it all goodbye.

The giant lumbered toward him, and Bolan stood his ground, content to wait it out and let the other guy expend his energy. Ten feet, and Bolan braced himself, requiring no artistic skill whatsoever to appear fatigued and winded. When the hulk had closed within six feet, the massive arms already reaching for him, Bolan ducked beneath the groping hands and put his weight behind a blow directed at the giant's solar plexus.

The jolt of impact raced up Bolan's arm and through his shoulder, but he had no time to think about it as a heavy forearm slammed across his shoulders, drove him down on all fours. There was a ringing in his ears, and Bolan realized the other terrorists were cheering his opponent now, encouraging him to destroy the brash American. The soldier caught his breath and tried to rise, but never got the chance.

A booted size fourteen caught Bolan in the ribs and emptied his lungs on impact, flipped him over on his back. The lights around him seemed to dim, and there were tiny, dancing flecks of color in his vision now. The ringing in his ears was deafening, and Bolan might have let it carry him away, except that he was conscious of the danger closing on him. The giant meant to grind his face, his ribs and spine beneath those combat boots, and he would do it if the soldier couldn't find a way to stop him.

A hazy glance was all it took to find his adversary bearing down upon him with a titan's stride. The move would take precision timing, and Bolan had to get it right the first time. There would be no second chance. If he miscalculated, he was finished.

Standing over him, the giant raised one foot, prepared to bring it down on Bolan's rib cage. Groaning with the effort and the pain it cost him, Bolan brought his knees up to his chest, already rolling over on his side, heels locked together as they pistoned out toward impact with his adversary's knee.

The giant bellowed, toppled, sprawling facedown on the rough-hewn stone. He might have pinned the Executioner beneath his weight, but Bolan had just enough strength to wriggle clear before the fall. It was a contest now to see which stunned combatant would recover first, and Bolan knew his adversary had the clear advantage. Still, he struggled to his hands and knees, ignoring dizziness, the spastic pain of battered ribs, and lurched erect with microseconds to spare.

His adversary had begun to snarl like a demented animal, and Bolan drew a twinge of satisfaction from the bloody face that turned to glower at him as the giant rose. The cheering from the sidelines faltered for an instant, and when it resumed, there was an angry, desperate tone about it, urging the champion to redeem himself.

Humiliation spurred the hulk into a headlong charge across the ring, long arms outstretched, hands aimed for Bolan's throat. The bastard might be capable of ripping off his head bare-handed, but the soldier didn't plan to let his adversary have the chance.

When ten feet lay between them, Bolan took a breath and held it, launched himself into a shoulder roll directly in the giant's path. There was a momentary, numbing impact as the boots collided with his tender abdomen, and then the hulk himself was airborne, howling with dismay before the jolt of impact slammed his jaws together, cutting off the sound.

The Executioner was on his feet this time before the thin, anemic cheering had a chance to die away entirely. Closing in on his adversary from his blind side, Bolan let the groggy giant struggle to his knees. It gave him better access to his chosen target as he raised one leg and slammed a boot heel home above the giant's kidney.

Pain convulsed the human hulk, his spine arching in his agony, and Bolan sidestepped for a roundhouse kick that snapped the big man's jaw and punched him over sideways. It would take a great deal more than that to keep him down, the soldier reasoned, and he was not disappointed as the giant struggled back to all fours, groaning with the effort, bloody spittle drooling down his chin.

There was no point in breaking knuckles with a slam to his face, so Bolan snapped another kick, from the giant's right this time, collapsing nose and cheekbone with a single blow. The big man tottered, almost going down, remaining upright by Herculean will alone. Bolan felt a grudging admiration for the guy, but knew that he was still in jeopardy until the fight was finished.

He put enough force in the final kick to kill an ordinary man, his heel impacting on the point where vertebrae and skull were joined. The giant gasped, a breathless sound, before he toppled forward on his face. Unconscious? Dead or dying? At the moment, Bolan didn't give a damn. *He* was alive—surrounded by the fallen giant's friends, unarmed, but still alive and standing. It was the best that he could have expected, in the circumstances.

Silence reigned throughout the gallery. A glance around the ring of stony faces showed the audience had roughly tripled during Bolan's contest with the human juggernaut. No smiles cracked those faces; most reflected disbelief, occasionally flavored with the anger of a disappointed child. They had been looking forward to the injury or death of the American intruder, but their noses had been rubbed in something else entirely. Some of them were shuffling away, returning to their duty stations now, and Bolan thought he recognized a couple of the demolitions men before they turned their backs, retreating from the gallery.

The others held their places, still surrounding Bolan, and he thought they might attack him as a group, annihilate him in an instant, but they made no move to strike. Instead, there was a ripple in the ranks, beginning from the rear, and they were parting, a human sea divided by the order of a modern Moses, who was still invisible.

The scowling face of Carlo Frenzi suddenly materialized at ringside. Frenzi took in the whole scene with one disgusted glance, paused long enough to shrivel Enzio Petrucchi where he stood. He then retrieved Belasko's coat and shoulder holster from the man beside him, handing them to Bolan with a mirthless smile.

"It seems that you have passed two tests this morning."

"Oh?"

"The test of the arena—" Frenzi swept a hand toward Bolan's prostrate adversary, still unconscious "—and my own examination of your background."

"Ah."

"If you are interested after this—" another glare of pure disgust at Enzio Petrucchi and the fallen giant "—I would welcome you to join our operation."

"Hey, that's what I'm here for." Bolan shook the hand that Frenzi offered, brushing past Petrucchi and the others as they left the gallery together. "I should really check back at my hotel, before they call the cops and tell 'em that I skipped out on the bill."

"No need."

"How's that?"

"The carabinieri have already called at your hotel. It seems they were alerted by your altercation in the nightclub, and they traced your lodgings . . . somehow. Weapons have been confiscated, and a car with, shall we say, suspicious luggage?"

"Dammit!"

Bolan had no doubt the Frenzi or his underlings had tipped police to Bolan's room at La Toscana. It would be a simple way to check him out, devoid of risk for Frenzi's people, painless either way it went. The confiscated weapons would increase his credibility among the terrorists, of course; their loss would also leave him at a disadvantage when the final showdown came, outnumbered and outgunned.

He had been up against the odds before, on every mission since his private, everlasting war began. Each time the odds were hopeless, and each time the Executioner had worked his magic, pulling raw survival from the hat and cheating death when it was hungry, anxious to deceive him. He could not ignore the odds forever, Bolan knew, but he was too damned far inside the present mission now to quibble over the percentages. He had no choice except to forge ahead, full speed, and let the devil take whoever lagged behind.

"It will be safer for you here, among your friends," the terrorist continued, seemingly oblivious to the ironic content of his words. "Security police are scouring the city even now. In any case, you have a job to do."

"A job?"

"It is a small thing, I assure you, but important, nonetheless. A man of your experience should have no difficulty whatsoever."

"Swell."

The "job" would almost certainly include another test of Bolan's loyalty and his ability to function under pressure. There was no point second-guessing Frenzi's plan; the soldier's only working option was to wait and see what happened next, find out what was demanded of him by his newfound "friends."

Except that Bolan, as Belasko, had no friends among the warriors of the catacombs. Petrucchi feared him and mistrusted him, might even envy him in some misguided way. The RJC's commander had a use for Bolan, but that did not make them friends by any stretch of the imagination. As for the remainder of the troops, they would not want to communicate with Belasko for the most part. He was an intruder in the fullest sense, a foreign mercenary thrust upon them arbitrarily for reasons that they did not fully comprehend. As such, he threatened their security, their share of any loot derived from future operations. And he had humbled their champion....

More than ample reason for any one of them to slip a blade between his ribs or blow his brains out if the opportunity arose. Among the rank and file, Belasko's death would scarcely cause a ripple, and his passing might ensure a larger share of booty for the soldiers who survived him.

Bolan would be doubly on his guard from that point on, but he could not allow the enemy to sense his apprehension. Any crack in the facade of gruff bravado would provide his adversaries with an opening, a signal that the time was right to strike against the interloper. Any show of weakness now was tantamount to suicide, and Bolan knew that he would have to keep his doubts, his apprehension, strictly to himself.

He still might manage to survive the tunnels. Tomorrow was never guaranteed to any man, and least of all a solitary soldier on the firing line. Today was all he had, and he would use it to his best advantage.

The soldier had a job to do for Carlo Frenzi. More important, he had a mission to accomplish for himself: Destruction of the viper in its nest, before the lethal reptile had a chance to lash out blindly, striking at the peaceful citizens of Rome.

9

"I owe you an apology, *signor*."

"How's that?"

"The incident that took place in my absence..."

Bolan shrugged. "Forget it."

They were seated in a chamber roughly twice the size of Bolan's cubicle, which served as Frenzi's office and his sleeping quarters. In the center of the room was a folding table, which Frenzi used as a desk, with more of the command post's ubiquitous camp chairs placed on either side. A standard issue army cot was folded up and standing in the corner. Lighting had been added, via an extension cable bolted to the ceiling; otherwise, the room was totally devoid of creature comforts.

"You are injured."

Bolan forced a smile.

"It's nothin'. I've had worse on R and R."

"Perhaps. But Enzio has flagrantly defied my personal instructions. Rest assured that I will punish him appropriately."

"Let it go. There's no harm done."

"You are too generous."

"Let's say I'd rather handle it myself."

A foxy gleam appeared in Frenzi's eye.

"I understand, and I approve...as long as *la vendetta* does not interfere with your assignment."

"Waitin' makes it sweeter. Now, about this job—"

"We are a young and growing army," Frenzi interrupted. "As with a child, an army in its infancy requires the best of care, particular supplies."

"And it'll need a whole lot more as it gets older," Bolan interjected.

"*Sì*. We understand each other." Frenzi hesitated for a moment, gathering his thoughts, and when he spoke again his voice had taken on the stilted tones of classic Roman oratory. "In my country's history, the bandits have emerged as heroes of a sort. We have our Guiliano and our mafiosi, though the latter have become perverted over time. They prey upon the people who have nurtured them through generations past. In time, we may be forced to deal with them."

"Good luck."

"Your country, I believe, has similar traditions?"

"Sure, we've got our fairy tales about Butch Cassidy and Jesse James, John Dillinger, you name it. And we've got the Mafia, the same as you. Don't bet on anybody dealin' with them, though, unless they make their bargain underneath the table."

Frenzi nodded, almost sadly.

"Our immediate priority is the collection of sufficient arms and ammunition to sustain the coming struggle."

"Well, from what I saw outside, you've got a decent start."

The RJC commander smiled and waved one hand in a dismissive gesture.

"It is nothing. For the movement I envision, we require ten times—a hundred times—what you have seen."

"Must be some movement."

"So it is. But every journey must begin with simple steps." He smiled, as if the mangled aphorism was original, and forged ahead. "Ironically, our secret movement needs publicity in order to obtain the weapons and matériel we require. It will be necessary to create an incident, demand a ransom.''

"Now you're talkin'."

Frenzi's smile was fading.

"I will not deceive you. We have made one previous attempt. A failure. There was some confusion at the point of the exchange. We lost the ransom. Three good men were killed."

"The hostage?"

"Also dead."

"That makes it sticky," Bolan muttered. "Smokin' hostages is murder on your credibility. Nobody's gonna front big money if you've got a reputation for the double cross."

"I fear that you may be correct, and so we shall not ask for money."

"Money or munitions, it's the same. They'll either let you whistle for it, or they'll put a SWAT team on the drop and blow away your pickup team."

"There is no drop, as you describe, no pickup team. The ransom we demand is abstract, rather than concrete, but nonetheless essential to our cause."

"You're losin' me."

"Our ransom is cooperation. The withdrawal of security police and other law enforcement officers from a selected area, upon command."

"That's great, if you believe what any bluecoat tells you on the telephone."

"Our target will have everything to gain by full cooperation, everything to lose by any slightest act of treachery."

"Let's spell it out."

"Of course."

The RJC's commander reached inside his jacket and produced a glossy photograph. The size and ragged right-hand edge told Bolan that it had been trimmed, and none too cleanly, from a larger photo. There, frozen for eternity on film, was a young woman of striking beauty, who appeared to challenge Bolan, even now, with eyes that were alive despite their flat reduction into black and white. The angel face was framed by raven hair that fell below her shoulders, and her low-cut evening gown revealed the greater portion of an ample bosom. She was hanging on to someone's arm, but scissors had excised her partner, leaving her in touch with only remnants of his severed arm.

"Not bad."

"Claudia Perrini. You are not a movie buff?"

"I never had the time."

"Claudia is the current goddess of Italian cinema. Her latest film is also doing well in France and Germany. There are persistent rumors of an offer from a major studio in Hollywood."

"Publicity."

"Of course, but there is yet another benefit. Her father, Salvatore Luciano, is the overall commander of security police in Italy. Claudia changed her last name at the urging of the studios, but they are close, this family. Whoever holds Claudia Perrini holds the reins of the security police."

"Not bad," the soldier said again, and meant it.

"With the present situation here in Rome, celebrities are very conscious of security. There may be certain difficulties."

"I get paid for handlin' the difficulties."

"But of course. We have the lady's address . . . a hotel on Via dei Cestari, near the Pantheon. We have her schedule, and we are informed of any unexpected movements. There are bodyguards, of course."

"You've done your homework."

"We cannot afford another failure. The embarrassment . . ."

He let the comment trail away, unfinished, but the look on Frenzi's face told Bolan that there was a hefty slice of ego on the line, along with any profit margin for the RJC. The bungled ransoming of Arthur Bishop had been felt, and

badly, by the upper echelons of the commando strike force.
Bolan wondered briefly whether Frenzi's explanation was,
in fact, the truth, if someone at the grass-roots level had
decided on a double cross unknown to his superiors. It
didn't really matter, either way; the murder of a hostage had
already placed the Executioner on Frenzi's track, and there
could be no backing off until the man, his private army and
his twisted dream had been destroyed forever.

"What's our schedule?"

"Claudia is attending a performance of the opera tonight. La Scala. When she reaches her hotel, you will be
waiting in her suite, together with a complement of revolutionary troops. There may be some resistance to your invitation from the bodyguards. I leave their treatment in your
hands. Above all else, our guest must not be harmed in any
way."

"I understand." He mulled over Frenzi's instructions for
a moment, hopefully concealing his surprise at the accelerated schedule. "Any objections if I pick the backup for
myself?"

"A wise decision, though you may not find a friend
among the soldiers here. I do not think Armand will live."

"His problem," Bolan growled, too stiff and battered to
affect remorse. "He bit off more than he could chew."

"Indeed. The others may despise you, but I think that
none of them will challenge you directly. I will order them
to follow your instructions. Still..."

"I'll watch my back," he told the terrorist commander.
"Always have."

"Another wise decision."

"Now, if you'll excuse me..."

"Certainly."

Alone again, among the vaulted shadows of the gallery
outside Frenzi's quarters, Mack Bolan turned the conversation over in his mind, alert for any hidden snares. The
scheduled snatch was not a trap per se; he knew that much

with certainty. If Frenzi had desired his death, the terrorist commander could have snapped his fingers and a score of gunmen would have volunteered to finish off the foreigner among them. No, the kidnap plan was not a double cross…at least for Mike Belasko. But the Executioner could not escape a sour feeling in his gut, a hunch that there was something very wrong about the setup.

Frenzi's knowledge of the girl, her family, could be obtained from any tabloid catering to movie buffs, of course. And there was nothing so remarkable about his penetration of the star's security. Corruption was a fact of life in Italy, as in so many other countries of the world—including the United States. A hotel concierge might be persuaded to divulge the crucial information for a pittance; information from the bodyguards themselves might cost a little more.

On second thought, he ruled out infiltration of the guards, convinced by Frenzi's offhand comment that he was expected to annihilate them at the first sign of resistance. And resistance was expected, right. A little blood would get the media's attention, might persuade the press and the authorities that the abductors of Claudia Perrini meant precisely what they said in any subsequent negotiations.

He would spare the lady's watchdogs if he could, but there had been no way on earth for Bolan to decline the job, no way for him to beg more time. If anything, Belasko would respond to confiscation of his car and weapons with a rush to earn more capital by any means available. The means, for now, were solidly in Carlo Frenzi's hands, and for the moment he was calling the shots.

But only for the moment.

Bolan would proceed with the assignment because he had no choice. He would attempt to minimize civilian casualties, protect the lady if he could, but it was necessary to preserve his cover for the moment, while he burrowed deeper into Frenzi's confidence and found out what the game was really all about.

One thing was certain: Frenzi didn't give a damn about the woman, movie star or not. His true concern was focused on the "ransom of cooperation" that he would demand of Perrini's father, the commander of the Italian security police. In Frenzi's terms, cooperation had to mean deliberate negligence, a blind eye turned at crucial moments, officers assigned to wild-goose chases while his revolutionary troops were free to carry out their duties as assigned.

It was the nature of those duties that eluded Bolan. When he knew the thrust and scope of Frenzi's master plan, he would be free to move against the bastard, stop him in his tracks. But in the meantime, he had to follow the orders that were passed along, no matter how bizarre or brutal they might seem. For now, he was a captive of the role he had assumed for the occasion, and he dared not let his adversaries look behind the mask.

The lady was a wild card, unexpected, coming out of nowhere. Bolan could not guarantee her safety, dared not let her presence in the catacombs distract him from his goal of destroying the RJC and Carlo Frenzi. He would help the lady if he could, but in the last analysis, a single life was nothing when compared to all the lives that might be thrown away should Frenzi and his mercenary liberation warriors walk away, to organize another operation somewhere down the line.

No matter how you looked at it, the lady was expendable. With any luck, she might come out of the kidnapping unscathed, her film career enhanced by the publicity. And if the worst should happen, if the soldier found no way of saving her, he could repay the bastards. With a vengeance, right.

He checked his watch. Long hours remained before the action, and he thought of Enzio Petrucchi, of his need to even up the score. For reasons of his own, the weasel had been bent on taking Bolan out, and he had tried to use the hulk, Armand, to do his dirty work. If Frenzi was correct, Armand was out of it for good, and that left Enzio, the shaky brains behind the sideshow operation, waiting nervously for retribution to descend upon him like the sword of Damocles.

So, let him wait. He was a zero in the scheme of things, a cipher in the death game Bolan had to play with Carlo Frenzi. If Petrucchi crossed his path again, the Executioner would deal with him; if not, then it could wait until hell broke loose beneath the streets of Rome, in Frenzi's secret underground. Whichever, Enzio Petrucchi was the least of Bolan's problems at the moment. As a threat, the little bastard didn't even rate.

He would have liked to speak with Hal Brognola, find out how the RJC had run his cover down. It would be helpful if he could identify their eyes and ears inside the carabinieri, before the roof fell in and every man was forced to scramble for himself.

It suddenly occurred to Bolan that if Frenzi had a man with the security police, he would be in a prime position to observe the commandant's reaction when a ransom bid came through. Whatever else the leader of the RJC might be, he wasn't anybody's fool. The guy was organized, damned right, and he had done his homework all the way. It made the soldier's job that much more difficult, but Bolan had no choice. He could proceed and hope for victory, or he could try to pull out now and kiss it all goodbye. Escape from Frenzi's stronghold in the catacombs was doubtful; any clean escape from Rome, with both terrorists and the authorities on his trail, would be impossible.

The gallery was stifling Bolan, suddenly, and he half imagined that he felt the weight of all humanity upon his shoulders, bearing down and threatening to crush him like an insect. He could only do so much. The rest of them, the handful who were conscious of his mission here in Rome, could not expect too much.

But he could try. Until it killed him. And with his final ounce of strength, his dying breath, the Executioner could try again. One man could make a difference, if he did his best and damned the cost in terms of pain and private sacrifice. One man could change the world—or some of it, at any rate—if he was willing to expend the energy, fulfill his duty to the limit and beyond.

The Executioner could make a difference, here and now. He could destroy Red Justice or expend his life in the attempt, and for the moment that was all that mattered. Here and now was the totality of his existence; there was no tomorrow, never would be, until every savage had been tamed or slaughtered, driven back beneath the stones from whence they had come purged with cleansing fire.

And *never* was the operative word, of course. The soldier's everlasting war would always be precisely that: a war devoid of final victory. His enemies were too prolific, far too numerous for any single warrior to annihilate them all. If he possessed a thousand soldiers at his beck and call, each man endowed with, say, a thousand lifetimes, Bolan might have had a chance to decimate the opposition. But the cannibals could never be exterminated while imperfect man himself survived. For the moment, here and now, it was enough to hold the animals at bay, to kill a few of them where possible and drive the others into hiding, aware that they would rise again some other day.

It galled the Executioner, this no-win situation so analogous to his experience in Vietnam. In Nam, the troops had been encumbered by the concept of "containment"; they were ordered to contain the enemy within his present boundaries, take him when he crossed the line, but never, under any circumstances, follow him across the arbitrary lines that politicians draw on maps. It was a losing situation from the start, but fifty thousand grunts had sanctified the losing battle with their lives, their blood, and there was no damned way on earth that Bolan would admit those lives were spent in vain. The savages *had* been contained, to some extent, until a call for "peace with honor" threw the portals open and invited them to roam at will, appropriating anyone and anything that caught their eye.

A similar defeatist attitude had turned the tide in ancient Rome, and Bolan recognized the lesson of the empire, yielding to barbarians by slow degrees until there had been nothing left to yield. If any single emperor had been inclined to stand his ground, to halt the raiders in their tracks and plow them under, how might history have been rewritten?

Riddles. And he had no time for mind games with the problems pressing close, demanding his attention. Reality was grim enough to keep the warrior occupied, and no mistake. Reality would kill him, if he lost his grip and let his mind go wandering too far afield.

The soldier had a duty to reality, to sanity and decency. From the beginning of his military service, he had recognized a warrior's first responsibility as the defense of civilized society. Protection of the weak and innocent, whoever and wherever they might be. A soldier who denied that duty, sold his gun out to the highest bidder, was himself no better than the savages.

A mercenary, in the truest sense, has sold his soul together with his services, surrendering identity, integrity and freedom of expression when he first accepts a check from his employer. Guns for hire were little more than hit men on a global scale, and if a few clung fast to personal morality of one sort or another, choosing sponsors with an eye toward goals and ideology, the vast majority were interested primarily in being paid, regardless of the source. The Executioner had known assorted mercenaries through the years; he had enjoyed the company of several and admired a few, but the majority were men apart, beyond the pale of normal understanding. Living always on the edge, they shared some traits in common with Mack Bolan, but the average mercenary's eyes were always looking inward, calculating odds and angles for his private benefit. If there was a potential profit, he would fight and risk his life; if either side was short on cash, allegiances were no more stable than a sand dune in the wind.

Frenzi would be watching Mike Belasko closely, Bolan knew that much. The RJC's commander would be used to handling the mercenaries under his command; he would regard Belasko as another hungry gunner from the same, familiar mold. An easy man to deal with, right, as long as you were picking up the tab.

But he was reckoning without Mack Bolan. Frenzi's calculations made no critical allowance for the Executioner, and while he might have some contingency to cope with traitors in the ranks, he would not be expecting infiltration by a warrior dedicated to his personal destruction, the destruction of his dream. When Frenzi recognized the error of his ways, it would be too late to turn back the clock, start the game all over from square one.

With any luck at all, it would be too damned late for Carlo Frenzi, period.

And would it also be too late for Bolan?

Standing on the shadowed gallery alone, he shrugged off the question as immaterial. A warrior's life was never the compelling issue in a desperate battle. There were always issues greater than the man himself, determinations of a cosmic nature to be settled by the outcome of a righteous war. If Bolan's fate decreed a dusty death beneath the streets of Rome, then he was ready to face the end. His only wish would be for time and strength to do his duty while he lived.

There was some life in Bolan yet, damned right, and while he lived, he would keep blitzing on.

10

Bolan's driver parked the Fiat four-door in a narrow alley that ran parallel to Via dei Cestari. Seated in the back, with two guns up in front, the Executioner had felt secure enough to study streets and landmarks on their drive, committing narrow side streets to his memory. If necessary, he could dump the escort now, retrace his path to the hotel on Via Dandolo and enter Frenzi's tunnel system there. If necessary. It would blow his cover and alert the terrorists to something dangerously wrong, but he could do it in a pinch. And with the backup he had chosen, Bolan knew that literally anything might happen.

He had bypassed Enzio Petrucchi in selection of his backup, a decision that had caused the weasel some embarrassment. Petrucchi had been glaring daggers at him when they left. It was the very least of his concerns right now, however, and he concentrated on the two men seated just in front of him, their craggy profiles faintly outlined by a street lamp two blocks down.

As Belasko supposedly knew no Italian he had requested gunners with a working knowledge of the English language, and had thereby narrowed down the field immediately. Of the thirty-odd commandos bivouacked in Frenzi's staging area, no more than ten spoke any English, and two-thirds of those were lost on simple phrases of command. The soldier had eventually chosen two with adequate vocabularies, standing by while Frenzi briefed them on the mission, making sure they understood precisely who was in command. Their promise to obey instructions hadn't meant a thing, of course; he read the open animosity in both their faces, and surmised that they were brooding over Belasko's handling of Armand.

The giant had survived for half an hour following his bout with Bolan, slipping deeper into a coma by the moment, finally giving up the ghost without regaining consciousness. For his part, Bolan wouldn't miss the bastard, but his comrades obviously took a different view. When Bolan moved among them now, they edged aside to let him pass, their faces filled with mingled awe and anger, fierce resentment and a trace of fear.

The backup guns were no exception, but their animosity toward Bolan had been tempered with an obvious enthusiasm for the mission. He did not believe that they would try to kill him in the middle of an operation ordered by Frenzi. He did not believe it, but he wasn't taking any foolish chances, either. He had kept the Fiat's backseat to himself throughout their drive across town, eliminating the potential risk of a garrote around his throat, a bullet shot behind one ear. The gunners might despise him, wish him dead, and that was fine...as long as they performed their tasks on cue. There would be time enough for them to try for him later, when he finally discarded the Belasko mask, and he would see then how they fared against the Executioner.

"Is time," the driver told him, dark eyes meeting Bolan's in the rearview mirror.

Bolan double-checked his watch and nodded. "Go."

They left the car unlocked, secure in the knowledge that pedestrians on Via dei Cestari would be tourists or affluent locals who confined their ramblings to the lighted street, avoiding darkened alleyways at any cost. The Fiat would be there when they emerged, complete with hubcaps, and the soldier was again impressed by that side of the Roman character.

The ancient city had its share of vermin, certainly—the sneak thieves, burglars and cutthroats, over all the Mafia—but after dark it was a damned sight safer than New York, Los Angeles, or any other stateside city he could think of at the moment. Rape was not unheard of, but its frequency did not approach the U.S. average of ten reported incidents per hour. Given the Italian temperament, the penchant for vendettas, murder was a problem, but the vast majority of homicides these days could be attributed to terrorists or mafiosi. Prosecutors finally had a handle on the latter problem, herding mobsters by the hundreds into giant cages, trying them en masse for their accumulated crimes and leading them in chains to serve their sentences, but terrorism was a problem momentarily without solutions.

Which, of course, was where the Executioner came in.

He would not solve the problem in Italy by eliminating Carlo Frenzi and the RJC, but it would be a start, the first decisive step along a bloody road that the authorities would have to follow, weeding out the savages wherever they were found, dispensing prison terms or simply wiping out the animals who had befouled the ancient majesty of Rome. In time, perhaps, they might achieve a victory of sorts, but Bolan knew from personal experience how fleeting such a victory might be.

A door had been left open to the hotel's kitchen area. They found a slender, surly kitchen worker waiting for them, shifting nervously from one foot to the other like a child with bladder problems. They were all alone inside the kitchen, with its ranks of shiny pots suspended overhead on hooks, and still the RJC's accomplice kept on flicking anxious glances toward the dining room, beyond a pair of swing doors. The beads of perspiration on his upper lip reminded Bolan of an artificial mustache carved from crystal.

"You are late," the contact stammered, nearly choking on the words.

"We're right on time," the Executioner corrected him. "Let's do it."

"*Sì.*"

He led them past the sinks, the massive grill and range with something like a score of burners, pausing at the swing doors to peer through windows made of murky Plexiglas. When he was satisfied, the little man conducted Bolan and his backup through the dining room and out again, along a corridor that led them to the service elevator.

"Here." He backed away, determined to proceed with them no farther. "Seventh floor, room 723."

"We know all that," the soldier snapped. He stalled a moment, waiting for the little guy to finish, and finally growled, "The key!"

Their contact jumped as if the Executioner had slapped him, digging frantically inside the pocket of his dirty apron, stretching out one arm to pass the key without approaching any closer to the man with the graveyard eyes. That done, he scuttled back along the corridor out of sight, a shadow blending with the other shadows of the hallway, swiftly gone.

The elevator was in better shape than that of Frenzi's lodgings on the Via Dandolo. It shuddered once or twice en route, but otherwise the soldier found it well maintained. He stood against a side wall, facing his companions, momentarily invisible to anyone who might be passing when the doors slid open at their destination. If Claudia Perrini had returned ahead of schedule, if her bodyguards were posted in the corridor outside her room, they might respond to the arrival of the elevator. If it happened, Bolan's vantage point would give him the advantage of surprise for something like a heartbeat, while the RJC commandos occupied his adversary's full attention. If, improbably, an ambush had been laid for them upstairs, the first barrage would take his backup, standing close together in the middle of the car, providing Bolan with a chance to reach his weapon, program the controls for a precipitate retreat.

If...

The elevator slowed, then grumbled to a halt on seven, thick hydraulic doors retracting with a hiss. He let the button men lead out, and when they were across the threshold, glancing off along the corridor in each direction, Bolan followed cautiously. The vacant hallway mocked him, sneering at the life-and-death precautions that were second nature to a soldier on the firing line. A set of numbers on the opposite wall, complete with plastic arrows, told him 723 was to the left, and Bolan moved in that direction, letting his companions watch the flank.

He hesitated outside Claudia Perrini's room, listening for a trace of human-generated sound inside. He knocked— again, more forcefully, when there was no response—and finally used the pass key, slipping through the doorway and into darkness with the backup on his heels. They remembered to lock the door behind them.

One of the commandos had his fingers on the light switch when Bolan called him off. The target and her entourage might be home early, might be on the street outside this very moment, and the briefest flash of light from windows overlooking Via dei Cestari would betray the presence of intruders in her suite. They dared not risk the lights, but Bolan compromised, resorting to a pencil flash just long enough for his accomplices to find the sofa, settle in with silenced pistols in their laps.

"Stay sharp," he growled, selecting for himself an easy chair that faced the door while granting him a clear peripheral of his associates. "And stay awake."

A wordless grunt from the direction of the sofa indicated that they had heard him, and Bolan left them to it. It would matter little if they fell asleep; on second thought, he might prefer it. There was nothing for the two of them to do until the target arrived, and Bolan didn't want them getting restless, trigger happy as they sat there stewing in the darkness. For a moment he could hear them whispering back and forth, but soon they both fell silent. Bolan's night sight was adjusting rapidly, and in the brooding darkness of the suite he half imagined that the terrorists were watching him, examining his profile, picking out *their* target. One of them was shifting on the sofa now, and scratching at himself . . . or was he reaching for the pistol in his lap?

Relax. The bastards might be borderline psychotics, but they weren't completely stupid. They would gain precisely nothing by eliminating Bolan now, and they had everything to lose. In his orders, Carlo Frenzi had been quick to stress the crucial nature of their mission, his determination that it should proceed without a hitch. If they returned without Belasko, Frenzi would demand an explanation, and despite their seeming competence with weapons, neither man appeared to be adept at thinking on his feet. They had to know that Frenzi would see through their lies and punish them for disobeying his instructions. And in Frenzi's world beneath the streets, the only punishment for disobedience was instant death.

So, it was settled. They would not attempt to murder Bolan here.

And yet, he watched them anyway.

An hour passed, then ninety minutes. Bolan stoically refused to budge, eyes flicking back and forth between the door and sofa, where his backup had begun to fidget restlessly. Accustomed to the hunt, the waiting that precedes a kill, the Executioner had learned to tame that restlessness within himself, to crouch immobile through the morning, afternoon and into evening. Waiting. For the enemy to show himself, the chosen face to fill the sniper's scope, enlarged to many times life size. Another heartbeat, and the swollen face would detonate like a grenade composed of flesh and blood, as if by magnifying it the sniper had somehow inflated it beyond the bursting point. So many ruptured faces that they all began to look alike with time. And time had always been the enemy.

Two hours. He caught the sound of voices now, from the direction of the elevator. One was certainly a woman's, laughing, and the other must be a man's. He snapped his fingers for the backup men, and they were on their feet as Bolan rose to take his place beside the door. From that position, he could cover anyone who entered, get the drop on any heavies who might follow Perrini inside.

Assuming that the laughing woman was Claudia Perrini, right. Assuming that the voices stopped outside 723.

Her key was in the lock almost before he knew it, and the soldier drew his weapon, praying that he would not have to use it. One of Perrini's bodyguards preceded her inside, his bulk obscuring the lighted corridor outside, one hand already fumbling for the light switch, calling up a blaze of artificial daylight in the living room.

The others crowded in behind him, Perrini's laughter winding down and stopping abruptly at the sight of three armed men. Her flanker had already closed the door, a broad smile frozen on his face as if he didn't quite know what to do with it in an emergency. He glanced at Bolan, swept the others with a steely eye, dismissing them with an expression of contempt. It took the guy perhaps a heartbeat to decide upon the most important move that he would ever make.

He lunged for Bolan, knowing there was no way he could ever reach the handgun slung beneath his arm. Both hands were reaching out for the Beretta, fingers curved like talons, and the Executioner retreated, loath to kill the man without good reason, swinging up his pistol for a solid blow against his adversary's skull.

Before he could deliver, Bolan saw the big man stumble, reeling from another silent impact, going down upon one knee. A scarlet blossom had unfolded sticky petals on his shirtfront, dribbling wetly, and the bodyguard was staring at it in amazement, square jaw working silently. Almost before Mack Bolan's mind could register the muffled popping of a silencer, round two exploded in the big man's face and punched him over backward, trembling into death.

His partner recognized the end of life and hope, already digging for his weapon, but the RJC commandos had him in their sights, unloading rounds in rapid-fire, at nearly point-blank range. The second bodyguard was lifted off his feet and slammed against the wall, rebounding with a boneless grace impossible for living humans to achieve. One outstretched hand grazed Perrini's cheek and left a bloody track, like crimson war paint on her alabaster skin.

Suddenly alone with murderers, the lady looked as if she was about to scream, and Bolan was beside her in an instant, one hand pressed across her mouth to hold the shriek inside. Above his hand, the eyes were flakes of emerald, alive with sudden terror, and the supple body pressed against his own was all that any man could ever want. The lady was a beauty, right, and Frenzi's censored photograph had scarcely done her justice.

"Not a sound," he cautioned, keeping his hand against her mouth, the sleek Beretta rising into Claudia Perrini's line of sight and staying there until her eyes registered comprehension. When she nodded jerkily, he took a chance and pulled his hand away. From where he stood, the Executioner could feel her trembling, and there was nothing sexy or arousing in her terror.

"You will come with us," he said, the tone admitting no refusal on her part. Claudia glanced from Bolan to his backup, to the bodies at her feet, and nodded miserably.

"*Sì.*"

He shot a scathing glance in the direction of the smug, self-satisfied commandos.

"Let's get out of here," he snapped. "And no more shooting, dammit!"

"Self-defense," the taller of them said, and smiled, already holstering his silenced automatic. Bolan had a sudden urge to push the smile back down his throat, and maybe grab a handful of his larynx in the process, but he couldn't spare the time. As it was, he pinned the bastard with a stare that bored inside his skull and set alarm bells ringing loud enough to take the cocky smile off the guy's face.

The soldier hesitated long enough to pull a handkerchief and wipe the bloody marks from Claudia's cheek. She flinched from Bolan's touch, still trembling, and there was something close to panic in the emerald eyes. But she was fighting it, controlling it, and he would give her that. She was hanging in there under pressure, and with any luck at all, the trait might be enough to see her out of this alive.

They double-locked the suite behind them, backtracked to the service elevator and a quick ride down. The dining room and kitchen were deserted now, their contact having split in search of safer ground. Outside, the crisp night air invigorated Bolan, overpowering the death aromas, kitchen smells, the lady's heady mix of panic and perfume. Upon reaching the Fiat, Bolan held a door for Perrini, snarling at the taller of the gunmen when he tried to join them in the back. Reluctantly, the shooter took his place in front of Bolan, twisted half around to stare with fascination at the movie star, while his comrade slid behind the wheel.

Before they started, Bolan slipped a black felt blindfold over Perrini's eyes. Frenzi had decreed that she must not be able to describe their route for the police. The blindfold was obligatory in this kind of operation, but the streets were dark enough that Bolan did not have to force her down onto the floorboards. Neither did he bind her hands, secure in the knowledge that a woman in a blindfold was unlikely to evacuate a speeding car.

The wheelman took them north along Corso Vittorio Emanuele II, doubling back southwest in the direction of the riverfront and Piazza Navona. He pulled the Fiat in behind a cheap café on Vicolo della Moretta, killed the lights and engine, bringing darkness down around them like a velvet curtain.

The café was closed, the parking lot and alleyway abandoned. Bolan stood beside the Fiat for a moment, sampling the night with every combat sense alert for danger, finally satisfied that they were in the clear. He reached inside to take the lady's hand in his and drew her to him, steadying her for a moment as she found her footing. She was reaching up instinctively to take off the blindfold when Bolan pulled her hands away.

"Not yet."

Before he could direct her toward the restaurant, the shotgun rider stepped in front of them to block the way. Peripherally, Bolan saw the wheelman circling around his flank.

"No hurry, eh?" the taller of the gunmen said as he leered, his eyes devouring the woman. "We have time for some amusement, no?"

"You called it right. The answer's no."

"I think the answer must be yes."

The gunner stepped past Bolan, reaching for the lady, clamping one hand on her breast and leaning in to kiss her as he forced her back against the car. Aware that number two was behind him, aching for a chance to take him out and share the woman with his friend, the soldier realized that he would have to keep priorities in order. And the first priority, right now, was on his flank.

The snap kick came from nowhere, Bolan pivoting his body, bending sharply at the waist and bringing up his left foot with the force of an Olympic swimmer demonstrating posture for sidestroke. He was dead on target with the flanker's face, his heel impacting on the would-be rapist's chin and lifting him completely off his feet before he had a chance to paw the silenced automatic out of hiding. Bolan could hear the crunch of shattered teeth, and then the guy was down, distinctly out of it.

At the sound of a stifled scream, the sound of shredding cloth, Bolan swung around to find the shotgun rider ripping at Claudia's gown. He had exposed one breast, and he had the woman pinned against the Fiat while he tried to work his free hand underneath her skirt. Bolan had no problem closing from his blind side, taking the bastard completely by surprise. A kidney punch turned legs to latex and the gunner folded, dropping to his knees. But he had taken other beatings, in the joint and on the street; he would survive the pain and deal it back in spades if Bolan gave him half a chance.

And so the warrior gave him no damned chance at all. The sleek Beretta was already in his fist before the shotgun rider had a chance to reach his own protection, with the silenced muzzle held rock-steady on a point between his rodent eyes.

"I'll bet your life that I can find the way from here alone," he told the punk. "Your choice."

The guy had to think about it for a moment, but he finally let his hands go slack, retreating from the open jacket and the pistol hidden underneath.

"I'll take the piece."

The shooter scowled. "I give my gun to no man."

"Fine."

He was already tightening into the squeeze when number one decided on discretion as the better part of valor. Holding out his empty palms as if the flesh would stop a parabellum round, the shotgun rider drew his automatic gingerly and dropped it at the soldier's feet. When Bolan had it safely tucked inside his belt, together with the fallen gunner's side arm, he was ready to proceed.

"You'd better give your friend a hand," he told the kneeling punk. "He'll have to gum his pasta for a while, but he can walk."

The hardguy spared a look of pure hatred for the Executioner, but hastened to obey his orders. When the battered terrorist was on his feet, one arm around his comrade's shoulders like a drunk returning home with a friend on New Year's Eve, they led the way with Bolan and the lady close behind. The place was locked, but Perrini's rodent-eyed attacker had a passkey and another moment found them safe inside the kitchen of the tiny restaurant.

"I'm gettin' tired of coming through the service entrance like a waiter," Bolan growled to no one in particular, preserving his Belasko image. "Let's get on with it—and no more fancy moves, or someone's goin' to wind up in tomorrow's antipasto."

The wheelman slumped against the stainless-steel sinks, his face already swelling as he cradled it in both hands and moaned through bloody lips. His partner found a trapdoor covered by a throw rug in the combination manager-accountant's office, hauled it open to reveal a metal ladder, rusty rungs descending into darkness.

"Ladies first?" the gunner offered, grinning crookedly.

"No time to stand on ceremony," Bolan told him. "Let's say sons of bitches first. That's you."

Another time, with even slightly better odds, the shooter might have tried it, but he dared not rush the soldier empty-handed. It was certain death, with no escape, and he was clearly not prepared to die just yet.

"Take this," the Executioner commanded, tossing him the pencil flash. "You keep it trained directly on the ground below the ladder, understand? One twitch, one move that makes me nervous, and you're history."

"I understand, *signor*. And I do not forget."

"That's two of us. Now move it, while you're still worth somethin' on your feet."

The gunner started down, the penlight in his teeth to free both hands for climbing. Overhead, the Executioner and Claudia Perrini watched the light descending, bobbing like a candle in the darkness of a tomb. A firefly in the bowels of hell.

He had already been there once, and now the soldier was returning to the underground, with prisoners and an expensive present for his master. Frenzi would be pleased about the woman. As for the rest of it . . .

The Executioner would have to wait and see, of course. For now, the darkness of the tunnel and the presence of an enemy at hand were adequate to occupy the soldier's mind. It was a long walk back to Frenzi's bivouac, and Bolan wondered which of them would make it there alive.

11

They moved along the tunnels two abreast, the battered gunners leading. The terrorist who had been snap-kicked on the jaw was weaving drunkenly and moaning to himself, dragging his feet on the stony floor as if each step might be his last. The shotgun rider carried Bolan's penlight, spinning gossamer illumination ahead of them, selecting forks to the left or the right at every branching of the tunnel. Perrini walked at Bolan's side, her eyes focused on her feet to make sure of her footing, but she edged closer to him each time a rat sped by scuttling for cover. She had tried to repair the tattered bodice of her gown, but now it was even more revealing despite her efforts, and the Executioner was apprehensive as to what effect her presence in the bivouac might have on Frenzi's soldiers.

As it was, the lady was the least of Bolan's problems. He was herding hostile captives through the tunnels at gunpoint, with an army of their comrades waiting at journey's end. If his victory against Armand had not inspired the other terrorists to take him out, this latest altercation, with his backup gunners on the snatch, might be the final straw. However Frenzi might react, the troopers of the RJC would take one look at Claudia Perrini and sympathize at once with Bolan's adversaries. If they tried to take her from him, or avenge their battered friends...

A bat swooped toward the lady, screeching, and Perrini leaped to Bolan's side as if he might envelop her and keep her safe from harm. He slipped an arm around her waist and kept her on her feet when she was close to falling, conscious of the burning glances the shotgun rider threw over his shoulder. Now the bastard must believe that Bolan meant to keep the woman for himself. It would be pointless to explain, and so much easier to put a bullet through the guy's skull, but Bolan meant to bring in the gunners alive—if they let him.

Lights shone ahead, and Bolan heard the challenge of the sentries seconds later. He allowed the shotgun rider to respond, and they were beckoned into the staging area. It didn't matter what the bastard told his comrades; Frenzi would be waiting for them, for the woman, and whatever happened next, it would be happening on Frenzi's order.

They were in a different staging area, of course, but it looked similar, if not identical, to Bolan. Men in khaki and OD fatigues, all armed, were engaged in cleaning or inspecting weapons and explosives. Vacant, hostile faces watched as they passed, all eyes returning to the woman, lingering, undressing her. Bolan had to check the names engraved on marble slabs laid into either wall before he could be certain that the bivouac had moved in fact.

But these were different soldiers, different weapons and explosives. Frenzi had at least two outposts set beneath the streets of Rome, and Bolan had no doubt there would be others. Flying squads of terrorists beneath the city, armed and ready to attack on Frenzi's order, sitting on enough C-4 to spread destruction far and wide, inflicting casualties Bolan did not even want to contemplate. The citizens of Rome, the tourists in her streets, had no inkling of their danger, had no way to prepare themselves, and once again he heard the voice of Arthur Bishop whispering in his ear.

No warning.

Bolan holstered the Beretta as a pair of sentries led them to Frenzi. The commander of the RJC was waiting for them in a Spartan "office" virtually identical to that in which he had conferred with Bolan earlier; the folding table, cot and chairs might have been shuttled from the other site to serve as props in Frenzi's private melodrama, bolstering his image of a revolutionary warrior in the underground.

"You were successful," Frenzi said, beaming as they were shown inside, already on his feet and circling the makeshift desk to greet them.

"More or less."

He tore his eyes away from Perrini, finally marking the condition of his gunners. "There was difficulty?"

"You could say that," Bolan answered. "Mutt and Jeff here killed the bodyguards for no damned reason. We could just as easily have stuffed them in the closet."

Frenzi shrugged. "What's done is done," he observed. "In war, we must expect some casualties."

"I guess we should expect some rape along the way, then. Right?"

The gunners stiffened as he spoke, and Bolan half turned, ready to receive them if they made a move in his direction. Frenzi did a double take on the woman, taking in the shredded bodice of her gown, and pinned his troopers with a burning stare.

"He lies," the shotgun rider blurted out. "Belasko tried to take the woman for himself. We held him back, and so received the injuries you see."

"It's gettin' deep in here," the Executioner replied. "If these two pulled me off anybody, how'n hell did I wind up with these?"

He took a chance and drew the captured automatic pistols from his waistband, passing them to Frenzi. The commander hefted one in each hand, as if weighing them, and Bolan saw him flick the safeties off with practiced ease. The soldier braced himself, prepared to move if Frenzi swung in his direction, wondering if he could make the draw and nail the guy before a lucky bullet took him out.

It would be close, no guarantees. But if he had no choice...

"It is discouraging to find dissension in the ranks," the commandant declared. "The plague of discord must be ruthlessly exterminated, wiped out at its source. The movement cannot tolerate such flagrant disobedience to standing orders."

Frenzi faced the battered gunners now. "You know what must be done."

The shotgun rider caught a glint of hope and grinned maliciously at Bolan, stepping forward to receive his weapon from the commandant. He kept on smiling as the first two silenced rounds punched through his rib cage, rocked him backward on his heels. The grin was like a death's-head grimace, stamped indelibly upon his dying face, until another bullet sheared his upper lip away, blasting through teeth and tissue on its way through to the brain.

The wheelman watched his comrade fall and finally recognized his peril. Bolting for the exit, he was clumsy off the mark, disoriented, dazed with pain and the effects of mild concussion. Still, a seasoned athlete in his prime could not have beaten the odds in this race, slanted as they were in Carlo Frenzi's favor.

Pivoting to bring the wheelman under fire, Frenzi raised both pistols, squeezing off in rapid-fire until the hammers fell on empty chambers. Cartridge casings clattered at his feet and pinged around the walls as Frenzi riddled the retreating figure. Impact punched the human target forward, slammed him face first into monolithic stone before he slid slowly to the floor.

At a shouted order from the commandant, burly riflemen appeared, surveyed the slaughterhouse without emotion and proceeded to remove the bodies. Bolan watched them go, their boot heels leaving drag marks in the slick blood, which was his backup team's only legacy. No longer interested, Frenzi dropped the empty autoloaders on the table, turning back to face Claudia Perrini and the Executioner.

"I must apologize for the behavior of my men," he told the lady, straight-faced. "It is inexcusable to take such liberties with one who is an honored guest."

Her voice was thick with the accumulated horror of all that she had seen so far. "Why have you brought me here?"

"All in due time, *signorina*. For the moment, rest assured that you are as safe with me as in your father's house. Provisions have been made for your security and safety while you are my guest. When it is time for you to leave, I will regret our parting."

Frenzi snapped his fingers and another pair of gunners filled the narrow doorway, then took up their stations, one on either side of the woman. Both were wise enough to keep their eyes on Frenzi and their comments to themselves.

"Escort the lady to her quarters," Frenzi snapped, "and see that she is comfortable." Once again he turned to his befuddled prisoner. "If I can be of any further service..."

"You may let me go. Return me now, this instant, to my hotel suite."

"In time, *signorina*," Frenzi purred. "All in good time."

They watched the lady being led away. When she was gone, the terrorist produced cigars and offered one to Bolan, lit them both and blew a plume of smoke in the direction of the low ceiling. Almost as an afterthought, he focused on the pools of blood that stained the ground, wincing with a newfound squeamishness that Bolan found completely unconvincing. Frenzi hadn't minded taking out the gunners who had tried to rape Claudia; on the contrary, he had seemed to enjoy it.

"Come, let's walk a bit while I have someone mop this up."

Outside, the gallery was sparsely populated. With the fireworks and theatrics finished for the evening, Frenzi's troopers off to bed or on about their tasks of waste disposal, peace and quiet reigned.

"You have done well," the terrorist told Bolan after they had walked some distance along the gallery in silence. "Another man might not have interfered with Fredo and Vincenzo. I believe you are a man of honor."

"I'm a man of orders," Bolan answered gruffly. "The instructions specified delivery unharmed. I couldn't see how gang rape fit the bill."

"Of course. But there were other feelings, surely."

Bolan pinned the RJC commander with a frosty eye. "The only thing that I've been feelin' lately is a little short of cash. I pulled your pinheads off before they had a chance to blow the operation, get it? All I give a damn about is payday."

"Very well. You will be anxious to complete your next assignment, then. It will bring payday closer for us all."

"I'm listenin'."

"It will be necessary to communicate with Perrini's father."

"Ever hear of telephones?"

"No good. The message must be absolutely confidential, and he must be totally convinced of our determination to proceed in case he should betray us."

Bolan knew the answer going in, but his charade demanded that he ask the question anyway. "So, where do I come in?"

"You will present yourself to the commander of security police and state our case. You will persuade him that compliance must be absolute in order to ensure his daughter's safe return."

"I don't suppose you'll come to visit me in prison?"

Carlo's laughter was spontaneous, apparently sincere. "There is no danger that he will arrest you. If you have not joined us safely in an hour after the appointed meeting time, we will eliminate his daughter in a most unpleasant way."

"Let's hope he buys it," Bolan growled.

"He will. Our Luciano is a fascist in his heart, but he adores Claudia more than anything on earth. It is a weakness we must utilize to our advantage."

"What's the pitch?"

"I beg your pardon?"

"Say I meet this Luciano. What's the story?"

"Ah. Allow me to explain precisely what I have in mind."

They walked, and Carlo Frenzi spelled out his plans for the soldier in minute detail. As Bolan listened, he could feel his stomach turning over slowly, and he wondered if he might already be too late. The scheme was organized on a broader scale than Bolan had imagined, more advanced than he would ever have suspected. He was caught up in the web, a fly ensnared by Frenzi's spider, waiting for the sting that would disable him and leave him helpless for the feast.

But as he listened, Bolan drew upon an inner well of grim determination, vowing to himself that Frenzi and the RJC would not succeed if there was any way on earth for one man, working on his own, to undermine the plan and bring its lethal mechanism to a grinding halt. There might just be a way...

But he was being premature. Before he had an opportunity to move on Frenzi, Bolan would be meeting with the chief of Italy's security police. Assigned to curb the rising tide of terrorism, Salvatore Luciano had a reputation as a strong administrator and an able soldier on the firing line. He had come up the hard way, through the ranks, and he had clashed with bands of armed fanatics more than once, emerging more or less intact while hearses carried off his adversaries. If scuttlebutt was accurate, the man was scrupulously honest, personally fearless when it came to risking life and limb.

But would he risk his daughter?

Carlo Frenzi seemed convinced that Perrini was the key; while she remained a hostage, under threat of death, her father would comply with the demands that might be made of him. Conversely, if the girl should somehow slip away, be reunited with her father, Luciano would be free to move against the RJC with every gun at his command. If Bolan, having brought the lady in, could now devise a way to get her out again...

But it was much too late for that, he realized. If Luciano's troopers were unleashed against the RJC, the end result would be disaster on a scale unprecedented in the history of modern terrorism. Frenzi and his men might be destroyed, but at what cost? If there was any other way around the stalemate, he would have to find it, soon, before the terrorist commander's deadline finally expired and left him sitting in the middle of a fire storm that would rock the world.

Accustomed to performing under pressure and with the odds against him, Bolan knew that there was nothing to be gained from worrying. Defeatist thinking was a lethal enemy of any soldier in the field; the battle could be lost inside a warrior's mind before he ever fired a shot against the enemy, and Bolan needed every ounce of confidence right now, if he held any hope at all of edging Frenzi's death machine off track. The one thing Bolan could not do, in any circumstances, was surrender to his enemies without a fight.

Above all else, he vowed that Frenzi would not live to profit from his scheme, would not escape to fight another day. The soldier contemplated taking out his adversary then and there, before they could be interrupted on the gallery, but there was too much information he still did not possess, which only Carlo Frenzi could supply. Without the information necessary to defeat his plan, the RJC commander's death would be meaningless. The juggernaut, once set in motion, would continue rolling on without him, driverless, until it self-destructed in a bloodbath that would make the ancient contests in the Coliseum seem like situation comedies.

In order to obtain the information that he needed, Bolan had to continue his role as Mike Belasko. He must meet Claudia Perrini's father and convince the chief of the security police to abrogate his duty for the first time in a twenty-year career. That much of it would be a bitter mission in itself, but it was nothing in comparison to the alternatives. If Luciano clapped him into jail or traced him back to Frenzi's hideout in the tunnels, there would be unholy hell to pay, and Bolan would not be alone in picking up the tab.

Claudia's life was riding on the Executioner's ability to sway her father from his duty, make him stand aside just long enough for Frenzi's secondary plan to take effect. If Bolan failed, the lady would be killed, as Frenzi had assured him, in a "most unpleasant way." Unfortunately, the lady's death would be the least of it, and while he hoped to bring her out alive, Claudia ran a distant third on Bolan's revised list of priorities.

The first priority was to prevent the RJC from executing Frenzi's plan, at any cost. The second was elimination of the man himself, together with as many of his mercenary troops as Bolan could accumulate within a given kill zone.

He scanned his memory for missions where the odds against him had been greater, the apparent likelihood of his destruction more extreme. There were a few, but all of them were in the past, and none meant more to Bolan than his mission in the here and now. If he had never heard of Carlo Frenzi or Red Justice, if his karma had not brought him here, the Executioner would be engaged with other enemies, on other killing fields, unmindful of a vicious threat to the Eternal City.

But he *was* in Rome. He knew the danger . . . and the private risks involved. He was already in too deep to think about evacuating, backing off the mission with his skin intact. The game had gone too far, and he was in for the duration, right. To death or victory, assuming that the two were somehow mutually exclusive.

He thought of Hal Brognola, wished he had some way of getting through to Wonderland in case the roof fell in. There would be little Hal could do, of course, from such a distance, but if Carlo Frenzi or a sizable contingent of the others got away, there might be opportunities for Able Team or Phoenix Force to even up the score in future.

Bolan put it out of mind, aware that Frenzi would be watching him each time he set foot outside the tunnels, double-checking through his spies and agents on the street, prepared to throw the doomsday switch at any inkling of a double cross. The terrorist commander might have eyes in Luciano's office even now, for all Bolan knew and he would have to play it straight right down the line.

Unless... It was no more than an idea, still unformed, but Bolan wondered if it might be possible to reach some private understanding with the chief of the security police. If Luciano would agree to play along with Frenzi, stall for time while Bolan worked the angles from within...

It needed work, and Bolan knew that he was running out of time. Tomorrow had already worked its magic transformation into here and how, and he was counting down the hours until he was face-to-face with Claudia Perrini's father.

No pessimist, Mack Bolan did not waste his time on futile optimism. Realism was the soldier's only game, and in the real world, you were forced to take the grief along with glory, spend an hour in the heat for every precious moment in the shade. The real world gave no quarter, took no prisoners, and no one on the face of Mother Earth was getting out of life alive.

The soldier's game was life and death, with no concessions to the weak, the lame, the ineffective. At the moment, Death was leading by a mile, and all the odds were in his favor, stacked against survival even for the fittest. Bolan could not fold, and he would have no opportunity to

HIT
THE JACKPOT
WITH GOLD EAGLE

Scratch off the 3 windows
to see what you'll get—FREE!

Then peel off Sticker, affix it to your Scorecard
and mail today to claim your Free Prizes!

IF YOU HIT THE JACKPOT, YOU GET 4 FREE BOOKS AND A FREE POCKETKNIFE

The free gifts shown on the slot machine Sticker are yours to keep forever—even if you never buy another book from Gold Eagle. But wait, there's more...

SCORE A BIGGER BONANZA AS A GOLD EAGLE SUBSCRIBER

Life is a game of chance, but you can be one of its lucky winners. How? By getting the world's hottest action-adventure novels delivered right to your home on a regular basis.

As a Gold Eagle subscriber, you'll rack up an unbeatable combination of benefits and privileges:

- You'll get 6 brand-new titles every second month (2 *Mack Bolans* and one each of *Able Team*, *Phoenix Force*, *Vietnam: Ground Zero* and *SOBs*) hot off the presses—and before they're available in stores.

- You'll save a hefty 12% off the retail price—you pay only $2.49 per book.

- You'll get our newsletter, AUTOMAG, *free* with every shipment.

- You'll get special books to preview or purchase at deep discounts.

YOUR NO-RISK GUARANTEE

As a subscriber, you can always cancel, return a shipment and owe nothing—so how can you lose?

RUSH YOUR ORDER TO US TODAY!

Yours FREE—this stainless-steel pocketknife.

Talk about versatile! You get 7 functions in this one handy device—screwdriver, bottle opener, nail cleaner, nail file, knife, scissors and key chain. Perfect for pocket, tool kit, tackle box. And it's yours free if it appears on your slot machine Sticker.

GOLD EAGLE READER SERVICE
YOUR SCORECARD

Did you hit the jackpot with 4 Free Books and a Free Pocketknife?

2 Gold Eagle Books

2 More Gold Eagle Books

☐ **YES!** I hit the jackpot. Please rush me the free gifts on the Sticker that I have affixed above. Then enroll me as a Gold Eagle subscriber with all the benefits and privileges outlined on the opposite page, including a no-risk money-back guarantee if I'm not satisfied.

166 CIM PAKA

Name _____ (PLEASE PRINT)

Address _____ Apt. _____

City _____

State _____ Zip _____

GOOD LUCK

draw a better hand before his bet was called. With luck, his hole card might turn out to be an ace.

No matter. There had been no choice for Bolan from the outset. There was no choice now.

"I'm in," he told the terrorist commander. "Set it up."

The Executioner was in, to the end of the line.

12

The Palazzo di Giustizia, Rome's Palace of Justice, stands beside the Tiber facing south. Completion of the massive structure took two decades, and the lag time is apparent in its architectural design. Colossal statuary, coupled with the bronze quadriga by Ximenes, mingle the baroque and classical traditions in a style that makes the palace one of Rome's best-known and most conspicuous modern buildings. Sweeping marble steps descend as if to meet the Tiber at Piazza de Tribunali, facing toward the bridge at Ponte Umberto and beyond it, to the very heart of Rome. Westward lies Castel Sant' Angelo, complete with antiquated courts and prisons that the palace has supplanted in this century. Farther west, but visible with effort from the steps, the Vatican stands stately and serene.

The Executioner felt none of that serenity as he prepared to climb those marble steps. He was about to put his head inside the lion's mouth, and he could smell the charnel breath already, reeking with the scent of death, which might turn out to be his own. The latest phase of Frenzi's plan could blow up in his face at any time, without a moment's warning, and there would be no way for the soldier to defend himself. Aside from walking straight into the headquarters of Roman law enforcement, he was going in unarmed, with nothing but his nerve and wits to see him safely out again.

Inside the lobby, Bolan paused a moment to observe the men and women who bustled around him, each preoccupied with errands that affected life and liberty for others. The carabinieri had their central office here, as did the leaders of the tough Italian security police.

He found a wall directory and crossed the vaulted chamber, passing through an open courtyard bright with shrubbery and flowers, on through other heavy doors and up a sweeping spiral staircase to the second level. Herein lay the private offices of Salvatore Luciano, chief of the security police. At the moment, though, the ranking cop would be a worried father first and foremost; Bolan was relying on that edge to see him through this task and safely back into the streets again.

He found the office that he wanted, let himself into a modest but well-furnished anteroom. The opulence displayed throughout the palace had not infiltrated here to any great degree, and Bolan took it as a part of Luciano's message to the world. Security police in Rome were more concerned with the reality of justice than the game, the glittering facade. They had a job to do, among the dirtiest available, and while the brass might be compelled to quarter in a palace by the Tiber, no one need suspect that Luciano or his men were going soft. If certain judges, ministers and law-enforcement officers grew fat and wealthy in the pursuit of criminals, it did not mean that Luciano's troopers were for sale.

He liked the man already, sight unseen, and that made Bolan's job more difficult. He must be the ruthless Mike Belasko now, intent on carrying through his mission at any cost to Luciano's life, his family. He had a message to deliver, and the man would have to listen to him, or Luciano's daughter would be paying for her father's stubbornness in blood and tears. Above all else, he had to make the chief of the security police believe that Carlo

Frenzi and the Red Justice Column were serious in each and every aspect of their threats, their bold demands.

No easy task, but Bolan was accustomed to the seemingly impossible. He crossed the empty waiting room and favored Luciano's secretary with his most engaging smile. She gave one back and granted that the chief inspector was available, already thumbing through the pages of a small appointment book.

"He is expecting you, Signor—?"

"Belasko," Bolan finished for her. "Actually, he's not, but I believe he'll want to see me anyway. I have a message from his daughter."

In the twinkling of an eye, the secretary's smile was twisted, swept away as if the Executioner had reached across the desk to slap her face. The flush of color had evaporated from her cheeks, and she was watching Bolan now as if he might be on the verge of transforming into something less than human. In her mind, of course, he had already made the change; the office staff would be aware of Claudia's disappearance, the assassination of her bodyguards, and they would be awaiting word from her abductors. There would be the usual whispered sympathies, averted eyes, each clerk and secretary praying he or she would not be tagged to play the messenger with that particularly brutal piece of news.

But he had dumped it in the lady's lap, and she was reaching for the intercom with trembling fingers, never taking eyes off Bolan, drilling him with a contempt more commonly reserved for child molesters and the tax man. Bolan took it, kept his hollow smile in place, unflinching. There was worse in store, by far, and he would take it as it came.

"This way." The secretary led him down a corridor to massive double doors that were handcrafted from mahogany. Her knock was furtive, almost birdlike, but it registered within, and they were summoned inside by a ringing baritone. The woman opened the doors and stepped into the room, followed by Bolan.

"Signor Belasko to see you," she announced faintly. The chief inspector waved her off, the heavy doors swung shut and they were finally alone.

Erect behind his desk, the chief inspector of security police was roughly Bolan's height but older, heavier where middle age was making inroads into a determined regimen of fitness. His mustache was thick, well-tended, flecked with gray that also showed around the temples. Eyes like bright obsidian bored into Bolan with a mixture of simple hate and curiosity.

"You are?"

"Belasko, Michael. You can call me Mike."

The false amenity produced no flicker of response from Luciano. "Please, be seated."

Bolan found a chair and settled into it. His grudging host did not sit down, but rather towered over Bolan with the desk between them like a glossy no-man's-land.

"You have a message from my daughter?"

"From her hosts." The soldier had to give him credit; there had scarcely been the shadow of a tremor in his voice. "She is secure in their hospitality, but growing homesick. I have been assigned to carry their expressions of goodwill to you and all your family."

"You are American?"

"I am."

"What has induced you to involve yourself in this affair?"

"You could say I'm a businessman."

"A mercenary?"

Bolan shrugged laconically. "Whatever."

"And your role in my misfortune?"

"I was with your daughter when she checked out of her suite last night."

The chief inspector stiffened slightly, but his face remained impassive. "You have just confessed to murder in the presence of a senior officer in the security police."

The soldier shook his head. "I don't believe that I've confessed to anything. The killers have been suitably disposed of."

"So, another murder, yes? Already you are facing life in prison."

"It's a chance I'll have to take."

"Which group of jackals do you represent? The Red Brigades? Jihad? The damned Albanians?"

"Red Justice."

"Ah."

It came out somewhere in the range between an exclamation and a moan. The chief inspector brought his hands together, his fingers interlaced in front of him, his elbows planted firmly on the desk as if to keep his hands from trembling. It was the worried father showing through at last, but there was steel beneath the deep pain, and Bolan saw the wheels in constant motion there, behind those flinty eyes.

"I should have realized. Your failure at the Naples cemetery must have been embarrassing."

The guy would never know how true that was, but Bolan let it pass. "We're here to talk about your daughter," he reminded Luciano. "Keep your fingers crossed, and maybe she won't be embarrassed like the boys in Naples."

"No escape," the chief inspector told him cryptically. "If harm is done to my Claudia, there is nowhere on earth that you can hide. Tell that to Carlo Frenzi."

Bolan didn't bat an eye when Luciano named the RJC commander. It was only common sense that the security police should have a line on active terrorists, perhaps a pair of eyes inside the group, and Enzio Petrucchi had already mentioned that the police would like to get their hands on Frenzi. Bolan wondered just how much of Frenzi's "secret" plan was really secret after all, but it was no time to begin a guessing game with Luciano, and he forged ahead.

"Your daughter's fine right now," he told the chief inspector, "and she'll stay that way as long as you cooperate."

"What are your terms?"

"One hundred million dollars, cash, with half in lire, half in deutsche marks. Three o'clock tomorrow morning is your deadline. You'll be given the directions for delivery by telephone."

"Ridiculous. How can you demand such a ransom? It is impossible for me to raise a fraction of that sum."

"Red Justice isn't askin' *you* to raise the money," Bolan told him flatly. "This is a demand upon the government of Italy."

For the barest fraction of a heartbeat, Luciano looked confused. "The state has ironclad policies against the payment of a ransom. You will find no sympathy for my Claudia in official circles."

Bolan shook his head. "You're still not with me. Your daughter's not the hostage here, she's just insurance, get it? Leverage. You try to throw a monkey wrench in Frenzi's plan, she suffers. You stand clear, the lady has no problem."

"But the money..."

"From the government," the Executioner explained. "Protection money. Payment keeps your city safe and sound. No pay, a major portion of the place goes up in smoke."

The chief inspector scowled. "Preposterous. We have security throughout the city now, at every major landmark. It would take an army to destroy one target."

"Frenzi has an army, but he isn't interested in fightin' any battles. Demolition's more his line, and he has charges buried at strategic points around the city, set to blow on schedule if he doesn't have the cash in hand. You miss the deadline, boom! No Vatican, no Coliseum, no Forum. Hell, for all I know, no Palace of Justice."

"Ridiculous. To plant such charges . . . No. It is impossible."

"I would have thought so, too, but I've been underground with Frenzi, and the charges *are* in place."

"When you say underground . . ."

"I mean precisely that. The catacombs, connecting tunnels, some of them improved the past few months by Frenzi's men. There's been a lot more going on down there than guided tours, Inspector. Frenzi has enough plastique to do some heavy damage, and with murder raps against him now, he doesn't have that much to lose."

"Assuming that I take you seriously—and I must advise you that your story sounds like science fiction—what is my involvement in this thing?"

"You play the middleman. Receive instructions for the drop and pass them on. Make certain that the boys in blue don't try to interfere and blow the whole damned thing. When time arrives, you make the drop."

"And my Claudia?"

"Will be safe as long as you play ball," the Executioner replied, and recognized the hollow lie before he spoke the words. "When Frenzi and the cash are clear, she'll be released on neutral ground, unharmed."

The chief inspector's face was etched in stone. "You realize that I could kill you now, in self-defense, or have you killed before you leave this room? One word, and you would never make it to the street alive."

The soldier nodded. "Sure, I know that. But it wouldn't be your smartest move today. We've all got deadlines, Chief. Mine calls for me to speak with Frenzi, from a pay phone in . . . eleven minutes. He'll have people watchin' me to make sure I'm not followed. If I don't check in, or if the lookouts spot a tail, things could get hot and heavy for your daughter in a hurry."

Luciano's frown reflected something other than the anger and contempt Bolan had become accustomed to. A trace of curiosity, perhaps.

"You speak of Carlo Frenzi and his men as if you stand apart from them, almost as an observer. I suspect you are not happy with your role in this affair."

He recognized the old policeman's trick and smiled. "I told you, I'm a businessman. I specialize in piecework. Pickin' up your daughter was a job, like comin' here to talk with you. Might be I wish that I was someplace else, but wishin' doesn't get it done."

"Indeed." When Luciano spoke again, his tone was almost wistful. "You must know that there is no escape from something of this magnitude. If Frenzi holds the power you describe, he will inevitably use it, for amusement if no other reason. He is not as other men."

The Executioner agreed with Luciano on that score, but he was running short of time and dared not overstep his bounds. "He's interested in money at the moment," Bolan told the chief inspector. "If you play it straight, there shouldn't be a problem."

"This will take some time."

"We understand that. You'll receive a call, let's say…two hours from right now. That gives you time to touch the bases, shake some people up, get their reactions. For your daughter's sake, I hope you make believers out of them."

"I promise nothing."

"Understood. But if you blow it…" Bolan left the statement hanging like a noose in front of Luciano. "Any message for your daughter?"

"Tell Claudia that I love her. I will help her if I can."

"Two hours, Chief. And let's not bother with a tail. You'd just be wasting precious time."

He closed the heavy doors behind him, passed the secretary without a backward glance, retraced his steps until he reached the street. Crossing the Ponte Umberto, he headed west to mingle with the crowds of tourists visiting the Vatican. The route was prearranged, with lookouts stationed here and there along the way, and Bolan did not deviate. He had to reach the phone booth across the piazza within minutes.

Checking in by telephone was a formality at best. He would not be reporting on his conversation with the chief inspector until he was face-to-face with Carlo Frenzi. Frenzi's paranoia led him to believe that every phone was tapped, each call susceptible to tracing, and the RJC commander wasn't taking any chances. Bolan would be shadowed for a mile or so, until he caught a taxi back to Piazza Navona and the small café that hid an entrance into Frenzi's underground. Debriefing would take place in Frenzi's office, deep beneath the bustling streets of Rome.

The soldier sympathized with Salvatore Luciano, recognized the worried father underneath the mask of staid professionalism. He could only hope that Luciano would submit, this once, without attempting any foolish countermeasures. Bolan had been gambling when he let it slip about the catacombs, but it had been essential that the chief inspector should believe in Frenzi's power to carry out his threat. Claudia's loss would be the least of it, damned right, if Frenzi started setting off his plastique at strategic intervals beneath the streets of Rome. An expert with the goop— or even lucky amateurs—might leave the ancient city with a close resemblance to the surface of the moon.

How many dead? The soldier didn't even want to think about it. Frenzi had proposed a cutoff time of 3:00 a.m., but if the ransom was not paid, he would be free to detonate the charges at his leisure, waiting for the crowded business hours, taking out assorted tourists, merchants, housewives as a form of retribution. Luciano was a stoic, but there had been something in his eyes when Bolan spoke about the tunnels. He could only hope the chief inspector bought it— or enough of it, at any rate, to keep his own commandos safely in their barracks and away from Frenzi's staging areas.

If not . . .

Then Luciano and the Executioner might well be witness to the second fall of Rome. It was a chilling prospect, and he did not dwell upon it as he shouldered through the drifting throngs of tourists, searching for the phone booth. If he missed it, even with the lookouts, Frenzi might assume that there was something wrong, reacting violently, irrevocably. And the chief inspector had been right about one thing: the RJC commander was a man apart, apparently divorced from the emotions of his fellow men.

Two minutes, and he had it now. Closing on the booth with loping strides, he found a callow, greasy youth already lounging in the shade there, the receiver tucked between his shoulder and his ear. The soldier stood in front of him and counted half a dozen heartbeats while he caught the kid's attention, pointing at his watch significantly, as an indication of an urgent call.

The punk ignored, him, turned his back, and now the Executioner was out of time. He snared the dirty collar of a shirt too long from the washtub and hauled the skinny wretch outside, immediately barging past him to appropriate the booth. A stream of hot invective wafted over Bolan, and the punk was working up his nerve to make a move when Bolan turned to face him, scowling, the graveyard eyes inviting reconsideration. With a final sneer, the kid retreated, seeking a safer environment. The soldier dropped in a coin, tapped out the number for a go-between who would communicate with Frenzi. A disgruntled voice responded on the second ring.

"*Sì?*"

"Belasko, clear."

"I tell."

The line went dead, and Bolan cradled the receiver, moving out. He had another good half mile ahead of him before he flagged a cab, which would deposit him a block from Frenzi's restaurant. If necessary, he could cut and run from there, but so far there had been no indication of a tail.

He hoped that Luciano played it straight, at least until the Executioner had found an opportunity to pull the plug on Frenzi's doomsday plan. There had to be a way, and he would find it, provided the authorities did nothing rash. Provided that he lived that long. The Eternal City's fate was hanging in the balance now, and Rome might not be so eternal after all....

13

Salvatore Luciano was devoted to the law. Not the abstract concepts of equality and justice, which were subject to an endless range of nebulous interpretations, but the law itself, as written down through generations that had gone before. The law was everything to Luciano, and he had pursued its rigorous enforcement from the time that he was old enough to fill a uniform. From childhood, the pursuit of criminals had been his life. In taking up the cause at twenty-one, he had fulfilled his destiny.

His father had been district prosecutor in Sardinia, a man who took his duties seriously in a region where the Mafia had thrived for centuries upon corruption and intimidation, murder and extortion. All of those were crimes, according to the statute books, and so Gaetane Luciano sought to jail the perpetrators, hauling them before reluctant magistrates, compelling frightened constables to drag them in repeatedly, regardless of their ages, wealth or social standing. When bribes were tendered, Prosecutor Luciano angrily rejected them and jailed the scum who came to him with hat—and cash—in hand. On one occasion, while visiting the courts in Naples to arrange for extradition of a prisoner, the prosecutor was accosted by a slim American whose name was also Luciano. Recently deported from America, the scar-faced Charlie Lucky had embraced Gaetane, called him brother, voiced the hope that they could work together amicably in the future. Livid,

Prosecutor Luciano spit in Charlie Lucky's face and walked away without a word. Incredibly, he lived to tell about it . . . but he did not live for long.

The ruling mafioso in Sardinia was Don Praetorio Carlino, an insatiable glutton who weighed in around 350 pounds when he was off his feed. Carlino's gluttony extended past the dining room, however, and encroached on other areas; his appetite for prepubescent girls was legendary, thinly covered by his wealth and the "esteem" in which his neighbors held the porcine mobster. It was said that no child under twelve was safe with Don Praetorio, but five successive prosecutors were unable to substantiate the charge. The sixth to try was Luciano's father, and it took him all of seven days to find Carlino in a hotel suite where he was "on vacation" with the daughter of a farmer from the neighborhood. The girl was nine years old, and she was nearly catatonic by the time a squad of policemen arrived with Luciano on point. Carlino was arrested on the spot, paraded through the streets to jail in saggy, boxer shorts and nothing else. He posted bail within the hour, and was huddled with his most accomplished guns by suppertime.

The gunners overtook Gaetane Luciano on the afternoon before Carlino's trial. They cut him down in broad daylight, firing seven shotgun blasts at point-blank range while scores of witnesses went briefly blind. The news reached Salvatore in Rome, where he was just a rookie on the force, intent on someday living up to the achievements of his father. Luciano took a leave of absence with permission from his captain, traveled south and spent a fortnight plying stubborn witnesses with wine. The effort cost him three months' pay, but it had given him four names—including that of Don Praetorio Carlino.

One by one, he took the gunners, going for them in his uniform and giving each the opportunity to peacefully surrender. To a man, they chose resistance, and he killed them all, sustaining gunshot wounds in his encounter with the third. Carlino sent a man to murder Luciano in the hospital, and that made four; though wounded, Salvatore disarmed the Don's assassin and employed the killer's own stiletto to engrave a ragged smile from ear to ear. In time, he went for Don Praetorio himself, a challenge to the mobster's honor that could never be ignored. Carlino waited for his adversary in the piazza where Gaetane Luciano had been slain. He wore a submachine gun beneath his coat, but never had an opportunity to use it. As the mobster tried to draw his weapon, Salvatore shot him once, between the eyes, and left Carlino leaking in the street.

Advancement with the carabinieri had been swift from that point on, and Luciano had become a local legend when the Mafia elected to ignore the death of Don Praetorio Carlino. It was easier, and far more profitable, to absorb the territories Carlino had accumulated through the years; as for the upstart carabiniere, he had closed a debt of blood and honor, which the Mafia could appreciate.

Back in Rome, the younger Luciano was promoted to detective at the end of his obligatory year's probation. As a plainclothes officer, he earned a reputation for tenacity in the pursuit of burglars, thieves and murderers, which made his entry to the case a prospect to be feared by local felons. For the next eleven years, his cases had a ninety-eight percent conviction rate, and it was said that Luciano never closed a case until the prison gates were closed behind the perpetrator. Violence seemed to follow Luciano, and in those eleven years he killed five more assailants in the line of duty: three were fugitives from murder warrants, and the other two were desperate thieves surprised by Luciano in the middle of a holdup. He became a favorite subject for the daily press, reviled or heralded depending on the personal persuasion of the editor toward law enforcement.

In the seventies, when terrorism came to Europe with a vengeance, Salvatore Luciano was among the first to recognize its danger. He dismissed suggestions that the Baader-

Meinhof, the Red Brigades and ETA were symptoms of a passing lunacy that would soon be forgotten, relegated to the garbage pail of history along with "flower power," miniskirts and Nehru jackets. Luciano recognized the peril months and years before his fellow officers, immediately pressing for the funds to organize a special antiterrorist commando force, equipped to wage guerrilla warfare if it should come down to that. A string of gruesome incidents would be required to drive his message home, but in the end, when Rome created the security police to cope with terror in Italy, the often-decorated carabiniere had been placed in overall command.

There had been no easy victories in Luciano's dirty war. His force was organized too late to save the life of Aldo Moro, but he had the satisfaction of extracting retribution from the Red Brigades, relentlessly pursuing them until the gang was now a shadow of its former self. When Baader-Meinhof gunmen fled from Germany to Italy in search of refuge, they discovered that there was no sanctuary in a war without official boundaries. Prison cells and special-weapons teams were waiting for them, and the few who wriggled through the net were glad to see the last of Luciano, happy to contend with the GSG-9 at home. In the pursuit of law and order, Luciano sent his troops against the Palestinians, the South Moluccans, Libyans, Iranians, assorted violence brokers drifting in and out of Rome from war-torn Africa. He treated all of them alike, and none of them was anxious for a second close encounter. In the media, which were fed up with revolutionaries and their half-baked causes, Luciano had become a hero. Lately there were public rumors that he might be named as minister of justice when the current minister retired in the near future.

For now, however, Luciano was the chief inspector of security police, with wars to wage on every side. He was familiar with Red Justice, certainly; the group had set up operations in his jurisdiction once before, abducting

Americans, and Luciano still could not forgive the way in which the business had been handled. It was not right for the Americans to send a special killer team—he could not credit rumors of a single man—and wreak such havoc on Italian soil. If there was violence to be done, it was the lot of the appropriate authorities to handle the dirty work. He had visited the embassy on that one and exchanged some angry words with the ambassador, convinced that the American was lying through his teeth when he denied all knowledge of the incident beyond what had been published in the press.

There had been certain benefits, of course, and for a time Luciano was convinced the RJC had been destroyed. The recent death of Arthur Bishop in a Naples cemetery had refuted any such illusion, and the bastards had his daughter now, expecting Luciano to react as any grieving father and forget his duty, crumble under pressure and submit to their demands. He had already telephoned the minister of justice, as instructed, leaving his superior to make the other calls. He had informed the minister of Mike Belasko's visit and the threat to set off plastique charges at strategic points beneath the Roman streets. He had not mentioned the abduction of his daughter, or the codicil to Frenzi's threat: that Luciano must restrain his men from taking any action while the ransom was delivered. He refused to tax the minister with problems of a private nature; rather, he would deal with them himself, in time, as he had dealt with the assassins of his father in Sardinia.

Claudia was as good as dead; he knew that much from grim experience in handling hostage situations. Terrorists occasionally freed their captives safe and sound, but it was the exception, rather than the rule. He had lost count of all the ransom drops, the desperate families with satchels full of cash to throw away, the shallow graves discovered later, snuffing out the final gleam of hope. By contrast, Mafia abductions were an exercise in chivalry: the hostages were treated reasonably well, were fed regularly and were murdered only in those cases where a ransom payment was refused. The face of crime had changed in Italy, and Luciano almost felt nostalgic at the passing of a simpler, if not gentler, age.

But they were bastards, all of them, and it had been his lifelong mission to pursue them, run them down and grind them into dust beneath his heel. The file on Carlo Frenzi lay upon his desk, open to the felon's rap sheet. The cocky mug shot grinned back at him in black and white. He would have put a bullet through that smiling face with pleasure, but he didn't know where Frenzi was. Somewhere underground, if Mike Belasko's story had the slightest credibility—but where? The chief inspector was familiar with the catacombs, the Vatican necropolis, but he had always pictured them as relatively small, restricted to a given portion of the city. He knew nothing of the other tunnels Belasko had alluded to, extending here and there beneath the streets at random, spun beneath the city like a safety net.

Except there was no safety there. A spiderweb, perhaps, and Carlo Frenzi was the lurking predator, prepared to feast on any human prey that might become entangled in his net. He had Claudia now, and in that certain knowledge, Luciano faced despair. He would not burden his superiors with mention of his private tragedy; they would commiserate and fawn around him for an hour or two, and then they would begin to question his ability to do a job where personal considerations were involved. If they could only realize it, they need entertain no doubts concerning the efficiency of Salvatore Luciano. With his daughter's life at stake, he would perform as he had always done, attacking where the enemy was least prepared, least able to defend himself.

And why had he not ordered officers to follow Mike Belasko? Why had he submitted to the mercenary's orders like a man intimidated? It was not Claudia's fate, he told himself, but rather the potential fate of Rome itself, the Eternal City, marked for demolition by a madman if security police

attempted to prevent the massive ransom payoff. Luciano
would not be responsible for such destruction, but he could
not let the terrorists escape with their extortion money,
either. It would run too much against the grain, require too
many changes in his thinking, in his very way of life.

'He would pursue Red Justice to the corners of the earth,
once Rome was safe again. When Frenzi's hidden charges
were discovered and defused, there would be time enough
to track the bastards into Switzerland, the Cayman Islands,
Rio de Janeiro—anywhere they thought that sanctuary
might be found from Luciano's wrath. He would do this for
the law, which he had served with every fiber of his being for
the past three decades. And if Frenzi's animals had harmed
Claudia, he would kill them.

Yes.

It might be murder, but there were so many ways around
the law these days. His uniform would take him far, and
there were methods of arranging for a suspect to resist arrest, appear to reach for weapons when he was, in fact, unarmed. It would be Luciano's one and only deviation from
the law, but he would owe Claudia that, at least. God knew
there had been little else between them for the past six years,
since Angelina's death. The job had claimed his time,
Claudia had been growing up alone and he was not especially surprised when she had run away from home. The real
surprise had come when he began to see her face in magazines, and later on the covers. When she made the move to
films, the chief inspector was astounded. Having seen her
only with a father's eyes, he had assumed her beauty was a
matter of perception, rather than established fact. The evidence displayed on screen had baffled Luciano, as the child
had baffled him when she was still at home. He had understood completely when she changed her name, and recognized that "art" was only partially responsible. Association
with a gung-ho counterterrorist could only damage the ca-

reer of an aspiring actress known as much for liberal politics as for her lines on screen.

Enough.

There was no time for maudlin introspection now, when Rome, the very heart of Italy, was being held for ransom by a pack of rabid animals. Although he had no formal voice in the decision, Luciano thought the government would pay. They had no realistic choice. If Frenzi was allowed to bring the city down around their ears, the government in power would be finished, individual participants discredited and hounded from the land. If Frenzi's threat was realized...

And if the government did not believe, in spite of Luciano's judgment, that Belasko had been truthful during their interview? What then? If someone at the top decided Frenzi and his animals were bluffing?

They would have to wait and see. Luciano was an observer now, compelled to wait for others to act, then respond to their initiatives. Whatever might come next, from compromise to Armageddon, Luciano had been sidelined.

But he knew how it would end.

In death.

For Carlo Frenzi.

For the RJC.

For Mike Belasko.

And for himself?

The chief inspector poured himself an unaccustomed glass of noonday wine and drank a toast to death.

"TOO BAD ABOUT Fredo and Vincenzo."

"It was terrible," Claudia answered, watching Carlo Frenzi pace the narrow cubicle. "It wasn't like the films at all."

"Too bad."

"You are unhappy?"

"I have pressing matters to consider."

She had never seen him act this way, and that surprised Claudia who had seen him virtually every other way across a span of eighteen months. It frightened her a little, most especially when coupled with the unexpected death of her companions back at the hotel, the effort to molest her that had only been prevented by the flint-eyed American. Carlo had been quick to punish her attackers, and while the reality of violence done before her eyes had sickened her, Claudia had known for months that Carlo's revolutionary lifestyle must incorporate a fair amount of homicide. The strain of violence had been part of the attraction, certainly, although she hesitated to admit it, even to herself. The heady scent of danger lent a new immediacy to their personal relationship, and it had never failed to turn her on. Tonight, the deaths of old acquaintances had put a new perspective on the matter, but Claudia still could not deny the old familiar stirring that she felt inside.

"I know a way to wipe those problems from your mind," she said, and stroked one slender hand across the canvas fabric of the cot. "A crude place, I agree, but still . . ."

"No time."

The brusqueness of his tone surprised her; it was like a slap across the face. At each of their encounters in the past he had been hungry for her, ravenous, unable to contain his passion. They had feasted on each other, gluttons seeking carnal pleasure, pausing only when exhaustion finally overtook them. As they had lain together, naked, sated for the moment, Carlo had explained his life to her in detail, spelling out his personal philosophies of liberation for the peasants of the world, and Claudia had begun to realize she loved him for his mind as much as for his body.

Well, almost as much.

He was an energetic, selfless lover, always letting Claudia have her pleasure first, before he took his own. His touch was masterful, unlike the fumbling of the college boys whom she had known, the furtive groping of producers and directors on the make. In time, Claudia had experimented with them all, but Carlo Frenzi stood apart, so different from the rest in every way. His zeal for liberating captive souls was simply one more aspect of the man she loved. Compassion for the masses, with an underlying trace of steel that would permit him to respond with violence if the neo-fascist state set out to crush him, to deprive the people of their due.

He explained all this when they had finished making love, in rented rooms and small apartments that belonged to some of Carlo's friends. Claudia never met his friends, as he had never fraternized with hers, for reasons of security. The enemies of freedom might be anywhere, he told her, and the very mention of her father was enough to make his comrades paranoid. Their love must be a closely guarded secret until Carlo could achieve the revolution that had been his goal since his days in prison.

Claudia knew about his past; they had no secrets from each other. Carlo had been frank about his background: rural poverty, a theft of meat to feed his family, the lawyer's promise that a guilty plea would spare him from a prison sentence. They were all liars, all the judges and attorneys who cooperated to suppress the common people. Carlo had been clapped into jail, surrounded by the worst examples of humanity, compelled to fight off homosexuals and scum of every sort to keep himself alive. In prison, he had learned the politics of revolution from others like himself, the persecuted souls who would emerge someday and lead the fight for liberation in Milan, in Naples, everywhere throughout the land.

The time in prison did not bother Claudia. Countless men and women were arrested every day on flimsy, fabricated charges, hustled off to dingy cells because the fascist state regarded them as dangers to stability. It was the same in Germany, in France and England, worst of all in the United States. She knew all this from listening to Carlo, reading the brochures and magazines he brought to her from time to time. It was an education for the daughter of a law-enforcement officer; she had been raised with black-and-white opinions in the area of crime, and was initially amazed to find that there were also many shades of gray.

Take robbery, for instance. Claudia knew it was illegal, and she had regarded it as wrong for nearly twenty years, but Carlo had supplied her with a new perspective. There were different sorts of robbery, he said. Some felons, like the mafiosi and *banditti* of the hills, were interested only in their personal enrichment, stealing from the wealthy and the poor alike to fatten their bankrolls. This was evil, and their kind would surely be exterminated with the coming of the revolution. Other thieves, however, had a different motive; they appropriated money from the rich and used it to support their liberation struggle, thereby giving back the wealth that had been sweated out of the common people in the first place. They were modern Robin Hoods, and history would rank them with the greatest patriots of Italy.

The same theory applied to the crime of homicide. For generations, the masses had been worked to death, their wages siphoned off to keep the rich in luxury, their sweat and blood like fertilizer for the rich Italian soil. When peasants raised a voice against the wealthy, men in uniforms were sent to hunt them down and murder them, their families, their neighbors. Members of the Mafia could murder with impunity because they paid police and prosecutors for the privilege. But the times were changing, and a fresh new wind was blowing through the land. Assassination, when selectively employed, could be a mighty weapon for the people. High officials who would not be moved by reason must be moved by other means, and if the means were terminal, that simply meant the problem was eliminated, wiped away like so much perspiration from the worker's brow. The execution of selected traitors was inevitable. In a war there must be casualties on either side, and Carlo was determined that his enemies should suffer more.

Claudia was disturbed at first when Carlo mentioned murdering her father, but with time she had become accustomed to the notion. Was he not the chief inspector of security police, responsible for heinous crimes against the common people and the revolution? Had his precious job not taken him away from home habitually while she was a child, in need of a father's love? Had not a trifling investigation taken him away from Angelina Luciano's bedside as the woman lay there dying, racked by cancer and tormented unmercifully?

Claudia owed her father nothing, had in fact abandoned him and his name to make her own way in the world. His death would mean no more to her than the devaluation of the yen... and yet, she felt a certain pang whenever Carlo mentioned eliminating the chief inspector, telling her how helpful she could be in a setting up the ambush.

She was helping Carlo now, but in a different fashion. The abduction had been his idea, and she had eagerly agreed, perhaps because she saw a way to strike back at her father, make him pay, while leaving him alive. Her ransom would support the revolution, purchase weapons, ammunition and medical supplies for wounded liberation fighters. Carlo would be proud of her, and he would show her in the special way she needed to be shown.

As now.

Claudia moved to stand in front of Carlo, cutting off his path before he could continue his pacing. The eyes that met her own were distant and distracted, faraway.

"I need you."

"Ah, Claudia."

"Now."

There was reluctance in his face, his manner, but it faded as she found him with her hand, the practiced summons that he knew so well.

"Claudia."

There, surrender in his voice, and it was music to her ears. His arms encircled her, his fingers searching for the zipper of her gown, and she knew that she was in control this time. It was her night, and she would drive the worries of the revolution from his mind, compel his concentration on the flesh that needed him, demanded him.

When they were finished in an hour or so, there would be time enough for Carlo to explain his problems and she would attempt to help him solve them. Claudia would do everything within her power for the man she loved, and for the revolution that was everything to him.

She pulled him down on top of her, ignoring squeaky protests from the army cot, unmindful of the fact that they had left the lights on, that the only door consisted of a flimsy curtain. Let the whole world recognize their love. Her father would be hurt, especially, and that was good.

That secret knowledge was, perhaps, the second-best sensation in Claudia's wide experience. The first . . .

She closed her eyes and melted into Carlo, let him plunder her as he would someday plunder Rome, in liberation's name. Her liberation had arrived. The rest would have to wait.

14

Some rear-echelon philosopher once characterized a combat soldier's life as hours of boredom, punctuated by moments of blind panic. He was wrong on both counts when it came to Bolan; as a sane man, he was often frightened, but the Executioner had never panicked, nor had he been bored. The action, living on the edge, had always been invigorating, and while waiting—ninety-five percent of any combat mission—there were always things to occupy his mind.

Like now.

He thought about Claudia Perrini in her lonely cubicle and wondered if there would be any chance for him to bring her out of this alive. He thought about her father, literally sitting on a time bomb, trapped between Red Justice and a government that might refuse to yield. The soldier felt for Luciano, sure, but there was nothing he could do or say to reassure the man, to raise his hopes that everything would turn out right in the end. Above all else, he thought about the charges Frenzi's men had planted at strategic points beneath the city. It could be a bluff, of course, but Bolan didn't think so. Frenzi was the sort who would delight in blowing up a city, turning monuments to smoking rubble, but the soldier didn't have to base his judgment on a madman's personality.

Explosives had been disappearing from the staging area. There had been several cases missing when he came back from abducting Perrini, others following his trip to see her father. There were other caches, Bolan knew, and more plastique for distribution through the underground. Enough, perhaps, to change the face of Rome forever. Frenzi would not hesitate to set the wheels in motion, that was clear, and it came down to Luciano now, the government of Italy. If the commander of security police convinced the minister of justice, if the other crucial high officials were persuaded of the need to pay, then Rome might stand awhile.

The waiting did not bother Bolan, but he felt a creeping sense of impotence as time slipped by without an answer to the question burning in his mind. How could he hope to find the hidden charges, scattered here and there around the city, wired and ready to explode upon command? Would Frenzi trust a timing mechanism, or would the explosives be connected to a central detonator under his control? The latter seemed a likely possibility, and it would make the soldier's task a great deal easier—provided he could find the mechanism and disarm it prior to Frenzi's deadline.

Rounding up the troops would be a separate problem. He could never hope to bring them all together, take them out en masse. He had already counted close to fifty guns; with two or three more staging areas—a minimum that he could not assume—he would be hopelessly outnumbered by the troopers of the RJC. The odds did not concern him, as he had prepared himself for death long years ago, but Bolan realized that it would be impossible to pull so many gunners in from scattered bivouacs. The sheer mechanics of it would defeat him, granting time and opportunity for countless problems to arise.

He had to concentrate on the explosives, and if he was incorrect in his assumption of a central detonating mechanism, he was finished from the start. Too many targets, right, and short of death, there would be no way of forcing Frenzi to divulge his secrets.

Rome could be a smoking wasteland, right, before he finished working Frenzi over.

Bolan's thoughts returned inevitably to Claudia Perrini. Absent since the scene in Frenzi's office, she would almost certainly be under guard in one of the secluded cubicles. It might be possible for him to reach her, speak with her, but to what end? He might console her with some empty reassurances, pretend that everything was going well and she would soon be free, but he did not believe it for a moment. Frenzi could no more afford a living witness than he could an infiltrator in the ranks. If Perrini was released, her testimony could doom Red Justice and condemn its leader to a life in prison.

At least five murders could be charged to Frenzi now, including Arthur Bishop and the goons who had attacked Claudia, but the evidence was slim to nonexistent. There were no surviving witnesses except for Bolan and the lady, half a dozen gunners who were neck-deep in the scheme themselves and therefore liable as accomplices. Without the girl, without Belasko, Frenzi faced a maximum of seven years on weapons charges, with time off for good behavior. Luciano knew his name, his record, but the chief inspector had no way of linking Frenzi to the kidnap plot with evidence admissible in court. He had not spoken to the terrorist commander, had not seen him, had no sample of his penmanship on anything incriminating.

Seven years, reduced to three or four if Frenzi kept his nose clean in the joint, and then it would begin again. In spades.

The Executioner had other plans, but he could not initiate his blitz before he had more information. If he canceled Frenzi's ticket now, the fate of Rome was up for grabs, and Bolan would not have that on his conscience, on his soul.

He thought of mingling with the other men, then passed off the idea as foolish. The general attitude toward Mike Belasko was a potpourri of fear, suspicion, anger and resentment. With a dash of blatant hatred, right, to heat things up. Without support from Carlo Frenzi, Bolan knew he wouldn't get the time of day from any grass-roots members of the RJC, and that left him precisely nowhere.

And for any warrior on a life-and-death assignment, nowhere is a deadly place to be.

He heard the scuffling footsteps, let himself pretend to be surprised. A khaki-clad commando with an automatic rifle in his hands was waiting when the soldier turned around.

"Signor Belasko, you will please to come with me."

"Why not?"

He trailed the gunner back along the gallery, through looming shadows that were constant, night and day. The soldier checked his wristwatch, found that Luciano's deadline for an answer from the government had passed just moments earlier. There would be news from topside, one way or the other, and the Executioner was being summoned to an audience with Frenzi where the fate of Rome would be revealed.

Four men were waiting when they got to Frenzi's office. Frenzi sat behind the makeshift desk, his face impassive, nodding stoically as Bolan entered. Enzio Petrucchi slouched in a camp chair in a corner of the cubicle, glowering at Bolan with his weasel eyes. The other two men were both in uniform, with the insignia of first lieutenant on their collars, side arms on their hips. A single folding chair stood empty in the middle of the room, and Bolan settled into it, prepared for anything, receiving minor comfort from the weight of the Beretta in its shoulder rigging.

Frenzi swept the tiny audience with eyes as black as coal. When he began to speak, his voice was taut with anger, on the verge of cracking.

"We have just received our answer from the fascist Luciano," he announced. "The state requires more time in which to ponder our demands. Their lackey begs our sufferance."

Bolan couldn't picture Luciano begging at the worst of times, but he was not especially surprised by the official stall. Somewhere along the chain of delegated power, someone had suggested that the threat might be a hoax, the charges nonexistent. Rome dared not be intimidated by an empty threat from two-bit terrorists. Red Justice was a paper tiger, clumsy at abductions, hopelessly incapable of pulling off so grandiose a scheme. More time would give authorities the chance to search for the hidden explosives, verify the danger or expose the grim charade.

More time.

The answer from on high had been predictable. So, too, was Carlo Frenzi's coolly furious response.

"We are compelled to offer an example," he declared. "The fascist insects must be taught a lesson if we are to deal with them from strength. Suggestions?"

Silence for a moment, then the older of the terrorist lieutenants raised a hand.

"Proceed."

"The Vatican?"

"Ambitious. I commend your zeal, but this must be our trump card. Premature destruction might produce unfortunate results."

The other uniform was fidgeting as if he had to use the bathroom. Frenzi finally deigned to notice him and nodded slowly, granting him permission to be heard.

"The Coliseum?"

Frenzi frowned and shook his head. "An empty shell. The target must be vital, a dynamic blow against the fascist state. We must impress the enemy with our determination to proceed at any cost."

A sudden light of inspiration dawned in Frenzi's eyes, a beatific smile emerging from beneath his scowl.

"I have it," he declared. "A target that will force our enemies to take us seriously. Leave me now! Wait, Enzio, I need you."

The lieutenants glanced at each other in confusion, rising slowly from their camp chairs. Enzio Petrucchi was already at his master's side, prepared to hear his orders, but he spared a gloating look of triumph for the Executioner as Bolan sauntered toward the door.

Whatever Frenzi had in mind, it would spell carnage on the streets, and Bolan was tormented by the thought that there was nothing he could do about it. Frenzi's choice of errand boys spoke volumes; he did not trust Mike Belasko well enough to let him have the mission, and his skilled lieutenants were to be held in reserve, against the possibility of Armageddon. Enzio was trusted *and* expendable, a combination that would make him perfect for a kamikaze mission on the streets.

It might be possible to throw the plan off track by taking out Petrucchi, but the move would cost the Executioner his cover and his life. Emerging from the musty cubicle, he saw the swarthy rifleman a few yards distant, watching him, and Bolan knew that the abduction of Claudia Perrini had not made him one of Frenzi's inner circle, after all. In Frenzi's eyes, he was a mercenary, plain and simple, paid to risk his life or take the lives of others, ever on the lookout for a higher bid. So far, he had performed as ordered, but the fat was in the fire now, and it would not hurt to keep an eye on Belasko as he went about his business.

When the time came, he would have to terminate the watchdog, but for now, the soldier's only option was to watch and wait. He had no realistic hope of scuttling Frenzi's "lesson"; he could only pray that there would be a minimum of senseless carnage. And, with any luck at all, he just might learn enough from the example to prevent the RJC from pulling off its master plan on schedule.

With any luck at all.

So far the lady had not smiled on him with any great conviction since his penetration of the underground. He was alive, but he had not deterred Red Justice from carrying out its mission on time.

The soldier might be forced to make his own luck.

Whichever way it went, the Executioner was tired of sitting on his hands. Soon now, those hands would find their grip on Carlo Frenzi's throat.

The soldier hoped it would be soon enough.

PETRUCCHI WATCHED the others leave, afraid that he might burst with pride before the last of them had cleared the room. Belasko had been fuming; he could see it in the mercenary's face when Frenzi passed him over, choosing Enzio to carry out the vital mission that would terrorize their enemies. Revenge was sweet, and would be sweeter still when there was time to deal with the American in private.

For the moment, though, Petrucchi's mission for the cause was everything. If Frenzi was impressed enough by his performance, he might be inclined to offer Enzio a battlefield promotion. Had he not dismissed the best suggestions of his two lieutenants, settling on Enzio instead? It was peculiar, granted, since Petrucchi had made no suggestions of his own. Had Frenzi chosen him through the simple process of elimination, as the only man who was not fool enough to blurt the first thing that had come to mind?

But, no. Belasko had not spoken, either, had not shamed himself in Frenzi's eyes. If anything, the mercenary's success at bringing in the woman should have made him Frenzi's choice. The fact of his dismissal, therefore, had been doubly heartening to Enzio. Petrucchi had been chosen on the basis of his courage, his dependability, his qualities of leadership.

Except that Enzio was not so sure about the courage. He had never been a hero, never been the first to throw a punch in any violent altercation. At the bar where he had met Belasko, Enzio had cowered in a corner while the big American took on the carabinieri by himself. Belasko recognized his fear, and so had passed him by when choosing men to kidnap the woman. Enzio despised himself for having cowered in the heat of combat, and he hated the American for calling him a coward with his eyes, his attitude. Petrucchi had arranged Belasko's match with big Armand to bring the mercenary down a peg or two and let him know what fear was all about...and now Armand was dead, while the American continued to stare at Petrucchi with contempt. He would be forced to kill Belasko soon, but first...

Petrucchi realized that Frenzi was already speaking, running down his plan, and he could only pray that nothing vital had been mentioned while his mind was lost in reverie. He dared not ask for any repetition, lest his master fly into a rage and throw him out, or worse, give the assignment to another.

"...perfect target for our needs," the commandant was saying. Had he named the target yet? "We are assured of tourists, probably some Americans. I am surprised I did not think of it at once."

Petrucchi kept his mouth shut while his stomach did a sluggish barrel roll. Already branded by Belasko as a coward, he could not permit the master to discover him a fool.

"Come, Enzio...can you not guess the target I have chosen?"

The weasel let his pent-up breath escape through teeth that ached from being clenched together. He was saved! If only he could put his mind on Frenzi's wavelength long enough to pluck the answer free and make himself appear the master strategist.

It came to him with sudden, crystal clarity, and Enzio was certain that their minds were perfectly in tune. When he revealed his prescience, Frenzi would be forced to recognize Petrucchi as his second-in-command, perhaps his equal. There would be no viable alternative.

"The Forum," he declared with perfect certainty.

The master's face was etched in stone. "You disappoint me, Enzio," he said.

Petrucchi wished the earth might open up and swallow him alive. A lightning bolt would do, impacting squarely on his skull, incinerating him before he withered from the force of Frenzi's gaze. The weasel hung his head and mumbled an apology, avoiding contact with the master's eyes by studying his pointed shoes.

"The tourists, Enzio. The women. *Think!* Where else in Rome might such an opportunity present itself?"

Petrucchi would have killed for a brochure of places frequented by foreign visitors. He knew them all by heart, of course, but now his mind had been wiped clean, as blank as a slate. He would be helpless if required to name his brothers.

"Via Veneto?"

He longed for death, already shriveling as Frenzi glared at him with undisguised contempt. Petrucchi rolled his eyes and waited for the end. If there was any mercy in the universe, it would be swift.

"The Trevi Fountain," Frenzi told him, making no attempt to mask the irritation in his voice. "You will agree it is the perfect choice?"

"Of course. Perfection!"

Enzio was mortified. The fountain would have been his next guess, certainly...if only it had come to mind. In fact, he thought it was no better than his own suggestions, but he would not dare to speak the thought aloud. Already, his stupidity had given Frenzi ample cause to doubt his choice of captains for the vital mission; nothing else must be allowed to keep Petrucchi from his destiny.

"The fascist state has chosen to dismiss us out of hand. We must instruct them in the error of their ways. Are you prepared?"

Petrucchi nodded, fearful now of even opening his mouth to speak. Suppose his voice should fail him altogether.

Would he stand there, gasping like a stranded fish? Instead, he nodded, listening intently while the master spelled his plan out in detail. He had two hours, maximum, in which to carry out the single greatest strike of modern Roman history. The Palestinians and Red Brigades would weep with envy when they heard of his achievement, grovel at the very mention of his name. At one stroke, Enzio Petrucchi would make history.

And afterward, there would be time to deal with the American, Belasko. He would know by then that Enzio was not a coward after all. The knowledge would unnerve Belasko, giving Enzio the edge he needed. And if all else failed he was prepared to shoot Belasko in the back.

It mattered little, in the long run. The important part was getting rid of enemies before they spread their poison, turning other minds against you, making others look at you with vague suspicion, thinly veiled distrust. The members of Red Justice would regard Petrucchi as a hero when his mission was completed, and he would not have Belasko laughing at him, spreading ugly talk behind his back. A soldier's honor was important, second only to his skill in combat, and while Enzio was more concerned with the illusion than reality, there was a point where both became as one. A warrior's reputation could ensure that he might never have to fight again, if it was fierce enough and universally accepted as the truth. A man could get along for years on reputation, but he dared not suffer enemies who slandered him and tore apart his reputation. A gunman who was criticized might soon be challenged, forced to prove himself again, and therein lay the risk.

For all his braggadocio, Petrucchi was a virgin when it came to killing. He had never taken a human life, although he had been present during an assassination, firing several bullets into empty space while others brought the target down, unmindful of his cowardice and faulty aim. The tales of his ferocity were so much bullshit, manufactured by Petrucchi as the situation might demand. The Trevi mission would provide him with an opportunity to prove himself spectacularly, brilliantly, surpassing anything that had been done before. When he was finished, none would dare contest his right to lead.

There would be time enough to deal with Mike Belasko then, when he had proved himself, and he would make the bastard sorry that he ever had insulted Enzio Petrucchi. Let the mercenary laugh at him, dismiss him as a coward and a joke. False confidence would be the man's undoing; ego would destroy him in the end.

And with Belasko gone, what then? The future lay before Petrucchi, bright with endless possibilities. When he had carried off the Trevi mission, Frenzi would be forced to take a second look at Enzio, forget about the bungled answers of a moment earlier and recognize his proved skill. If he refused to recognize the man Petrucchi had become... well, it was not uncommon for a revolutionary group to suffer vacancies in leadership along the road to liberation. Vacancies that would be filled by men of grit, intelligence and daring.

It was premature, of course, to think of ousting Frenzi. That would take some expert planning, possibly collusion with some others in the ranks. And it might not be necessary, after all, if Frenzi simply recognized the fact of Enzio's achievement, his superiority above the rest. That done, it might be months before Petrucchi thought of usurping Frenzi.

There should be some reward for such a warrior as himself, and while he listened to the master's explanation, memorizing every detail, Enzio began to rack his brain for suitable suggestions. Cash, of course... but that was so mundane, and they would all be drawing shares of the enormous ransom when it was collected. Status in the group... but that would soon be his in any case, the natural result of his performance under fire.

The woman.

In a sudden flash of genius, Enzio was certain what he wanted—what he *needed*, yes—to make his life complete. The woman would be his reward for bringing off the Trevi strike as planned. He need not mention it to Frenzi in advance; there would be time enough when he had demonstrated his ability to make the fascists bow their heads in terror. Enzio could see it now, the master with an arm around his shoulders, while the others crowded close to clap him on the back or merely touch his clothing. Frenzi turning to him with a dazzling smile, inquiring whether there was anything, some trifle, that the hero of the hour might desire.

And Enzio would have an answer ready for him, yes, indeed.

They had to kill the woman, anyway; it would not matter if he used her for a while before the soldiers dragged her off to outer darkness and disposed of her remains. Petrucchi might just volunteer to do the job himself, when he was finished with her, demonstrating for the record that he was not hampered by emotional entanglements. It would be like the icing on the cake.

But he was being premature. The Trevi mission was his first priority, and if he bungled there, if he should fail . . .

The old self-doubts were with him once again, in force, dispersing Enzio's illusions. He was unblooded as a soldier—would be until he finished with his business at the fountain and returned in safety to the tunnels. In the meantime, there were preparations to be made, supplies to be obtained, security to be maintained.

Success was far from guaranteed. The job could blow up in his face, destroy him in an instant if he let his guard down, let his dreams of future glory interfere with hard-and-fast reality. He pushed thoughts of the woman from his mind, sent Mike Belasko packing with a shrug, dismissed all thoughts of bucking Carlo Frenzi for his leadership position in the RJC. Such dreams could get him killed if they were premature, and Enzio had not begun to live.

15

They had been trudging through the tunnels for an hour, but in surface distance, Bolan estimated that they might have covered no more than a thousand yards. With Carlo Frenzi in the lead, they had ascended through the galleries until the street was just above them. Bolan half imagined voices, street sounds, though he knew with perfect certainty that nothing could be heard inside their tomblike passageway.

He had no inkling of their final destination. Frenzi had insisted on Belasko's presence for the big event, but otherwise he had been silent on the nature of his coup, the time and place when he would offer his example to the world. It would have made no difference in any case; cut off from all communication with the outside world, the Executioner would have no opportunity to warn authorities. He was alone, and he would have to play it out that way, relying on the cards in his hand.

He could have executed Frenzi, might have taken him at any time along their trek and iced the terrorist commander's backup gunner, as well. But Frenzi's death would be a wasted gesture if his scheme was in the works already, if his demolition team was set to move without him in the case of intervention by police. And there was more at stake for Bolan here than any single target Frenzi might select. If Frenzi bought it prematurely, Bolan would be forced to scramble blind for answers on the placement of the other charges. If he moved too quickly...

"Here."

A rusty ladder was bolted to the wall where Frenzi stood, ascending into darkness. Carlo led the way, with Bolan trailing and his backup gunner bringing up the rear in silence. By the time he had topped the ladder and found a place to stand, a panel had been opened in the wall, permitting access to a dark and musty cellar. Frenzi turned to face him with a cunning smile.

"The basement of St. Luke's Academy, on Via della Stamperia. Fortunately, it is closed for restoration. There will be no workmen here today."

They climbed a rugged staircase to the ground floor of St. Luke's Academy, and Bolan realized that it had been—would be—a gallery of portraits. All the artwork had been stripped from walls in need of plasterwork and painting, but their marks were left behind in clean rectangular designs, outlined by the accumulated grime of generations. Bolan wondered at the missing workmen, finally remembering the time. They would have knocked off for the day, retreating to their homes or favorite nightspots to forget about the dust and drudgery of working for a while.

"This way."

He followed Frenzi through abandoned rooms with scaffolding along the walls, the tools of carpenters and masons resting where they had been dropped at quitting time. Tomorrow, St. Luke's Academy would ring with hammers and the voices of the workmen once again, provided that it was allowed to stand.

The soldier took another look around the place, decided that it could not be the target. Frenzi had been looking for a mark that would attract attention, someplace where a crowd of tourists could be placed at risk, convincing the authorities to take Red Justice seriously. Blowing the academy would raise a dust cloud, cause some traffic problems if the walls fell toward the street, but there was something missing. The demolition of St. Luke's would get the government's attention, but the Executioner was certain that it would not be enough for Frenzi. Carlo needed blood, and he would never find it here today.

A marble staircase took them to the second floor to more empty rooms awaiting the attention of the workmen, but their destination was a ladder tucked away inside a walk-in closet used for storage of custodial supplies. A trapdoor opened onto the roof of the academy, and Bolan followed Frenzi through the hatch, the other gunman like a shadow on his heels.

From topside, Bolan had a sweeping vista of the Quirinal—the highest of the seven hills of Rome. Almost due south, two hundred yards distant, stood the Quirinal Palace, official residence of the Italian president. For half a heartbeat, Bolan wondered whether Frenzi might have lost his mind entirely, but the soldier let himself relax a fraction when he found the terrorist commander and his lackey facing eastward.

Toward the Trevi Fountain.

He recognized the target instantly, and Bolan felt his stomach tightening. The workmen of St. Luke's were finished for the day, but there were hours of daylight left, and tourists flocked around the ornate fountain, snapping shutters, posing for the photo of a lifetime. From no more than sixty yards away, the Executioner could see them plainly, watch them turn their backs in the direction of the fountain, tossing coins across their shoulders in response to ancient superstition. One coin guaranteed another trip to Rome, according to the legend, while a second gave the visitor one wish. Traditionally, that was used in seeking love or happiness, and Bolan wondered whether any of them here today were wishing for survival.

Frenzi turned to Bolan, beaming with self-satisfaction. "Is it not perfection? Could there be a finer choice for our example?"

Bolan shrugged, endeavoring to keep it casual. "I guess."

His tone caught Frenzi by surprise and cracked the gunman's plastic smile. "You have some reservations?" Carlo asked, suspicion heavy in his voice.

The soldier tried to sound disinterested. "Not really," he replied. "It just seems like a lot of trouble for a fountain and some tourists pitching pennies. If you're gonna get these guys pissed off, you might as well go all the way. Why not blow up the president, for instance? He's a sitting duck right there, no more'n a hundred yards away."

A momentary silence hung between them, then the terrorist commander's frown exploded into hearty laughter. Bolan tried a smile on, didn't like the feel of it and let it slide.

"What's funny?"

Carlo Frenzi shook his head and took another moment to compose himself. "I do not laugh at you, *signor*. I simply find your brash, direct approach refreshing, stimulating. Sadly, we may not proceed along the course you propose, for two important reasons. First, direct assaults upon the government have never been effective here in Italy. If anything, they seem to strengthen the resolve of those in power, make the fascists see themselves as martyrs in a holy cause. Tourism is the life of Rome. A strike against the so-called innocents will serve us better than assassination of the president and all his ministers combined."

"The second reason," Bolan prodded.

"Ah. The tunnels," Frenzi said, as if that cleared up everything.

"Explain."

"Our network is extensive," Frenzi answered, "but it does not cover every street and alleyway in Rome, by any means. Whole districts are excluded, closed to travel underground. The tunnel that we followed here continues for another block or so, then terminates in solid stone... What you Americans would call the dead end, *sì*?" He turned and pointed southward, toward the presidential palace. "In between our tunnel and the palace lie a hundred meters of impenetrable stone. We have no ready access to the target. The same applies to the Palazzo di Giustizia and certain other bastions of the fascist state. For now, if we desire concealment we are bounded by the limitations of the tunnel network, forced to strike at targets that are readily accessible from underground."

The soldier understood, and with that understanding came a glint of hope. If Frenzi's troopers were confined within the tunnels, limited in their selection of potential targets, then there had to be whole streets and neighborhoods in Rome that were excluded from the hit list. Frenzi did not have an infinite variety of targets to choose from, though the range might still be very large indeed. If Bolan's theory was correct, the terrorists would also shy away from catacombs and tunnels open to the public, even if their secret passageways might somewhere intersect. That theoretically ruled out the Vatican necropolis, various catacombs under the Appian Way, some others in the so-called "African" district, northeast of Villa Borghese. Bolan realized that he was aware of tunnels only in the Trastevere district, on the Tiber's western bank, and in the midtown east-west stretch between the Quirinal and Piazza Navona. There would almost certainly be others—one of Frenzi's officers had mentioned demolition of the Coliseum—but their number and the ground they covered were not nearly as extensive as the Executioner had feared.

Which meant precisely nothing if he could not pin down specific targets, if he couldn't get a better handle on the situation.

"Time."

He moved along the rooftop railing to stand at Frenzi's side. Frenzi pulled a compact radio transceiver from the pocket of his coat, adjusting it to the designated frequency. Bolan had an urge to slap the walkie-talkie from his hand and send it spinning to the street below, but he restrained himself. Impetuous behavior would destroy his cover, and while he was confident of his ability to take the gunners by surprise, eliminate them both before they had a chance to reach their holstered sidearms, he was back at his original predicament: no Frenzi, no aversion of the fire storm that Red Justice had in store for Rome. No chance to pull his mission off successfully.

If Bolan tried to save the Trevi Fountain and the people in the piazza he might sacrifice the whole city to the terrorists.

Disgusted with the options that were really no damned choice at all, the Executioner thrust both hands deep into his pockets, commanding them away from Carlo Frenzi's throat.

"Time."

Frenzi could feel the old excitement mounting in his stomach, tingling along the nerve synapses, spreading through his body like the flush of too much wine. It was a heady feeling, and one he experienced at moments of supreme accomplishment, when mortal risk and vast reward were balanced on a razor's edge, the end result too close to call.

He was addicted to the thrill of danger, had been since the days of childhood thievery when the pursuit, the risk of capture, had been more important than the stolen merchandise. As an adult, when burglarizing shops and homes, he had been constantly on edge, suspended in a near-orgasmic state that lasted while his life and liberty remained at risk. The feeling had been rare of late, confined as Frenzi was to the commander's role, condemned to play the strategist while others carried out his orders, but he had almost achieved it with the execution of Claudia's would-be rapists, and the thrill was with him now full force. He wondered idly why no woman had been able to inspire such passion in his flesh, but it was pointless to concern himself with whims of nature, and he put the problem out of mind.

In front of him, no more than fifty yards away, was the Trevi Fountain. Without straining narrowed eyes, he could make out the sculpted form of Oceanus in his chariot, with sea horses and tritons in the yoke, the figures of Abundance and Salubrity on either flank. He counted off a hundred tourists prior to losing track, and estimated twice as many pressed around the fountain, tossing coins and snapping photographs. An equal number milled aimlessly within a radius of twenty yards, waiting for an opening, a chance to join the crush.

And it was perfect, as he had known it would be.

Just beneath the fountain, in a tunnel hammered out of living stone, Petrucchi and his demolition team would have the plastic explosives in place, the gelignite arranged and tamped so that the force of the explosion would be channeled skyward. There would be enough to breach the sidewalk, split the pavement of the street. Enough to...well, they would just have to wait and see.

In retrospect, it was a blessing that the government had tried to stall for time. In theory, Frenzi's plan was perfect, foolproof, but the Trevi mission was the first and only test of his ability to ravage Rome with high explosives set beneath her streets. If there was any problem with the charges—if they should prove too weak, too strong; if they should fail to detonate at all—his men would have a second chance to get it right before his final deadline for the ransom drop. If Trevi was a failure, it would only guarantee long-term success for Frenzi's scheme, and he could always find another makeshift killing ground to teach the fascist running dogs a lesson in diplomacy.

He cast a sidelong glance at the American, Belasko, as he raised the radio to his lips. The mercenary had a certain reckless daring typical of the Americans, but there was something else, a vague and insubstantial something that prevented Frenzi from completely trusting him. The RJC commander had insisted that a backup gunner should accompany them, not because he feared an ambush by police, but rather to protect his back from Mike Belasko.

Not that Frenzi feared the brash American, far from it. It was just that nothing, no one, must intrude upon his plans this close to the culmination of a dream. If there was treason in Belasko's heart and mind, it would be simple to dispose of him, eliminate the minor threat before proceeding with his master plan. The mercenary could not harm him now.

Petrucchi and the others should be clear. If not, it would be their misfortune. Frenzi held the radio's transmitter button down and spoke a single word.

"Proceed."

Across the Trevi piazza, outside the Church of Saints Vincent and Anastasius, a young man with a hearing aid received the message, slipping one hand in the knapsack that he carried, fishing for the detonator hidden there. Another moment passed, then he must have found it, flashed the lethal signal in an instant, for he was already moving across the piazza, south on Via di Pilotta.

Frenzi felt the blast before he heard it, a vibration rising through the ancient structure of St. Luke's beneath his feet. Downrange, the tourists at the site felt it more immediately, falling silent in a heartbeat's time, surmising that they were experiencing an earth tremor. The group at ground zero never had a chance to change their minds.

Before his eyes, the fountain, its surrounding pavement—everything—was catapulted skyward with a roar that startled Frenzi, stole his breath away. The water from the fountain was a geyser now, all muddy as it mingled with the earth and shattered stone that had been hurled aloft.

And bodies. Bits and pieces of them. Others were still intact but airborne like rag dolls in a hurricane. A veil of smoke and dust obscured their awkward tumble back to earth, but Carlo Frenzi had already seen enough to know that they were dead on impact. On the blast's perimeter, the living staggered, limped or dragged themselves away in search of succor, any respite from the hellish ringing in their ears. They crawled through shattered windows, the blood from lacerated hands and knees already mingling with the flow from twisted, mangled bodies that would never rise again.

The carnage instantly reminded Frenzi of a scene from Dante's *Inferno*. The ragged voices of the maimed and dying were like subtle music to his ears. He braced both hands against the parapet and leaned far out above the sidewalk, breathing deeply, savoring the acrid smell created by the holocaust, the stench of burned human flesh.

From somewhere in the distance came the sounds of sirens, drawing closer by the second. There was no time left to savor his accomplishment, but Frenzi had already seen enough to rate the strike as an unqualified success. The government would listen to him with a new respect from this point forward; they would look at Trevi piazza and imagine other landmarks, other tourists, rising in a cloud of dust and flame if Frenzi's ransom payment was denied. The world would understand that members of the sick establishment had forced this deed on Carlo Frenzi, forcing him to act before they would respect him as a man.

The bastards would respect him now, by God! They would begin to shiver and quake at mention of his name. The liberation fighters of a dozen countries would be after Carlo Frenzi, hat in hand, beseeching him to guide them, share his genius in pursuit of this or that exalted cause. And all of them would have to pay.

They dared not trifle with him now. In retrospect, it was a pity that his first demand had been so modest, but the hundred million would be adequate ... for now. In time, as Frenzi's needs increased, there would be other demands, larger payments, but he was a man of honor, and he would not gouge the enemy when they were humbled at his feet. A hundred million dollars would do very nicely as an appetizer for the feast to come.

He pocketed the radio transceiver, turned to face his two companions on the rooftop. Giovanni, a gunman whose IQ was roughly equal to the caliber of weapon in his shoulder holster, beamed at Frenzi, muttering, *"Bravo! Bravisimo!"* Belasko, on the other hand, was looking faintly ill; the color had evaporated from his cheeks, his shoulders slumped, as if someone had punched him in the stomach and he did not have the energy to fall.

"You disapprove?"

"Who, me?" Belasko shook his head without conviction. "Just seems wasteful, like I said before."

"Perhaps. But they will listen to us now, believe us when we tell them that we hold the power to destroy the city, strip three thousand years of Roman history away like so much garbage."

"Maybe," the American replied, a trace of animation creeping back into his face. "And, then again, you might've kicked the hornet's nest, you follow? They might just be *so* pissed off, they'd rather risk it just to fry your ass."

The sirens were in the near distance now, and Frenzi felt the need to be away, but he could not allow Belasko the last word.

"I know the Roman mind, *signor*. To these men, history is everything, tradition a religion in itself. To save their monuments, their icons, they would offer up their wives and children on a silver platter. Anything that we demand is ours."

"I hope you're right," the mercenary grumbled, turning from the parapet to start the long walk back. "'Cause if you're wrong, you just stepped in deep shit."

THE URGE TO THROTTLE FRENZI, lift him overhead and cast him down to Via della Stamperia like a bag of leaking garbage, almost overwhelmed the Executioner for several seconds after the explosion. It would be so easy, and so satisfying as his body struck the pavement, twisted, broken, lifeless. He would take the dimwit gunner first, of course, perhaps with a karate chop across the larynx, sealing off his breath forever, leaving him to strangle while his master took the dive alone.

The soldier wanted Frenzi's blood so badly he could almost taste it in his throat . . . but he would have to wait. The damage was already done in Trevi piazza, but the worst still lay ahead for Rome if Frenzi was permitted to continue with his plan. The Executioner imagined Trevi piazza and its carnage multiplied a dozen times, the streets awash with blood and hazy with the dust of subterranean explosions. He might stop it yet, but only if he let the bastard live a little longer. Long enough, perhaps, to hang himself and scuttle his demented scheme before it could be carried through.

It was a long walk back, and Bolan heard the agonizing voices even after they were safely underground, when it was physically impossible for sound to penetrate and reach his ears. He saw the twisted bodies, airborne, tumbling back to earth in pieces, staining shattered pavement with themselves on impact. Trevi Fountain's unleashed flood would never wash that stain away. It would require more blood, and as he followed Frenzi through the winding tunnels, rodents scuttling like furtive messengers around their feet, Mack Bolan had the perfect source in mind.

Bolan knew the sequence of events from this point on. Another contact with the chief inspector of security police. More threats against his daughter and against the city, citing Trevi piazza as conclusive proof of Frenzi's grim commitment to proceed. The message would be relayed on through Luciano, up the ladder of command, and this time they would promise payment, begging Frenzi's pardon for the earlier confusion. Payment might or might not be intended, but they would go through the motions, either way.

And in the meantime, Luciano's soldiers would be scouring the catacombs, attempting to discover Frenzi's hiding place.

They would get nowhere from the Trevi piazza, Bolan realized. The blast would certainly have sealed that tunnel off, and any effort to retrace it from the surface, ripping up the streets and sidewalks, would be much too obvious. Already, sources in the media would be at work constructing stories of a gas leak, anything to head off panic that might sound the death knell of the Roman tourist industry.

Another deadline might be fixed by Frenzi, or if he was in an unforgiving mood, he might maintain the old one: 3:00 a.m. The drop would not be specified just yet; no point in giving Luciano excess time to lay an ambush at the site. A bagman would be chosen from the ranks... or he might choose a mercenary who was paid to risk his life on missions that were tantamount to suicide.

The prospect of his selection to retrieve the ransom payment did not bother Bolan. He did not intend to let things go that far—not after they had gone so terribly awry already. Any confrontation at the drop, the slightest evidence of a double cross, and Frenzi would be primed to detonate the other charges placed at strategic points along the tunnel network. He might decide to detonate them anyway, and for that very reason, Bolan knew that he would never leave the underground again until his enemy had been eliminated, Frenzi's fantasy—or Rome itself—reduced to ashes in the end.

So far, the game was too damned close to call, and Bolan was not making any forecasts. It could still go either way, he realized, and either way might spell a sudden, bloody finish for the Executioner.

16

Salvatore Luciano stood outside the Church of Saints Vincent and Anastasius, watching as ambulance attendants went about their grisly business. Wounded victims had been removed to hospitals immediately, sirens braying in the stillness that was so unnatural for Rome. When all the living had been evacuated, bodies and body parts were photographed from every angle by forensic teams, their placement charted on a large-scale map, which might be used as evidence if anyone was ever brought to trial for the atrocity. The lab men came prepared for anything, in starched white jump suits, hip boots insulating them from blood and the continued overflow of the fountain.

Luciano wondered when someone would get around to turning off the water, then decided it didn't matter. If they let the flood run long enough, perhaps it would begin to wash away the stains left by the carnage, blot out memories of bodies twisted, broken, like a giant's cast-off toys.

Perhaps.

Discovery of a shattered tunnel under the piazza had confirmed the chief inspector's greatest fear. Belasko had been truthful in his brief description of a hidden network beneath the streets of Rome. Unknown to Luciano, to the general populace, subversive vermin had been scuttling beneath their feet like termites for—how long? A year? Two years? For decades? Were there any other vital secrets the chief inspector of security police was yet to learn?

Luciano shook his head, immersed in self-disgust. Undoubtedly there were such secrets, and their mere existence marked him as a failure in his mission to protect the state, the population, from precisely this sort of disaster. If the tunnels had been known to Luciano earlier, his options would have varied widely, but he had no options now. He could not trace the tunnel revealed at this site, not without demolishing the streets in each direction—and what then? If additional tunnels were discovered, should he send his officers to root the bastards out? Rely upon the military, with its less than sterling record? Risk a firefight in the underground that might ignite the very charges he was seeking to defuse?

No options, and it galled him that the likes of Carlo Frenzi should be in control, dictating terms to Rome. He had no doubt that this was Frenzi's work; a phone call to his office at the moment of the Trevi detonation had confirmed as much, describing the atrocity as "an example to the fascist insects," but he would have known in any case. The stall for time had been a gamble, and the gamblers had lost. If Rome was to be salvaged, they would have to pay while time remained.

He would advise the minister of his opinion, and in no uncertain terms. The choice did not reside with him, of course; he was a go-between, what the Americans would call a middleman. The fact that Frenzi had abducted Luciano's child was irrelevant, still unknown to his superiors. The double murder in Claudia's suite would be investigated by the carabinieri in due time, but for the moment, every man in uniform was concentrating on Red Justice and the greater threat to Rome. If Frenzi could destroy so many lives without a backward glance, as an example, then he was no doubt capable of worse. If he could not be found—and Luciano had already given up on that—then his demands must be fulfilled.

And after payment, they would wait to learn if Frenzi was a terrorist who kept his word, or whether he would set the charges off to spite his enemies, as an expression of supreme contempt. A third alternative was equally disturbing: Frenzi might accept the cash, but only as a first installment, leaving the explosive charges where they were or moving them around strategically, to keep the government guessing, keep it paying through the nose. The bastard might become de facto king of Italy if he was not unearthed and eliminated, but the search would have to wait.

The chief inspector thought about Claudia, and as quickly pushed the image of her smiling face away. He had no time for any personal concerns. Claudia might be dead already, and if not, she would most likely be eliminated once the ransom was collected. Luciano felt her loss already, with a chilling certainty that left him cold and dead inside. It did not matter what became of him now; his wife and daughter both were gone, wiped out by circumstances and by forces he would never understand. What made the human cell explode into malignancy? What drove a man to turn against his species with the fury of a demon in the flesh?

No matter. There were surgeons to pursue malignant cells, and Luciano was a surgeon in his own right, set to track the human scum within society. His mission was their eradication, and it mattered little in the long run whether Luciano's targets were shot down or brought to trial and locked away for years. He personally favored permanent solutions, but they were so difficult to come by in the modern day. As soon as one fanatic was eliminated, half a dozen others rose to take his place, and Luciano wondered how much longer he could stand against the rising tide of filth.

Not long.

This case would be his last, in fact. There would be questions, certainly, about the lack of warning in the Trevi massacre, and Luciano had no answers. He could salvage something from it yet, if he could drop the net on Carlo Frenzi and his comrades, but it might take time. The chief inspector wondered whether he would be allowed to lead the hunt at all. A scapegoat might be necessary after this terrorist incident, and who better than the man in charge of gathering intelligence on terrorists? It must be Luciano's fault; if he was on the job, performing satisfactorily, he would have known about the tunnels years ago.

It did not matter if they dumped him now. If word came down today, this instant, he would gracefully submit his resignation. And continue searching for the bastards on his own. The job, per se, meant nothing to him, but his mission was a sacred trust. He would destroy Red Justice, throttle Carlo Frenzi with his own bare hands, and if it meant a term in prison, Luciano was prepared to live within the walls. And if the search should cost his life, that, too, was insignificant, as long as Luciano had an opportunity to face the savages who had unleashed such carnage in the streets of Rome.

If he could find Claudia, bring her safely home... But no, he dared not hope too much. She might be dead already, and false hopes would only slow him down when there was need for swift decisions.

Death was Luciano's comrade now, his only comfort. He could feel the Reaper, standing close beside him on the marble steps, surveying Carlo Frenzi's handiwork. And in his heart, he knew the Reaper was appalled.

They would work well together, Luciano and the Reaper. They had certain common interests now, and Luciano hoped his newfound comrade might be able to unearth Red Justice, sniff the scum out amid the catacombs.

Luciano tore his eyes away from the piazza, concentrating on the task at hand. He had a call to make, and once again he would advise the ministers to pay at once. They might or might not listen to him, but the matter would be in their hands once Luciano had fulfilled his obligation to report. From that point on, until the ministers made up their minds, the chief inspector would be on his own. There were inquiries to be made, the usual suspects to be rounded up for rough interrogation.

If the ministers were rational, if they decided to submit, he would demand the privilege of carrying the ransom himself. It was a long shot, certainly, but it might be his one and only opportunity of making contact with Red Justice in the flesh. From that point on, he would be walking with the Reaper, taking all his cues from Father Death, and either way it went, the Reaper would be waiting for him in the end.

GOOD LUCK WAS RARE ENOUGH in Bolan's war, and he was never one to put the lady off when she came calling unexpectedly. He made the terrorist communications center quite by accident—or fate, perhaps—while hiking back from the latrine. A heavy curtain had been pulled aside, providing ventilation for a cubicle approximately twice the size of Bolan's quarters, and he had a glimpse of some sophisticated radio equipment set against the opposite wall. A chunky gunner dressed in olive drab was operating earphones clamped atop his head. The guy was passing orders on to other groups of soldiers in the underground.

Bolan ambled over, taking full advantage of the guy's preoccupation, and lounged in the open doorway, acting casual while he took in the whole setup. It was a wireless set, and with the winding tunnels, that meant boosters placed strategically throughout the network, able to receive a message from the major staging areas and pass it on. A breakdown anywhere along the line would compromise the outlaw army's critical communications system, isolating separate bivouacs from one another, leaving Frenzi out of touch with soldiers on the firing line. It was a weakness—a potential weakness, anyway—and Bolan filed it in his mind for future reference.

More interesting at the moment was a map of Rome, that was suspended from the wall with strips of masking tape. The map was a commercial one that was usually sold to tourists, but another artist had supplied a few additions of his own with felt-tip pens. The revised edition portrayed the undulating tunnel system that traversed the city's face, obscuring streets and landmarks, bridging rivers and canals, bisecting public parks. The soldier was immediately heartened by their limited extent; as he had thought, there was a cluster in the Trastevere district, a more convoluted network in the heart of Rome, connecting Via Veneto, the Quirinal and other points with Piazza Navona . . . and that was all.

No tunnels to the south or east. No penetration of the terrorist malignancy beyond the limits he had traversed on foot with Frenzi or Petrucchi. Straining, Bolan picked out streets and landmarks, memorizing points where tunnels started, where they dead-ended. The network could be sealed, if the authorities were swift enough, meticulously thorough in their search for hidden exits. Bolan could supply them with a starting place—the café in Piazza Navona, the hotel on Via Dandolo—but he could not begin to estimate how many other shops or homes might have an entryway concealed beneath the floor, behind a basement wall. It would be Luciano's job to root out the vermin, exterminate them as they stood, bewildered, in the light of day.

He was distracted by assorted colored stars that had been pasted to the map, above the black lines that represented the tunnels. One was blue, three others green, the final seven red. The soldier made another scan, and felt the short hairs rising on his neck as Frenzi's simple color code revealed itself in crystal clarity.

The blue star marked the bivouac in which he stood; it was the rough equivalent of mall directories in the United States, with their illuminated arrows stating, You Are Here. The green stars indicated other staging areas—the one on

Viale di Trastevere marked the bivouac where Bolan had
been forced to kill Armand—which made the total four in
all. That gave the RJC a hundred and fifty gunners, more
or less, and Bolan didn't like the odds.

The seven red stars interested Bolan most. Each one was
pasted next to a major landmark, that was readily accessible above the winding tunnels, and he had no doubt that
they were targets, marked for demolition if the ransom
payment was refused. His hunch was instantly confirmed
when Bolan spied a red star plastered next to the Trevi piazza, pointed arms extending like the runnels of a blood-
stain from the massacre that he had witnessed earlier.

Scratch one, and Bolan swiftly memorized the other targets. One red star beside the Coliseum. Another at the Roman Forum. Number three atop the Pantheon. A fourth
appended to the Arch of Constantine. A fifth outside Santa
Suzanna, on Via Veneto. A sixth appended to the Church of
Saint Cecilia in Trastevere. The demolition of a single target would be catastrophic, both in terms of history and human life. Destruction of them all at once would rip the very
heart from Rome, leave untold hundreds dead or dying in
the rubble.

Bolan slipped away before the operator noticed him. He
ambled along the gallery, ignoring the resentful and suspicious eyes that followed him past other cubicles. The gunners were like animals in cages with the doors removed, still
nervous when he came to venturing outside. He passed them
by without a second glance, already concentrating on the
problem of his newfound knowledge and the method of
communicating it to Salvatore Luciano.

When the answer came, it was simplicity itself. The execution would be hazardous, but Bolan had no viable alternative. He dared not leave the tunnels on his own, but there
was still an outside chance that he could send an emissary.
Bolan's note, entrusted to the woman, would tell her father
everything he had to know about the tunnels, targets, Fren-

zi's plan of operations. It would let the chief inspector know that there was someone on the inside, working toward destruction of the terrorists, and while he could expect no quarter from a raiding party of security police, there was a possibility, however slim, that he might slip away in confusion.

If he lived.

He fished a notepad and a ballpoint from his pockets, spent five minutes spelling out the details he had memorized from Frenzi's map. An estimate of troop strength was included, but the raiders would be on their own once they set foot inside the tunnels. In the meantime, he would have to find the lady and make sure that she got out.

During the hike with Frenzi to the Quirinal and Trevi piazza, Bolan had noticed several places where rusty ladders had been bolted into the tunnel walls, ascending into darkened air shafts. He surmised that they were passageways, with entrances concealed in shops, cafés, providing escape hatches for the gunners if they should be taken unaware by enemies. The nearest exit—if, in fact, it was an exit—was located no more than a hundred yards beyond the troops' latrine. If he could spring the woman on some pretext, walk her back along the gallery until they reached the nearest ladder, he could have her on the street inside half an hour. Once Claudia cleared the tunnels, it would be no time at all until she reached her father, passed Bolan's message on and set the wheels in motion for the demise of the Red Justice Column.

While he was waiting for the cavalry, there would be time enough to blow the radio, take care of Frenzi and his officers, create enough confusion to prevent the terrorists from following cohesive plans. With any luck, he might survive just long enough to reach an exit hatch himself.

But first, the lady, right. And there was no time like the present.

Bolan moved along the gallery until he reached a block of vacant cubicles. The solitary rifleman outside a cubicle halfway down the line betrayed where Claudia Perrini was being held. Bolan took the path of least resistance, sauntering directly toward the gunner with an air of confidence, as if he knew precisely what must happen next.

The rifleman regarded Bolan with suspicion. He had not been witness to the contest with Armand, but word had traveled fast, and everyone in the encampment must have been conscious of the fact that Mike Belasko had betrayed two compatriots, leading to their executions. He had not been popular among the terrorists to start with, and right now his stock was at an all-time low.

The sentry frowned and raised an inquiring eyebrow.

"Don Carlo wants the woman."

As he spoke, the Executioner glanced along the gallery in each direction, checking for witnesses to the confrontation. They were alone. Stepping closer, smiling confidentially at the gunner, he drove the stiffened fingers of a hard right hand into the sentry's solar plexus, twisting up beneath the sternum, searching for his spleen. The guy was doubling over, gagging, when a rising knee collided with his forehead, nailing him between the eyes and straightening him again. His head lolled back against the stone wall, his throat exposed. Bolan drove the knife edge of his hand against the man's windpipe with lethal force, then brought his hand up in a choke hold and held it there for the thirty seconds that it took the sentry to die.

Claudia Perrini was reclining on her cot as Bolan dragged his burden through the doorway. Scrambling to her feet, she stared from Bolan to the lifeless sentry, back again, eyes wide, uncomprehending in her sudden terror. Bolan kept his distance, kneeling as he eased the dead man into a prone position, but he raised a finger to his lips and cautioned her to be silent.

"Listen carefully," he cautioned. "I am not with Frenzi, do you understand? I mean to stop him if I can, but I need your help. Your father's help."

At mention of her father, Claudia frowned. "You are with the security police?"

The soldier shook his head. "Not even close. We have a common goal in your release, prevention of a general massacre in Rome."

"What massacre?"

"No time for explanations now." She cringed from Bolan as he closed the gap between them, halting when her shoulders met with hard, unyielding stone. "This information will permit your father to arrest the man responsible for your abduction."

"*You* abducted me!"

"We're out of time." He tucked the folded note into her cleavage. "I have to get you out of here right now."

"You are releasing me?"

"I'm trying, lady."

Bolan gripped her wrist in one big hand, and she did not resist him as he led her toward the door.

PETRUCCHI HAD BEEN FOLLOWING Belasko for the better part of an hour. Gobbling aspirin for his headache, he had wandered out onto the gallery in time to see the mercenary pass, en route to the latrine. With all that he had seen and done this day, with all the accolades from jealous comrades, Enzio was not convinced that it was time for him to face Belasko one-on-one. Still, if he saw an opportunity to embarrass the American, it couldn't hurt. And Belasko turned his back just long enough...

The headache had returned full force, and Enzio retreated into shadow, lounging back against the wall while the American relieved himself. His ears still hummed with the concussion of the Trevi blast, and even after bathing from a bucket he could not erase the pervasive smell of dust.

He wondered if the smell would ever leave him, even when he finally left the underground.

There had been several moments, at the fountain and immediately after, when Petrucchi was convinced that he would die. Arrangement of the charges had been left to others, the technicians, while he stood uneasy guard against the nonexistent possibility of ambush. No one knew about the tunnels, no one could have learned their plan in time, but it was still Petrucchi's mission, and he stood the watch as if a hostile army might barge in at any moment. Watching the technicians, he had tried to visualize the consequence of any slight mistake, the smallest error: fire and thunder, rushing out to swallow him alive, incinerating Enzio before he even had a chance to scream.

But the reality was infinitely worse.

When they had finished rigging wires and detonators, they retreated through the tunnels for perhaps a block, still close enough to register the impact when it came. The detonation would be executed from above, and Frenzi used his walkie-talkie to advise the surface man that all had been prepared. The answer was a cryptic monosyllable, and they had settled down to wait.

Despite his state of readiness, the tension that had set his teeth on edge, the blast succeeded in surprising Enzio. He had been glancing at his watch, concerned that it might be a minute slow, when he was staggered by the shock wave, fairly deafened by the crack of doomsday. Images had blurred together in an instant: the technicians, sprinting back along the tunnel with their heads down, seeking cover; a boiling wall of smoke and dust advancing through the tunnel now at breakneck speed, enveloping Petrucchi, blinding him before he had a chance to turn and run. He stumbled, sightless, through the roaring maelstrom, suffocating, falling to his knees and struggling to rise again before the ash and dust could bury him alive.

Somewhere behind him, they had lost the tunnel. It had been anticipated, planned for, but he wondered now if the shock waves might not bring the ceiling down on top of him, or seal off his retreat at some point farther on. He might be crushed, or walled up in a tomb to die of thirst while rescue workers searched for wounded victims not a hundred yards away. The irony had forced demented laughter from his throat, and he was laughing when the others found him, doubling back to see what had become of their superior.

Of such were legends born.

Already, tales of Enzio the laughing devil had begun to circulate among the ranks. Before the hour was out, it would be common knowledge that he laughed at danger, courting death on missions the average terrorist would never dare attempt. They were awaiting casualty reports from Trevi piazza, but Petrucchi knew the numbers would be awesome. He had entered history today, and he could ask for nothing more...except, perhaps, for the opportunity to deal with Mike Belasko.

He was trailing the American on his return from the latrines. Belasko had not noticed him, and Enzio hung back, content to know the mercenary could not lose him in the tunnels. He was watching when Belasko paused outside of the communications room, moved closer for a look inside. Petrucchi could not hear if any words were passed between the operator and Belasko, but it didn't matter. Vague, unformed suspicion was already stirring in his mind, and it began to take on concrete form when the American produced a pen and notebook, scribbling rapidly for several moments, finally pocketing the items and moving on.

Suspicion was already verging on alarm when Mike Belasko passed his sleeping quarters, moving along the gallery toward the empty cubicles. All empty, save for one, and Enzio was trembling with anticipation as he watched the mercenary strike up a conversation with the sentry who had been detailed to guard the woman. The American was getting nowhere with his small talk, but the speed of his assault amazed Petrucchi, turned his stomach sour at the thought of facing such a man, alone in mortal combat. He was watching from the shadows as Belasko dragged the dead sentry out of sight, and suddenly he realized that he had been presented with a golden opportunity.

Whatever the American might have in mind, he clearly was not acting with the knowledge or support of Carlo Frenzi. Gathering intelligence from the communications room, assassinating one of Frenzi's troopers, seemingly intent on rescuing the woman, Mike Belasko had already sealed his fate. The only question still on tap concerned his captor: who should bag the mercenary, reap the credit and reward that would be sure to follow the exposure of an infiltrator in the ranks?

Who else, if not Petrucchi?

Enzio was trembling again as he released the heavy Astra automatic pistol from its shoulder holster, flicking off the safety, drawing back the hammer with his thumb. He was prepared to kill Belasko on the spot, but given any choice at all he would prefer to take the prisoner alive to Carlo's chamber. With the girl in tow, he would present his case to Frenzi, watch the master's face light up with admiration of his genius, his powers of observation. It would be a double coup, and who could ever seriously doubt Petrucchi's leadership with such a weight of evidence to back him up?

He scuttled forward, hesitating at the door, eavesdropping on the muffled conversation from within. As he suspected, the American was planning to release the woman; worse, he was providing her with information for delivery to her father, chief inspector of security police in Rome.

Petrucchi whipped the curtain back, stepped through the open doorway, Astra automatic leveled at Belasko's chest.

"I hope I am not interrupting anything," he said, and smiled.

The line was lifted from a movie he had seen, in which effete Americans played bedroom games and wallowed in their money for an hour and a half. It pleased him, in the circumstances, but he was completely unprepared for the response.

"Get Carlo!" Perrini snapped, retreating from her would-be savior, stabbing an accusatory finger at Belasko. "This man is a traitor to the cause!"

17

Carlo Frenzi leaned back in his camp chair, propped up his feet on the corner of his makeshift desk. Belasko and Claudia Perrini stood in front of him, defiance written on the mercenary's face, a kind of feline satisfaction in the woman's eyes. Petrucchi stood beside the woman, trying to assume the posture of a leader, while a gunner with an AK-47 covered the American. Belasko's custom-tooled Beretta lay on Frenzi's desk, within his reach if he should care to pick it up and put a bullet through the big man's scowling face.

"You have betrayed my trust," he told Belasko, proud that he was able to conceal the anger, keep it from his voice. "Claudia's loyalty—and Enzio's astute perception—have prevented you from doing mortal damage to the cause."

"Too bad. I'll try to get it right next time."

"There will not be a next time, I assure you." For the second time, he read the note Belasko had entrusted to Claudia, saw the details of his master plan spelled out in words that had been meant for hostile eyes. "I must congratulate you on your skill at gathering intelligence. You have been very thorough."

"It was nothin'."

"Sad, that you should die for nothing." Frenzi crumpled the note and let it fall. "You realize that it will be impossible for me to spare your life," he told Belasko. "I can offer you a swift and painless death, but in return you must provide me with the name of your employer, your assignment, contacts."

The mercenary smiled and shook his head. "I'll pass."

"I think that you will tell me everything, *signor*... Belasko, is it? Might there be another name, perhaps?"

"What difference does it make?"

"To me? No difference." It was Frenzi's turn to smile. "I will enjoy the process of extracting all your little secrets, one by one."

"Whatever turns you on."

"Indeed."

"I guess you need a break from killin' tourists, eh?"

"Enough."

Claudia had been staring at Belasko, but she turned to Frenzi now, a look of consternation on her face.

"What tourists, Carlo? What is he—"

"Enough!"

Belasko's smile was frozen into place, but it had never reached the tall man's graveyard eyes. Those eyes were fixed on Carlo Frenzi now, although the traitor's words were aimed at Perrini.

"Didn't lover boy explain about his 'lesson' to your father? Ask him what went down at the Trevi Fountain earlier this afternoon. How many dead? A hundred? More?"

"Be silent!"

Frenzi's gunner moved from behind Belasko and took a short step forward, swung his rifle butt against the mercenary's lower back. Belasko staggered, went down on one knee. The rifleman was poised to strike again when Frenzi raised his hand magnanimously, warding off the second blow.

"What is he saying, Carlo? Tell me!"

"You forget your place, Claudia." Frenzi's voice was stiff with anger, as cold as ice.

"My place?" He saw the color rising in her cheeks and recognized the warning signs of an impending tantrum. "What is my place, exactly?"

From the floor, incredibly, Belasko had begun to chuckle. "Guess that blows the sisterhood and liberation line," he said.

At a nod from Frenzi, the rifle butt swept downward and struck a jarring blow to the mercenary's skull. Belasko folded like a straw man suddenly deprived of his supports, and Frenzi swept one hand above his prostrate form, a gesture of dismissal and contempt.

"Dispose of him," he growled—and reconsidered instantly. "No, wait! I wish to speak with him once more before he dies. Confine him to his quarters, under guard. No need to rush the execution, after all."

Petrucchi and the rifleman took hold of Mike Belasko's arms and dragged him through the curtained doorway, out of sight. Another moment, and the scuffing sound of boot heels on the stony floor was lost. The RJC commander turned his full attention to Claudia Perrini, anger rising in his breast at the sight of her defiant face.

"You have embarrassed me in front of my subordinates. I cannot tolerate such insolence."

"*You* cannot tolerate? I do not recognize you, Carlo. We are equals in the revolution."

Frenzi's laughter was explosive, genuine. It took the woman by surprise and she recoiled a hasty step before she found the nerve to stand her ground.

"Equals? Dear Claudia, you delude yourself. I *am* the revolution. Have you not learned that by now?"

"What happened at the Trevi Fountain, Carlo?"

"An example for the fascists. They resisted my demands, and I provided them a lesson in reality."

"*What happened?*"

Frenzi sniffed and glowered at her from across the table. "I will not be questioned in this way. You are an agent of the revolution. You will follow orders and be silent unless spoken to.''

He had expected tears, but there was only rage in Claudia's eyes. "You treat me like a child," she exploded, "a cheap possession. I am not your plaything, Carlo."

"Really? Then I must apologize for underestimating your performance as an actress. I was totally convinced."

"You bastard."

"But of course. You sound surprised, Claudia. Was there ever any doubt?"

"I trusted you."

"You *needed* me," the terrorist corrected her, already circling the table. "In your sterile life of fantasy and meaningless affairs, you needed someone vital, someone real. The cause supplied you with a reason for existing, going on from day to day. I made you feel alive."

"You make me feel unclean," she spat at him, retreating now until her shoulders nudged the wall and she could go no farther.

"Ah? Since when? Was it revulsion that you felt last night? Again this morning?"

"Bastard!"

"We've established that." Another stride, and she was now within arm's reach. "But come, you waste my time with histrionics. There is no audition here. Feel free to speak your mind."

"I hate you."

"So. A pity. I will miss you, little one. But it will pass."

"What will you do with me?"

"What would I do with any hostage who attempted to escape? Another lesson for your father, yes? But first, I think my troops might fancy some diversion...a reward for work well done."

She sprang at Frenzi with a kind of savage desperation, claws outstretched to rake his face, but he had seen it coming and he sidestepped, going low, inside, a clenched fist coming up beneath her breastbone, emptying her lungs and dropping Claudia to her knees in front of him. It was the old familiar pose, but with a difference now, and her subservience, her helplessness, excited him. He brushed the hair back from her face with artificial tenderness, then seized a handful of it, twisted, pulled her head back sharply. His excitement was immediately heightened by the panic in her eyes.

"Once more for old times' sake, before you meet the others, eh, Claudia?"

BOLAN WOKE UP RETCHING, with a drill team practicing maneuvers on the inside of his skull. He probed the scalp with gentle fingers, instantly rewarded by another stabbing pain from lower down, in the direction of his kidneys, and the scene in Frenzi's office flooded back with crystal clarity. He had the hulking gunner's face in mind, and vowed to pay him back with interest if the opportunity arose.

Provided that they didn't kill him first, of course.

There was no doubt that Frenzi meant to see him dead; the only questions that remained were when and how. A simple bullet would suffice, but if the master of the RJC had an easy death in mind for Bolan, he would never have awakened from his beating. There was still unfinished business left between them, questions the terrorist would hope to answer, scores to settle from the way in which Bolan had deceived him from the start.

He sat up slowly, cradling his head in his hands until the throbbing had receded to mere agony. No other sudden pains; at least the bastards hadn't worked him over while he was unconscious. If the Executioner could stand, if he could fight, he had a chance.

There was no viable alternative, and Bolan would not entertain the notion of surrender. Frenzi might destroy him absolutely, but it would not come without a fight, and if the terrorist got close enough, he would be sorry for the second chance he had given Mike Belasko.

If.

The soldier spent another minute working on his equilibrium and finally made it to his feet. The room gave one last fling, complete with heaving floor and spinning walls, before it settled down and the Executioner was able to examine his surroundings. Smaller than the other cubicles he had visited, the room was bare—no cot, no chairs, no folding table. Faint illumination was provided by a naked, grimy bulb suspended from the ceiling, but the fifty-watter couldn't hold its own against encroaching shadows. Bolan did a rapid scan to satisfy himself that there were no potential weapons in the room, then shifted closer to the door.

This one was made of heavy wood, and had been set into the stone by carpenters who had known what they were doing. There was no knob on the inside, but the door was locked; the soldier tried his weight against it, getting nowhere fast. The door fit flush against its stony frame on every side, with no room even to insert a knife blade—if the Executioner had had a knife.

Petrucchi had relieved him of his side arm prior to Bolan's audience with Carlo Frenzi, and the extra magazines were also missing from his shoulder rigging. Likewise his belt, with his concealed push-dagger built into the buckle and the slim, built-in garrote that Bolan had worn around his waist. Unless he had an opportunity to capture hardware from his enemies, whatever fighting Bolan did from this point on would have to be bare-handed.

The soldier reflected that he might have taken Enzio Petrucchi if it had not been for the surprise of his betrayal by the woman. By the time he realized precisely what was happening, the weasel had him covered and was shouting down the gallery for reinforcements. Bolan could have risked a shoot-out, trusting in the little gunner's lag time, knowing he would lose, but dead-end gambles weren't his style. The

audience with Frenzi bought him time. He was alive, and
while he lived, there was a chance of pulling off a few surprises on his own.

The girl had been a ringer from the start, of course. He
knew that now, but knowing didn't make it any easier to
take. He wondered idly whether she had been surprised by
the annihilation of her bodyguards, or whether she was just
a better actress than he had supposed. In retrospect, her
anger during Bolan's final meet with Frenzi had seemed
genuine, and there had been no motive, then, for keeping up
the pretense. Carlo had not told her everything, by any
means, and if the soldier read Claudia accurately, she would
not be pleased with the atrocity at the Trevi Fountain. Revolution and the people's war were trendy topics at a cock-
tail party, fun to kick around with other young sophisticates
while smoking grass or sipping wine, but it was something
else entirely when the stench of death was in your nostrils
and the blood of innocents was on your hands.

Bolan knew—had known—a host of others like Claudia
Perrini. College students, for the most part, long on high
ideals and principle, if short on common sense. They saw a
world of troubles, sought a way to change it for the better,
now, and all too often ran afoul of others who would take
advantage of their trust, their wide-eyed innocence. Back
home, the SDS had started out protesting segregation and
had wound up staging riots, sniping at policemen, bombing banks, all in the name of "peace." How many hundreds,
even thousands of American and European youths had been
seduced by their ideals into subversive and felonious activities? The Red Brigades and Baader-Meinhof used their kind
for cannon fodder, drawing off the hostile fire while older,
seasoned members made the scores that counted. In Bel-
fast, there had never been a paucity of young and eager soldiers for the IRA, prepared to spend their lives if necessary
for the cause. The Palestinian commandos had a long, dis-

honorable history of duping young idealists, converting them to zealots, martyrs, in a cause they never fully understood. The method wasn't new with Carlo Frenzi and the RJC, by any means, but Bolan never grew accustomed to it, and he never found forgiveness in his heart for those responsible.

He wondered briefly how the terrorists had hooked Claudia. Her relationship with Luciano might provide a portion of the answer; it was not unusual for a policeman's son or daughter to rebel against authority at home and in the outside world. Claudia's own involvement in the motion picture industry, her proximity to fantasy, might be another factor, blurring her perceptions of reality. But there was something else—a hurt, perhaps—in her voice and in her eyes when she discovered Frenzi's move at Trevi piazza, which bespoke more personal involvement. It would not surprise the Executioner to learn that she was Frenzi's lover, voluntarily cooperating in her own abduction with an eye toward raising money for the cause. As so much excess baggage, she would not have been forewarned about the Trevi massacre; it would have come as an appalling and complete surprise.

He wondered what the lady might be going through right now. Would she attempt to reconcile her gut reaction to the massacre with any feelings she might have for Carlo Frenzi? Or would the discovery of her exclusion from important plans be shock enough to make her reconsider, take another searching look around her at the savages she had adopted as her family? It could go either way, the soldier knew—or it might go nowhere at all. If Claudia challenged Frenzi openly, she was likely to be killed before she could disrupt the operation. She had made some points with Frenzi by betraying Bolan, but it wouldn't matter if she stepped on Frenzi's ego, tried to undermine his operation.

Bolan put the lady out of mind. Whatever happened to her now, she had quite literally asked for it, the moment she enlisted with the RJC. And she was on her own, for now; the Executioner was locked into a struggle for survival that he dared not lose. Not only his life, but the fate of Rome was hanging in the balance, dangling by a tattered thread. And Carlo Frenzi held the razor, sharpened and shiny, ready for the stroke that meant destruction for Mack Bolan, for an ancient city, for a way of life.

It was possible that the demolition of selected Roman landmarks would not jeopardize the government. If the explosions were detonated at 3:00 a.m., Frenzi's deadline, there would be few, if any, casualties. But the annihilation of historic structures such as the Pantheon, the Coliseum, the Roman Forum, might be fatal to the city's spirit—never mind the loss of tourist revenue, the fire storm of publicity that would follow hot on the heels of a strike of such dimensions. Never mind the critical embarrassment for politicians more concerned with their reputations than the city they were sworn to serve. Such massive vandalism might irreparably scar the soul of the Eternal City, and Bolan vowed he would do everything within his power to avert that tragedy.

He would do everything within his power. And for the moment, all that he could do was sit and wait. The muffled voices from the corridor beyond his door informed him that the sentries were posted in pairs. They would be armed with automatic weapons, certainly, and even if he could devise some ruse to sucker one inside, the other would most certainly remain alert and out of reach, prepared to blast away at the first sign of trouble. Nothing would be accomplished if he died inside his tiny cell, before he could find a way to pull the plug on Carlo's plan to savage Rome.

The soldier found a corner, and settled down to wait, praying that Frenzi would be coming for him soon, before the deadline. If his adversary failed to show, then the Executioner's mission would go straight to hell.

Mack Bolan checked his watch. Still time to spare, but he could hear the numbers falling, ticking off his life, the life of Rome. The soldier closed his eyes and concentrated on the inner darkness, looking for solutions. And finding only blood.

CLAUDIA PERRINI HUDDLED on her cot beneath a scratchy woolen blanket, knees drawn up to her chest, her body racked with pain. The rape by Carlo had been bad enough— a violent travesty of what they once had shared together, joyfully—but afterward, the man had gone berserk. Instead of sating him, the violent sex had seemed to light a different kind of fire in Carlo; cursing at Claudia, he had kicked and beaten her unmercifully while she had cowered at his feet. She had believed he meant to kill her, then and there, but Carlo's rage had disappeared as suddenly as it began, and he had called for two of his soldiers to drag her out and place her in her cell. Then he had posted guards outside the door.

Her evening gown was in tatters now, and Claudia kept the blanket wrapped snugly around her due more to late-blooming modesty than to ward off the subterranean chill. She was not bashful when it came to showing off her body; Claudia's films had universally included nude scenes, and she had been known to strip at parties when the hash or liquor was particularly fine. But now, in these surroundings, after her experience with Carlo Frenzi, she felt different . . . exposed.

She knew that Carlo had been serious when threatening to let his soldiers have her. He might do it yet, if she could not devise some method of escape. She did not know how many soldiers he commanded, but the numbers were the least of her concerns. Carlo had made her feel used, unclean, like something from the gutter. In her mind, the swift release of death seemed vastly preferable to more suffering, prolonged indignities. If she could escape from Carlo, from the tunnels, then she could find sanctuary. But with whom?

Her father, yes.

How often he had warned her, lectured her, about her life-style? She had angrily defied him, never passing up an opportunity to raise the specter of his failure as a husband, as a father. He had let her mother die in loneliness, preferring to put his time and attention into his career, the chase. But now she wondered if he had been so wrong. If there were men like Carlo Frenzi in the world, prepared to murder in their own self-serving cause, must not someone be ready to oppose them? Had her father's marathon pursuit of criminals been something other than the game she had imagined? Could it have been a burden? A duty he could not have refused?

Her jumbled thoughts moved on to the American, the man they called Belasko. He had led the team that had abducted her, at the hotel, and had defended her when Carlo's men had tried to assault her. He had not participated in the murder of her bodyguards, and he had tried to free her from captivity, alert her father to the danger that was hanging over Rome. He had tried to help her, tried to help the city that she loved. She had betrayed him, very likely had caused his death, and for that crime there would be no forgiveness.

She had glimpsed Belasko's note before Petrucchi snatched it from her and delivered it to his commander. The information had puzzled her: bombs beneath the Pantheon, the Coliseum, other Roman landmarks. Carlo had never hinted at such a plan; she had agreed to the abduction scheme on his assurance that the government would eagerly provide the ransom payment he demanded, money that would put the revolution on a solid footing, help him work for all the starving peasants everywhere. She would be safe with Carlo, the obligatory death threats empty words designed to frighten the authorities, her father in particu-

lar. It seemed amusing, with the barest hint of danger to
provide excitement . . . and an opportunity to wound her father, as she fancied he had wounded her.

But all of that had changed abruptly, and Claudia saw
that her abduction was a smoke screen, a diversion for her
father and his men. The target was—had always been—
Rome, and Frenzi planned to hold the city for ransom, or to
bring it down around their ears. He was insane, she realized that now, and marveled at the youthful ignorance that
had allowed him to deceive her. Claudia had believed herself to be sophisticated, worldly, capable of handling the
best—and worst—life had to offer. Now, she realized that
she had been a child, intent on playing grown-up, carelessly
mistaking sexual experience for *life* experience, naively
swallowing the line that Frenzi had handed her. In her con-
ceit, she had believed that she was vital to "the revolution," letting vanity and love obscure her vision, blind her
to the truth. The secrecy surrounding her affair with Carlo
Frenzi had been his idea, and while she did not doubt his
statements that the police were searching for him, she now
believed there was another reason why he had avoided
meeting any of her friends, insisting that she never mention
their relationship to anyone. He knew that a more objec-
tive person might reveal him as the liar that he was, expose
the rot behind his slick facade.

And she had fallen for it, all the way. In childish naïveté,
she had believed that Carlo loved her, valued her opinions,
trusted her with secrets that he told to no one else. In her
stupidity, she had become his mindless tool for the destruction of a city that she loved, a weapon to be used against the
father who had loved her from the moment she was born.

But she might be a two-edged weapon yet, for Carlo
Frenzi. She might cut both ways before he had an opportunity to share her with his troops. Claudia was an actress,
and a better one than the reviewers sometimes gave her
credit for. She had been playing out a role with Carlo up to

now, and all the world had been her audience. It might be time, she thought, for certain rewrites on the script, a drastic alteration of the plot, together with her character. There might still be a chance to save the show before it closed, due to the extermination of the players.

It would be her most difficult role, Claudia realized, without the stand-ins and assorted stunt performers to protect her from a hazardous performance. She was on her own, with no alternative except submission and the ultimate indignity of a passive death.

The lady steeled herself for the performance of a lifetime, knowing that it probably would be her last. Whatever happened next, no matter what the critics had to say, she was prepared to give it everything she had.

18

Carlo Frenzi lit a thin cigar and watched the smoky spiral as it rose above him, flattening against the ceiling. Champagne would admirably suit his mood, but he permitted no intoxicating beverages inside the tunnels, and was thus compelled to settle for a mug of bitter coffee. Later, when his business was concluded, there would be an opportunity for celebration—but his business wasn't finished yet, by any means.

The fascists had agreed to pay, as he had known they would. His agent on the street had spoken once again with Luciano, offering assurances that the Trevi Fountain had been only one of several targets marked for demolition if the ransom payment was delayed or finally denied. The chief inspector of police had been most anxious to oblige, and his superiors had also been impressed by Frenzi's demonstration. There was no more foolish talk of delays in gathering the cash. His deadline would be met, and Luciano would be carrying the payment personally.

Frenzi considered it something of a bonus to meet the chief inspector, watch him grovel like a servant, but of course he would not be within a mile of the secluded drop zone. Luciano would be meeting with an errand boy, a flunky, while the brains behind Red Justice remained behind in the safety of his tunnel network, ready to unleash the holocaust at first sign of treachery.

And there was this business with Belasko. Blood would have to be spilled. Somehow, the security police or yet another agency had infiltrated Frenzi's gang. He trusted Lupo's background check on the American—although the bastard would be getting no reward for this one—and he was conscious of the fact that records could be altered, even fabricated, to reflect a personality that might, in fact, be nonexistent. If Belasko was a mercenary—if he *was* Belasko—then the government had bought him out for this assignment, waiving prosecution in some sticky case, perhaps. It was known to happen all the time in the United States, and European agencies were learning from America's example. The employment of a Yank had been a stroke of genius, allaying Frenzi's suspicious nature by insertion of a foreigner where an Italian agent would have normally been used.

Of course, the operation might be an American concern from start to finish. Red Justice had abducted one American already, and the CIA or someone else might have decided it was time to ring the curtain down. Belasko might not be with the security police at all, which only made him twice as dangerous. He had to be dealt with properly and promptly, but before he died, there were some answers Frenzi wanted, information that was vital to his own survival.

When he finished with Belasko, Frenzi would know the man's employers and their game. He would be able to decide on countermeasures to protect himself and his fortune, if the hounds decided to pursue him. And they would; he knew that much with crystal clarity. With what he had in mind for Rome, the bastards would be forced to hunt him down.

And he had made preparations: the new identity was waiting for him, like an empty suit of clothes needing only to be filled. But if there was an unknown enemy outside Rome, then his plans might be undone at any moment. He must guard himself against surprises, hold the edge that was his only sure protection for the future. If his adversaries ever got ahead of him, in thought or action, he was finished. Doomed.

Belasko had the answers—some of them, at any rate—and it was time for Frenzi to begin extracting them. The mercenary would resist, that much was clear. In fact, the terrorist was counting on it. If he yielded easily, without a fight, it would have spoiled the moment, ruined Frenzi's lesson to Belasko's sponsors. By resisting, even though resistance would be futile in the end, Belasko would provide a grim example for the others who might follow him. It was a certainty that others would be sent, but if their confidence was shaken at the outset, if they were infected with the germ of fear, then Frenzi would be capable of dealing with them when the moment came. He might decide to let the infiltrator live, his grim existence a perpetual reminder to the others if they dared match wits with Carlo Frenzi.

He drowned the cigarette in the tepid coffee, rose and left his makeshift office, moving down the gallery toward Mike Belasko's cell. Outside the guards were whispering back and forth. They immediately fell silent once they were aware of his approach, snapping an approximation of attention with their rifles slung.

"We must move him to the kitchen," Frenzi told them, catching a significant exchange of glances and a hint of trepidation. He did not begrudge his troops the normal fear response, as long as they were more afraid of him than any other man.

The taller of the sentries rummaged in a pocket for a key, then bent to unlock the door. His partner moved back and slightly to the left, his automatic rifle leveled from the waist, prepared to pour a stream of point-blank fire across the threshold if Belasko attempted a rush. Unmindful of the risk, secure in his ability to handle the American imposter,

Frenzi pushed on past the sentries, leading through the doorway as soon as it was opened.

Mike Belasko sat in a corner, a grim expression of defeat stamped into his features. There would be fight inside him yet, but at the moment he was hurting, feeling sorry for himself, and Frenzi's years in prison had provided him with insight into handling beaten men. He might attempt conciliation first, resorting to the harsher methods only if he failed through "kindness."

"It is finished," he informed Belasko, conscious of the slight exaggeration. "Your employers have agreed to my demands. Apparently, they have no interest in your fate."

"That's life."

"Indeed. While life still remains, you have an opportunity to pay them back for their disinterest. Together, we can make them wish that they had not been born."

"What's in the deal for me?" Belasko asked.

"Survival," Frenzi lied. "Perhaps a bonus, if your information pleases me."

The mercenary shook his head. "No sale."

"You leave me no alternative."

"There are alternatives to everythin'."

"Not this time. Come with me."

Belasko scrambled to his feet with energy surprising in a man who seemed so docile moments earlier. He turned toward Frenzi, might have lunged for the man's throat, had not the sentries intervened, their automatic rifles pointed at his chest.

"Your choice, *signor*. If you prefer to die immediately, rest assured that it can be arranged."

Belasko shrugged, appearing to relax. "No rush," he said. "I've always planned on trying it the hard way."

ENZIO PETRUCCHI GLANCED both ways along the gallery before he lit a cigarette, inhaling deeply, leaning back with shoulders pressed against the cool, smooth surface of a marble slab. He did not recognize the occupant by name, no more than he had recognized the voiceless tenants of this world beneath the streets. Despite his Catholic background, he was no believer in the afterlife and did not fear the dead. His troubles always emanated from the living, and another of his enemies was being dealt with at the moment, rendered permanently harmless by the butchers Frenzi kept on staff.

He had not been invited to the execution, though he might have asked, and Carlo surely would have granted him a ringside seat. In fact, despite his hatred for the big American, Petrucchi had a weakness of the stomach when it came to torture, and he feared embarrassment that might erase his other great achievements of the day. It would not do for him to wilt before the sight of blood. Not after Trevi. Not with the American prisoner because of Enzio's swift thinking, his reactions to an obvious emergency.

He dared not reveal weakness in front of the others. They would turn upon him like a pack of wolves, remorseless, unforgiving. It would make no difference that he had already proved himself this day, with deeds surpassing anything the others might have done. One sign of weakness and they would devour him, make Enzio an outcast in the very group for which he had already risked his life.

But he had other plans, in any case. It was a night for celebration, and Petrucchi had devised the perfect gift with which to honor his accomplishments. While Frenzi was preoccupied with the American's interrogation, Enzio would claim Claudia Perrini for himself.

It would have been a risky proposition earlier, when she was under Carlo's protection, and Petrucchi was reminded of the troopers who had tried to have their way with her, the swift and final punishment they had received. But Enzio had marked the shifting winds, observed the change in Frenzi's attitude when the woman questioned him about the incident at the Trevi Fountain. After the American had been dragged away, Petrucchi had remained outside of Carlo's office, one ear pressed against the blackout curtain, listening. At last he understood the woman's double role, her close relationship to Frenzi, which was suddenly unraveling as they began to argue, snapping back and forth at each other. He was listening when Carlo promised Perrini that the troops would have her, still listening when Frenzi claimed her one last time, the sound of violent rutting as loud as cannon fire to Enzio, inflaming him until he had been forced to turn away. But not before he inched the curtains wide enough to peer inside.

The famous Claudia Perrini would be his, and Carlo would not mind because he had already marked her as a present for the troops. As one of Frenzi's closest confidantes, it was entirely fitting that Petrucchi should be first, especially considering his great successes of the afternoon. Because of him, the fascists had agreed to pay the ransom as demanded. Because of him, an infiltrator in the ranks had been exposed before he could cause irreparable damage to the operation. Never modest at the best of times, Petrucchi saw himself now as heroic, set apart from the other members of Red Justice. He would claim the sweet reward that was his own, then pass her to the others in a show of generosity befitting his greatness. It would be the least that he could do . . . but Enzio would claim her first.

Provided he could make himself perform. The hero of the hour had a problem in that area, as with the sight of blood. From adolescence, he had lacked the courage to approach a woman, win her for himself and claim the prize that waited at the end of courtship. He might still have been a virgin if the prostitutes of Rome were not so readily available, their rates so reasonable. With "working girls," Petrucchi merely had to walk along the street, or park his car at any one of several well-known intersections, and the women came to him, performing the aggressive role traditionally reserved for men. He was not tongue-tied when with a prostitute, felt no compulsion to amuse her with his wit, the lies he habitually told to make himself seem stronger, more courageous than he was in fact. A whore was interested in money, and it did not matter to Petrucchi if she faked her pleasure in their coupling. He had given up on any illusions of his own desirability, content to take relief where he could find it, paying cash for services received.

Until today.

This afternoon, Petrucchi had already proved himself a warrior to be reckoned with. Tonight, he meant to prove himself a man in other ways. He would possess the star of films and television, make her kneel before him. When he was finished with her, she would beg for more—or, at the very least, admit that Enzio had been the best in her experience. She would acknowledge his superiority to the other men, confess her need for him…or she would pay the price.

He slipped a hand inside his jacket, drawing reassurance from the Astra automatic in its shoulder rigging. He would hold the weapon in reserve, a last resort, in case Claudia proved too stubborn. She was not a novice in the art of love; Petrucchi knew that much from sitting through her films repeatedly in dingy theaters, ignoring puerile dialogue and waiting, breathless, for the moment when she would reveal herself. If he had known of her relationship with Carlo Frenzi…

What?

Would he have dared to intervene? Assert himself in competition with the master? Petrucchi knew the answer, and it brought a flush of anger to his cheeks. If he had known about Claudia's personal relationship with Carlo Frenzi, he would certainly have kept it to himself, done nothing. Her probable rejection would have frightened him beyond the threat of any violence from the RJC commander. Death was sometimes preferable to shame, and Enzio did everything within his power to shun them both.

But she could not reject him now. She would accept the hero of the hour because she had no choice. No one but Frenzi dared oppose him, and the master would be occupied with Mike Belasko for at least an hour. Enzio suspected that the mercenary would not be an easy man to break, and while he had the strength to bear his pain in silence, Enzio would not be interrupted with Claudia.

The musty odor of the catacombs annoyed Petrucchi, and he hoped that he would soon be free of them forever. With his portion of the ransom in hand, he would be able to assume a new identity, go on to bigger, better things, no longer trapped in Frenzi's shadow. With the reputation he had earned that afternoon, he would be welcomed by the most prestigious criminal fraternities, accepted from the outset as a man of leadership, courage and ruthlessness. Enzio could name his price from this point on, and others would consider it an honor if and when he joined their ranks.

On second thought, he might create a fighting cadre of his own, selecting warriors only like himself, prepared to go the limit for a worthy cause. The cause, of course, would be their own enrichment, and there was no limit to the things they might achieve. Once Rome had paid a ransom, why not Paris, London or Madrid? Why not New York or Washington, D.C.? A man was only limited by lack of nerve and confidence; with grim determination and commitment to success, all things were possible.

Petrucchi stubbed his cigarette against the nearest marble slab and let it fall to the ground. The dead were not susceptible to insult, and he cared no more for them than for the living. At the moment, Enzio cared only for himself, the satisfaction of a hunger that had grown demanding, irresistibly.

He moved along the gallery with long, determined strides, ignoring other troopers as they passed him with a nod, a cautious smile. They had been forced to reconsider Enzio, revise their first impressions of the man whom many had regarded as a simple errand boy for Carlo Frenzi. They would see him differently in future, treat him with the respect that was his due. As for Petrucchi, filled with self-importance, he might not see them at all.

Right now, tonight, his eyes were for only Claudia Perrini. Fantasy was about to become reality, a dream was about to come true, and Enzio had no time for distractions. Women would be falling over him, no doubt, when he was rich and famous, but the gunner might not have a chance like this again. To *own* a woman, soul and body, even for an hour, was an opportunity few men ever had. Petrucchi could not face himself if he allowed the moment to escape, to pass him by.

Tonight, he would possess a rising star of the Italian cinema. Tomorrow, the world would be his hunting ground.

The hunter stalked in silence, shunning contact with his comrades as he continued along the gallery. He felt their eyes upon him as he passed, and he recognized their envy, gaining strength and confidence with every stride. His conquest of Claudia would be yet another lesson for the rank and file. She would compare the others to Petrucchi, when they came for her in turn, and none would measure up. It was his fate to be a man apart, superior in every way.

It was his destiny.

CLAUDIA KNEW WHAT she had to do. It was distasteful to her, but the circumstances left her with no alternative. If sex could save her now, she would employ the only weapon left at her disposal. If submission to another foul indignity meant life, instead of death, then she was ready for the sacrifice.

In many ways, it was no different from her film career, her life in general. Sex had always seen her through, on screen or off. The promise of delights that might be fulfilled had made Claudia what she was today. And what was that, precisely? Earlier, her answer would undoubtedly have been "a star." But now, after having reevaluated her life, she wondered if she had been a fool. How many of the men whom she had teased or finally satisfied regarded her as something other than a piece of meat? How many thought of her with love, respect or anything except a casual contempt?

Tonight, with raw survival on the line, Claudia knew that sex might save her life, if she was able to perform on cue, convince her one-man audience that she was his and his alone. If lust could override the bastard's built-in fear of Carlo Frenzi, she had a chance.

But she would have to try, in any case. Surrender was unthinkable, and if she had a choice between one soldier and the pack . . . well, it was really no damned choice at all. She must dismiss the pain, the unfamiliar feelings of embarrassment, and save herself. Now. Before time ran out.

The sentry was her only hope, and Perrini had to make her move before he was relieved by someone else. He was an ugly man, and it would be impossible to make him think that she had fallen for him at a glance, but she had a backup plan in mind. Sex now, and money later, with a promise of her silence if he helped her to escape. She would agree to testify on his behalf if he should be arrested with the others, swear that he had risked his life to free her.

It was a lie, of course, but she was counting on the minimal intelligence that seemed to be the predominant feature of the troops in Carlo's private army. They were common criminals, perhaps more vicious than the average, but there were no geniuses among them, and Claudia felt assured that she could win the sentry over, given time.

And time would be her greatest enemy tonight. Each passing moment brought her closer to the fate Frenzi had in mind for her; each heartbeat brought them nearer to the destruction of the city that she loved.

If Claudia could escape, she would alert her father, tell him of the targets that had been listed in Mike Belasko's note. If there was time...

Belasko.

The American had risked his life to help her, and he was suffering because of it. Because of her betrayal. Blinded by the love she had felt for Carlo Frenzi, Claudia had betrayed her only friend within the catacombs, and when she fled, she would be leaving him to die.

Unless she took him with her.

It was risky, and it would require a change in plans, but there was still an outside chance that she could pull it off. If she could win the sentry over, convince him of the wealth and pleasure that awaited him once she was free and safe once more...

The blackout curtain rustled softly and was pulled aside, revealing Enzio Petrucchi in the doorway. He was smiling at her, staring with a hunger that she recognized all too well. It was the look she had frequently received from producers and directors, leading men in every film she had made, assorted VIPs who did their thinking with their balls and bankrolls. Claudia knew the look, all right, and knew that she could handle Enzio if she was cautious.

"I wanted to be certain you were comfortable," he said. His dark eyes ricocheted around the tiny room, returning to her cleavage, where he stared fixedly.

"Comfortable? Here? You must be joking, Enzio."

It would not hurt to put him on a first-name basis from the outset, let him feel the intimacy grow between them as she played the old, familiar part.

"If there was something I could do..."

"Perhaps there is." She pressed a finger to her lips and moved to stand beside him, letting one breast graze his arm deliberately. When she leaned in close to whisper in his ear, her breath was like a warm caress upon his neck. "We must be careful of the guard," she said.

"I have relieved him. We are quite alone."

The on-screen power of her eyes was legendary, and she turned it on now full force.

"Then we can speak in confidence?"

"Of course."

"I wish to get away from here, as soon as possible."

"Claudia—"

"Carlo has gone mad. He means to kill me, I am certain of it." She did not have to fabricate the tremor in her voice, the fear behind her words. "I do not want to die."

Enzio said nothing, but his hands had come to rest upon her hips, and Claudia felt the first small twinge of victory. She crowded him, kissing close.

"He means to let the others have me, Enzio. All of them. Is there nothing you can do to help me?"

"I cannot betray the movement."

"Nor will I! I gave you the American, and this has been my thanks." Her lips had formed into a sexy pout. "He hurt me, Enzio. He could not satisfy me, so he hurt me, like an animal."

She felt him stir against her; she pressed herself against the bulge in his fatigues. His weasel eyes were straining to explore the secrets of her cleavage, and his hands were inching slowly downward from her hips, in the direction of her buttocks. Claudia let her arms encircle him beneath the open flak jacket, inspiration jolting her as one hand brushed against his shoulder holster and the automatic pistol it contained.

"I need a real man, Enzio. A man who can protect me now. I would be grateful."

"Ah."

"So very grateful."

Claudia wedged a knee between his thighs, one arm moving up to encircle his neck, the other snug and warm against his shoulder rigging, underneath the jacket. Pressed against him now, she let her lips graze his, an invitation.

"Will you help me, Enzio?"

"Claudia—"

"Please?"

The knee slammed home against his scrotum, grinding hard against the pubic bone, as Claudia's teeth clamped on his lower lip. She tasted blood, released him as he doubled over, moaning loudly. He turned into dead weight in her arms, but in the heartbeat after contact she had freed his handgun from its holster, stepping back to level it directly at Petrucchi's face.

"I will not wait for Carlo's jackals, Enzio. You have a choice: assist me now, or I am forced to kill you and go on alone."

He knelt in front of her, hands clasped against his wounded genitals, blood drooling down his chin. Several moments passed before he found his voice again.

"What is it that you want of me?"

"An escort, nothing more."

"I cannot walk."

"Then you will have to die."

"No! Wait!" He fanned the air with outstretched hands, as if his open palms could stop a bullet. "Another moment, and I will do anything I can. I know the exits."

"Good. But first, we have another stop to make. We will be taking the American."

There was a spark of fury in his weasel eyes, behind the overriding pain, but Enzio was wise enough to keep his mouth shut. Claudia knew the he could not be trusted, but he was her only hope of saving the American and finding a way out of the labyrinth. Still, if he tried to trick her . . .

She would kill him, yes. And do the rest of it alone, if need be. If she lived. She had watched the curtain rise, and she was on. She only prayed that she would be alive tomorrow, for the reviews.

19

Frenzi's kitchen was a converted columbarium with its urns removed from the niches on the walls and stainless-steel serving tables bolted to the floor. Electric ranges were employed to heat the food, which seemed to come primarily from cans, and bottled water made up for the lack of plumbing. As he entered, flanked by gunners, Bolan saw that one long serving table had been cleared of pots and pans, its surface gleaming softly in the artificial light. From rings affixed to each stout leg, a set of manacles hung limp and empty, waiting to be filled.

The turkey-doctors were already waiting for him, burly men in splattered aprons, blank of face and cold of eye. The Executioner had met their kind before, in other charnel houses, and he knew what they were capable of doing to the human body, to the mind and soul. An expert could prolong the agony for days or weeks on end, employing stimulants and antiseptics, cauterizing as they worked, transfusing blood if necessary to preserve the mangled shell that once had been a sentient man or woman. Frenzi's butchers had no medical degrees, that much was obvious, but they would know enough to keep him conscious, keep him screaming, while the RJC commander asked his questions.

Right.

"Allow me, please, to introduce Guillermo and Arturo. They will be performing for our entertainment…if you still refuse to answer my extremely simple questions."

"Funny thing. I feel a case of lockjaw coming on."

"I have the cure, *signor*. If you will please disrobe…"

"I'd rather not. There seems to be a draft in here."

The terrorist was smiling as he turned toward his gorillas. "Strip him," Frenzi ordered, stepping back to give the hulks access.

They closed in swiftly, circling, and Bolan edged backward, toward the serving table that was still piled high with pots and pans. Another moment and he nudged against the metal, cutting off retreat. He reached back blindly, found a skillet and was ripping off a brutal backhand when the butchers rushed him simultaneously.

Bolan clubbed the nearest of them squarely in the face, rewarded by a crunch of cartilage, a grunt of pained surprise. The turkey-maker tottered, sliding to his knees, and Bolan was already turning to confront his number two when his assailant threw a flying tackle into Bolan's ribs with crushing force, both of them reeling and rebounding from the stainless-steel table in a rain of cookware.

Sucking desperately for breath, Bolan felt the skillet slip through his numbed fingers. He was on hands and knees, already struggling to rise, when massive arms slipped underneath his own and locked, fingers intertwined behind his neck. The Executioner was lifted like a rag doll as he flailed with his feet in hopes of striking the guy's groin or a kneecap, but his heels rebounded from a pair of thighs as thick and seemingly insensitive as truck tires.

From the sidelines, Frenzi's gunners rushed the two combatants, while Don Carlo covered all concerned with an AK-47 tucked beneath each arm. The khaki soldiers got a lock on Bolan's flailing feet, stepped back to pull his legs apart. Each in turn delivered a resounding kick to Bolan's groin.

The Executioner went limp in the butcher's grip, then struggled vainly to control his stomach muscles. He retched painfully. His latest meal came up, almost intact.

Before he knew it, hostile hands were pulling off his shoes and tugging at his slacks, his underwear. Bolan tried to bring his knees up, give himself some minimal protection, but the muscles in his legs would not respond. The butcher suddenly released him and he fell on his hands and knees, flesh torn on rough, unfinished stone. As he writhed in agony the hands were at him once again, divesting him of jacket, shoulder holster, shirt. When he was stripped, the Executioner was lifted bodily and carried to the vacant serving table, stretched out with his naked back against the cold stainless steel. He struggled ineffectually as manacles were fastened on his wrists and ankles, locking him in place upon the altar like some Aztec sacrificial victim.

Would they cut his heart out? Bolan wondered. The burning pain in his genitals was threatening to carry him away, and Bolan concentrated on the feel of icy metal pressed against his flesh, commanding battered nerves to mute their message, give him room to think. It worked, but only to a point, and Bolan was coherent in his pain when Frenzi came to stand beside the table, smiling down upon him.

"Merely a prelude, I assure you. There is so much worse to come, unless you answer all my questions truthfully."

The soldier's smile was closer to a death's-head grin. "We've come this far," he said. "I'd hate to miss the floor show."

Frenzi snapped his fingers, and a carving knife was pressed into his open palm. He held the blade aloft and turned it slowly, let it catch the meager light, refracting little sunbursts into Bolan's eyes. He ran a thumb along the edge to test its sharpness, then applied the blade to Bolan's throat, allowing Bolan to appreciate it for himself.

"So easy," Carlo purred. "With just a simple motion I could end your life...but that would be too quick, too merciful."

"We wouldn't want to spoil your reputation," Bolan told him.

And the blade began to move, descending, creasing Bolan's sternum, veering left to probe around a nipple, pricking. Back on line to trace the hollow of his navel, edging lower.

"Perhaps I should relieve you of your suffering, *signor*." The twelve-inch blade wormed in between his thighs and twisted, balancing Bolan's scrotum on the razor's edge. "The Bible says if thine eye offend thee, it should be plucked out."

Bolan swallowed the obstruction that had formed spontaneously in his throat. "I'd call that view short-sighted," he answered.

Frenzi threw his head back, laughing, and withdrew the knife blade with a twist that left the soldier straining at his chains. He felt the sudden, sticky warmth of blood on the inside of his thighs, but it was still a trickle rather than a flow, and Bolan guessed that there had been no lasting damage done.

Not yet.

"I hope you do not break too easily, *signor*. I have been looking forward to your last performance, and it would be such a shame to cut the moment short."

He passed the knife in front of Bolan's face again, delighted with his pun and with his power over Mike Belasko. Bolan wondered briefly if the RJC commander would participate himself, deciding that he might, but only after others had prepared the way. He wondered also whether he could go the distance, stick it out until the butchers finally got tired enough or mad enough to let him die. If he began to spill, there would be relatively little damage done; the access codes at Stony Man had been revised a hundred times or more since Bolan's exit from the program, and he had no inkling of the key. He knew some names—Brognola, personnel from Able Team and Phoenix Force—but it would all be meaningless to Frenzi, useless to the RJC. The warrior's unofficial status was his best defense in case of capture; as an outlaw, acting on his own, he was not privy to the secrets of the inner circle. He could talk his head off, and it wouldn't hurt a goddamned thing.

But he would play it out in silence all the same.

"Arturo, if you please."

Apparently, Guillermo would be sitting out the early action while his seconds tried to clean the skillet's imprint off his face. The soldier wished them luck and concentrated on the scowling hulk that loomed above him on his right, the eyes like marbles boring into Bolan's own.

Before the butcher could begin, a runner barged into the kitchen, breathless, calling Frenzi's name. He did a double-take at the sight of Bolan stretched out on the table, and he paled a shade when big Arturo hit him with a scathing glare.

"Don Carlo...I am sorry, but...a message for you."

"I am busy," Carlo said, dismissing him.

"The message is from Lupo. He insists that it is urgent."

Frenzi stiffened, cursing underneath his breath. The Executioner saw something very much like sadness in his adversary's eyes as Carlo shrugged resignedly.

"Unfortunately, I must miss the overture. But rest assured that I will join you for the main event." He faced Arturo over Bolan's prostrate form. "I want the name of his employer, any details of his mission, outside contacts. If he has communicated with the police, we must be ready to defend ourselves."

"It shall be done, Don Carlo."

Frenzi turned away and swiftly disappeared from Bolan's field of vision. Looming over him, Arturo was no longer scowling; now he wore a gap-toothed smile that instantly reminded Bolan of a hungry crocodile. The hulk bent lower, closer, so that the sour breath washed over Bolan, working on his queasy stomach.

"So," the butcher said, "let us begin."

THE PAIN WAS NOTHING in comparison to Enzio Petrucchi's shame. His lip had ceased to bleed, the swelling scarcely noticeable now at a distance, and the throbbing in his groin—so brutal moments earlier—had eased enough that he could walk with only the suggestion of a limp. It would be something else, entirely, if he should be called upon to run, but the external pain was trivial, inconsequential, next to his intense embarrassment. To be deceived, disarmed by a malicious female hostage, taken prisoner and marched along the gallery for all to see; it was enough to make a strong man hang his head and weep from sheer humiliation.

Of course, his plight might not be obvious to those who passed them on the gallery. Claudia kept one arm looped through his own, her other hand tucked under, out of sight, the Astra automatic's muzzle grinding hard against his ribs. He knew that it was cocked, the safety off, and even if he had the nerve to test her, make a move, she could not miss at such a range. In his imagination, Enzio could feel the bullet boring in between his ribs, perhaps deflected by initial impact, tearing lungs and liver, stomach, pancreas, intestines—everything. He would be dead before he hit the ground. But even that might be a blessing, in the face of his humiliation should he live.

What explanation could he offer Carlo? Had he been within his rights, approaching the woman in her cell? And would it matter, when the others saw how badly he had bungled the attempted rape?

Petrucchi made a silent vow that should he live, he would restrict himself to prostitutes in future. They were safe, affordable, no strings attached. Not like the others: women with ambitions and desires of their own, prepared to fight if necessary for their dignity and honor. Women were the root of evil in Petrucchi's world, and it was only fitting that his darkest moment should be orchestrated by a scheming female.

They were heading for the kitchen, though Claudia didn't know it yet. Belasko had been taken there for questioning, and Frenzi's butchers should be getting down to work by now, eliciting the answers to a host of painful questions. Claudia could not be prepared for what was waiting in the kitchen; she might falter, let her guard down just a fraction, granting Enzio the space he needed to escape.

But it would not be good enough. He would accomplish little, grappling with a woman there, in front of Frenzi and the others. If he let her take him in at gunpoint, he was finished. If he found a way to take her out before they reached the kitchen, though, it might be possible to cover his incompetence, erase his failure. He would have to kill the woman, certainly, and there was still the sentry who had seen him enter Perrini's cell. He could not trust the man to keep his secret, even with a bribe beneath his belt, but anything could happen in the tunnels, and Petrucchi had no qualms about eliminating one more witness to his personal disgrace.

The woman was the problem now, or more specifically, the pistol she held against his ribs. If he made any move against her, she was sure to fire, and if he waited . . .

It was no more than a hundred yards to the kitchen now, and Enzio was desperate. He drew a ragged breath and held it, praying that his hands would cease their trembling before he was betrayed by nervousness. Another step, one more, and he had fixed his eyes upon a rough spot in the floor, a sort of pothole where a man might stumble, lose his balance.

Now!

The lurching sidestep carried Enzio away from Claudia, jerked his arm out of her grasp. He wobbled, nearly falling, closing off his mind to angry protests from his groin, recovering before he lost it all and lunging toward her with his hands outstretched to grasp the pistol. He could take her now...

But she was there ahead of him, reacting smoothly to his gambit, rapidly retreating as he made his awkward lunge. His fingers closed on empty air as Perrini brought the pistol slicing down, across his face. The impact opened up Petrucchi's cheek and knocked him sprawling, blood already splattering his jacket as he fell.

The woman stood above him, legs spread wide as if in mocking invitation, both hands wrapped around the Astra, with its muzzle aimed directly at his face. The gunner saw his death in Claudia's eyes, and knew she would have killed him on the spot, without remorse if it would not have raised a hue and cry along the gallery.

"Get up," she gritted, "and walk ahead of me. Six paces."

Enzio was scrambling to his feet, already searching for another way to save himself. "If someone sees us—"

"Then you die," she told him simply, in a tone he recognized as deadly serious.

He had no voice with which to answer her, and so he led the way once more, acutely conscious of the weapon aimed between his shoulder blades. The woman would not be a marksman, but she did not need to be at such a range. If he should break and run, or turn upon her, rush the gun, it would be difficult to miss a man-sized target, even in the semidarkness of the catacombs.

His opportunity had come and gone; Petrucchi knew that he had blown it. He would have to wait until they reached the kitchen now, and pray that her surprise, her horror at the spectacle, would help him find an opening, another chance to seize the gun and punch a bullet through the woman's smirking face. No matter that his shame would be revealed to Carlo and the rest; at least he could redeem himself to some degree by stopping the woman at the kitchen threshold, well before she could effect Belasko's rescue.

Clearly, it was what she had in mind. Petrucchi could not fathom female logic; Claudia had betrayed the bastard in the first place, when he tried to set her free, and then she quarreled with Carlo over the American, as if his life had some significance. Incredibly, she was prepared to risk herself, when she could easily have reached the exit ladders on her own, to help a man whom she, herself, had doomed to a painful death.

Petrucchi scowled at womankind in general, his eyes fixed firmly on the tunnel ahead. If any other troops appeared, he was a dead man, and it had been—what, how long?—since they had passed another living soul. Too long, and there were still more cubicles to pass before they reached the kitchen.

Enzio began to weep, and cursed the woman for revealing his intrinsic weakness. He was not a hero after all. He was an idiot, and everyone would know it when he stepped into the kitchen with Claudia Perrini at his heels, the pistol leveled at his spine. If he survived, they would humiliate him, scorn him as a fool who did his thinking with his gonads while his brain accumulated dust. Don Carlo might expel him—worse, might have him executed as an example to the rest.

But he could show them all, once he disarmed the woman, blew her brains into the stainless-steel cookware. While he was about it, Enzio could spare a round for Frenzi, for the other witnesses. It would be his word then, with no prospect of contradiction from the dead, and he could hear the story now. Claudia had escaped from custody—the careless sentry would be blamed, of course—acquired a weapon, tried to free Belasko in the midst of his interrogation. She had opened fire on Frenzi and the others, killing them before Petrucchi put a bullet through her brain. Enraged, grief-stricken by the death of valiant comrades, he had finished off Belasko as an afterthought.

And it would work. With no survivors to contest his claim, Petrucchi would remain the hero of the hour, Frenzi's obvious successor as commander of the RJC. He would be duty-bound to carry out the final wishes of his friend and comrade, seeing to collection of the ransom payment...and, with cash in hand, he would be free to seek the good life elsewhere, free of memories, reminders that his own incompetence had brought the near-disaster down upon him in the first place.

He could save it all: his life, his reputation, dreams of future glory. But he must disarm the woman first, eliminate the threat of sudden death that walked behind him, clinging like a dark, malignant shadow. Enzio could be a hero once again, if he did not become a corpse beforehand. Either way, his fate was waiting for him in the kitchen, with Belasko. With the butchers. With Don Carlo.

CLAUDIA HAD EXPECTED Enzio to make a break, had mentally prepared herself to kill if need be, but she had not known that it would be so easy to outwit the man a second time. He might have been shaky from his injuries or merely awkward, but his vain attempt to seize the pistol had been laughable. When she had clubbed him, opening his cheek, Claudia had experienced a sense of power vastly different from the self-importance she had grown accustomed to in recent months. Fawning was one thing; life-and-death control over another human being was something else entirely. When she struck at Enzio, prepared to kill him, she was also striking out at Frenzi, at the other men who had taken advantage of her even as she told herself that she had been using them.

She felt a little safer with Petrucchi several strides in front, but at the same time, Claudia knew the danger of discovery was greater still. She meant to kill Petrucchi if they met another gunman on the gallery, defend herself from that point on as best she could. She cherished no illusions of surviving in an all-out battle with the terrorists. She had a working knowledge of the pistol in her hand from an adventure film that she had made the year before, but she had never fired a loaded gun, had never tried to harm another human being before this night, and when the magazine was empty, she was finished.

If she lived that long.

They might be creeping up behind her even now. She darted a quick glance over one shoulder, scanning the shadows of the catacombs. An army might be lurking there, for all she knew, but Claudia had no choice. She had to help Mike Belasko if she could. And if the two of them survived her rescue effort, they would find an exit from the tunnels. The American had memorized them, she remembered. He had told her so, before she had given him up to Carlo and Petrucchi.

He must hate her, but if she could rescue him he might forget about his anger long enough to take her with him, lead her to the streets and daylight once again. He could not be so cruel, so heartless, as to punish her by leaving her behind. Claudia concentrated on her memories of Rome—the sights, the street sounds—pushing every other thought away and out of mind as she proceeded through the semidarkness, trailing Enzio, the captured pistol leveled at his back.

If it came down it it, would she have nerve enough to kill him? Killing someone in a film would be vastly different than the reality. There were no makeup men to fake the wounds, the blood. No coffee break between the cuts, when all the dead got up to share a sandwich or a cigarette with their assassins. This was real, and if she squeezed the trigger of her pistol now, Petrucchi would not rise again at the director's order. The enormity of her predicament was staggering, but she could not retreat. She could proceed, or stop and wait to die. If death was waiting for her up ahead, among the shadows, then she really had no choice at all. She preferred to meet it with defiance, instead of sniveling and begging for her life. She would not go without a fight.

At sixty yards, she recognized their destination. Enzio had not forewarned her, but she knew, somehow, that Mike Belasko would be taken to the kitchen. There was light, sufficient room for several men to move around—and all the tools required for an interrogation. She did not want to think about the pain he might have suffered thanks to her. No screams were audible as yet, but did that mean she had arrived in time . . . or that she was too late? Had they begun work on the American? Or were they finished with him, wrapping up his corpse for quick disposal down an air shaft?

Claudia did not care to think about the consequences of arriving on the scene too late. Belasko's death would be her fault, of course, and she would certainly have doomed herself, as well. By wasting time in her attempt to save a dead man, she would miss her only chance to find an exit, stumbling into Carlo's clutches, helpless in the face of his assembled troops.

But, no. She was not helpless. She was armed, and in possession of a hostage. Claudia knew that Carlo would not lift a finger on behalf of Enzio, but she could use him as a shield, let him absorb the first few rounds while she attempted to revenge herself on Frenzi. If she could be granted one clear shot at Carlo, certain of a killing hit, she would be satisfied. She had betrayed her father and the city of her birth; her life was finished, ruined. She did not deserve to live, and if her death could serve a purpose by wiping out the blot of Carlo Frenzi . . .

But Claudia had no wish to die. Not here, not now. So much of life still lay before her. So much that she must tell her father, begging his forgiveness. If she died before she could explain, he would despise her memory. She would be branded as a traitor in the darkest hour of modern Roman history.

No matter. If she had an opportunity to mitigate the damage she had done, eradicate the menace to her city, then it made no difference what the people thought of her in retrospect. It mattered only that they were alive to think of her at all, that Frenzi's plan was blocked before the city was transformed into a charnel house.

And she could kill. The lady had no doubts about it now. Petrucchi might be the first to die, unless she had a clear shot at Carlo going in. Above all else, she wanted Carlo in her sights, the smirking face lined up before her like a bull's-eye, waiting to be drilled between the eyes by lethal rounds.

Petrucchi halted at the kitchen doors, as she had known he would. He turned to face her, nodding toward the open doorway. It was one of three that served the kitchen, and from where she stood, Claudia couldn't see a thing except for folding tables stacked against the opposite wall. She gestured with the automatic, silently commanding him to lead the way inside. He shrugged, was shuffling toward the doorway, when he suddenly reversed his track and rushed her, snarling like an animal.

Claudia shot him in the face at point-blank range. The force of impact knocked Petrucchi off his stride, no longer growling as a portion of his jaw was sheared away. Somehow, incredibly, he kept his balance, glaring at her balefully, advancing in a stagger. The second bullet took him in the chest and knocked him backward off his feet, but there was no time left to check the dying man for vital signs.

Her slim advantage of surprise was gone, and she would have to go with guts alone from this point on. Prepared to kill, almost prepared to die, Claudia Perrini stepped across the threshold into hell.

FROM HIS POSITION on the table, Bolan heard the stovetop burners heating slowly, clicking as the temperature increased. He had already watched the butcher laying out his tools, arranging them around the largest burner so that blades and tines and skewers would be heated equally. Before the chef was finished, he would doubtless use them all, and preparation was the most important part of any recipe.

The Executioner had tried to mentally prepare himself for what was coming. He had been interrogated in the past, confronted with the possibility of a slow and savage death, but no man ever really knew his limits until they were tested in the fire. He would not break immediately, but with time and patience anything could be achieved. The warrior knew enough of pain, of torture, to believe that he would cheerfully confess the Kennedy assassination somewhere down the road, if only it would ease the pain for just a moment.

But it did not have to go that far. The butcher was a simple man, unschooled, without the training of a master at his craft. If he could be provoked, he might get careless, let his turkey slip away in the release of death before the session went too far, before Bolan felt his will begin to crumble. It was worth a shot, in any case. And at the moment barring intervention of the gods, it was the soldier's only play.

"I've got it," he announced to no one in particular, rewarded as the butcher turned to face him, frowning in his curiosity. "I knew that you reminded me of something."

"Eh?"

"Hell, yes. It's a pig." The soldier grinned good-naturedly.

The butcher scowled at Bolan, storing up the insult, turning back to watch his implements as they began to glow a fiery red.

"Okay, so maybe I was wrong," the warrior taunted. "Come to think of it, you don't look much like a pig. More like a tub of pig shit, really. Say, what *is* that smell?"

The big man lunged at Bolan, struck him with a solid backhand to the face that left motes dancing in his field of vision. Sausage fingers tangled in Bolan's hair, and his head was lifted from the stainless-steel table, twisted toward the butcher. Through bleary eyes, he saw the massive fist already poised to strike and wondered if the blow would be enough to kill him.

Suddenly, from somewhere to his left, came the crack of pistol shots. The butcher twisted, dropping Bolan's head, already circling toward the stove and his array of weapons. Frenzi's riflemen were scrambling for their guns, laid aside when they were detailed to clean up the second chef. They hadn't reached the AK-47s yet, when Bolan saw Claudia Perrini in the doorway, sighting down the barrel of an automatic pistol, squeezing off instinctively in rapid-fire.

The nearest gunner took a round between the shoulder blades, the impact adding to his own momentum and propelling him along in double time. He reached the weapons, lifeless fingers sliding over steel and polished walnut stocks before he folded, taking both guns with him, trapping them beneath him on the floor. His partner tried to roll the body over, groping for his rifle, but he never really had a chance.

The lady was a natural. Round two impacted squarely in the gunner's chest and lifted him completely off his feet. His shoulders struck the other serving table, bringing down an avalanche of pots and pans on top of him like some peculiar funeral monument.

The butcher with a skillet imprint on his face was out of it, but his companion had already reached the stove, scooped up a carving knife. His arm was cocked to make the pitch when Bolan shouted out a warning, and the lady pivoted to bring him under fire.

Three rounds at twenty feet, and it was over for the chef before he hit the floor. Mack Bolan watched as the life ran out of him through holes in stomach, chest and throat, the greasy shirt and apron staining red by stages. Finally, as if the pull of gravity had grown too powerful to be ignored, he toppled forward, landing on his face with an impressive crunch that he would never feel.

The manacles were held secure by means of simple latches, and the lady had them open in another moment. Bolan noticed that her hands were trembling, but he couldn't fault her there. Outside, he saw a huddled body in the corridor, and that meant four for four. The lady had a right to tremble, sure, and Bolan knew that she would never be the same again . . . assuming that she lived to see another day.

"I owe you one," he told her simply, scrambling for his clothes. Her automatic's slide had frozen open on an empty chamber, and he gently pried the weapon from her hand, discarding it, collecting a replacement from the body of a fallen rifleman.

She took the AK-47 that he offered to her, listened briefly as he showed her how to operate the weapon, nodding that she understood when he was finished. Bolan took the other rifle, tucked an automatic pistol in his belt and jammed his pockets full of extra magazines.

They were already out of time, and he could feel the numbers falling now. If Frenzi heard the gunfire, he might flash a signal to the other staging areas at once, commanding them to detonate their charges. If Bolan could not prevent the terrorist from sending off that message, bringing hellfire down around their heads . . .

Then he could die in the attempt.

20

Lupo's message had been less than startling. The fascists were prepared to pay, as Carlo had already known, and Chief Inspector Luciano was delivering the ransom personally. Frenzi made a point of thanking his informant, did not mention that the "news" had been delivered by another source some thirty minutes earlier. Let Lupo cherish his illusions, think that he was Frenzi's only pair of eyes in the security police.

In fact, three separate officers were on the payroll of Red Justice, and while Lupo was the highest-ranking of the three, he was not irreplaceable, by any means. If he should ever grow too greedy, too ambitious, it would be a relatively simple matter to eliminate him, wait for someone else to fill his post in turn. And if the new replacement could not be suborned with sex or cash or any of the other usual means, he could be bypassed, certainly.

In any case, Frenzi would have little need of paid informants once the ransom was safely in his hands. He would be leaving Rome, abandoning his native Italy, perhaps forever. Carlo Frenzi had a sudden urge to see the world, to let the world see him. A man of some sophistication, prison record notwithstanding, Frenzi knew that he could get along at any level of society. He needed only cash to join the ranks of the elite, and it was coming to him soon. Mere hours, now, and he would be among the richest men in Italy, perhaps in all Western Europe. It mattered not that he would be compelled to change his name, perhaps his face; it was the color of his money that would count among the friends he planned to make in Paris, Monte Carlo, St. Moritz.

As for the people's revolution, it could get along without him. He was tired of all the military trappings, anyway, and if he ever felt the urge to launch another war for profit, there were always would-be warriors waiting in the wings. His troops might be a problem, but with foresight, any obstacle could be avoided. Enzio Petrucchi would be picking up the ransom, taking all the risks in case the fascist Luciano had some kind of double cross in mind. When Enzio was clear and running free, with ample time to check for any tails or problems with the cash itself, they would regroup at Carlo's safehouse to divide the loot.

He had secured Petrucchi's loyalty, his silence, by appearing to engage him in a master plan to dupe the others, leave them empty-handed while the two of them divided the hundred million down the middle. Enzio, in fact, would never live to spend a penny of the ransom, but his life would be expended in a worthy cause: the personal advancement of Don Carlo Frenzi.

At a single stroke, the terrorist commander would outstrip his friends and enemies in the Italian underworld, achieving in a moment what the rest of them could only contemplate in drunken fantasies. The Mafia would envy him, and if he stayed in Rome, they would undoubtedly come calling, sniffing after Frenzi's cash with bogus wishes "for his own protection." If he had been more courageous, more foolhardy, Carlo might have stayed to face them down, but he had nothing left to prove where manhood was concerned. He had already earned a place in history, and he would not allow the greedy jackals to deprive him of his just reward.

He was halfway to the kitchen, the communications shack behind him and his thoughts already focused on a pleasant interlude with Mike Belasko, when he heard the gunshots.

Two, at first, immediately followed by another burst. He knew where the shots had come from, knew that something had gone unexpectedly and desperately wrong with the interrogation of the mercenary.

Carlo's first reaction was to reach the kitchen swiftly, find out what the hell was going on, but caution intervened. If the American had somehow armed himself, it would be suicidal to confront him empty-handed. Frenzi seldom carried weapons in the tunnels, trusting in his sentries, but there were certain special items in his makeshift office, just in case. He doubled back and reached the cubicle, plunged inside.

A stout footlocker rested against one wall, its lid secured with a hasp and padlock. Frenzi fumbled with the key, his fingers trembling with excitement—it could not be fear; he would not entertain the thought—and finally got it open. Scooping out an M-16, complete with a 40 mm grenade launcher mounted underneath the barrel, Carlo fed a magazine into the receiver of the assault rifle, pocketing two more against emergencies. He primed the launcher with a can of high explosives, locked the breech and slung the heavy combo weapon from his shoulder on a strap of military webbing.

Reaching the gallery he saw that his troops were scrambling from their quarters like a swarm of rats evacuating flooded holes. The sound of pistol fire had been replaced by automatic weapons now, and Frenzi wondered idly if the catacombs could stand a running firefight. He would soon find out, and if Belasko had a chance to summon the authorities, then it would matter little whether Frenzi stopped a bullet or the roof caved in on him. Either way he would be dead, his dreams of wealth and glory shattered on the horns of circumstance. By one accursed man.

He would not let Belasko ruin everything that he had worked for through the years, the dream that he had cherished during endless prison nights and wasted days. If the

American unraveled Frenzi's dream, he must be made to pay in blood. If he could not be made to suffer slowly, he must be eradicated, root and branch, so that no trace of him remained.

A high-explosive charge and three magazines of 5.56 mm rounds should be ample for the task. If not, then Carlo was prepared to do the job bare-handed, with his teeth, if necessary. Let the mercenary-turned-informant tamper with his dream. And let him feel the full, unbridled wrath of Carlo Frenzi as a consequence.

The gunners milling around him were confused, disoriented, and he called a dozen of them into rough formation, organized a flying wedge of sorts and sent them off ahead of him, in the direction of the kitchen and the ringing gunfire. It would do no harm to let Mike Belasko expend a little energy before Frenzi made the kill, and his commandos were expendable, in any case. The more of them who were eliminated now, the fewer there would be to worry Carlo later, after he absconded with the cash.

He double-checked the safety on his M-16 and switched the weapon's fire-selection lever into automatic mode. There would be no opportunity for sniping with precision in the murky tunnels. Carlo would rely instead on saturation fire, and if a few of his subordinates should accidentally be taken down along with the American... well, soldiers in a combat situation must expect to suffer casualties.

Prepared for anything except defeat, the terrorist commander trailed his men along the gallery to face his nemesis and save the remnants of his dream while time remained.

BOLAN STITCHED two startled gunners with a fiery figure eight and blew them both away, not bothering to check the pair for vital signs. Alive or dead, they were no danger to him now, and Bolan had no time to spare. He ran with Claudia at his heels, deliberately turning east, away from the communications room and Frenzi's office, knowing that the counterpunch would come from that direction. Bolan had another route in mind, but the success or failure of his ploy depended now on speed, as well as chance encounters with the enemy.

Don Carlo's bivouac was on the lowest level of the catacombs, with two more galleries above, the levels linked by stairways etched from living rock. They reached the nearest staircase unopposed and Bolan led the way, ascending to the second-level gallery. Behind him, Claudia labored on the narrow steps, intent on keeping up, the automatic rifle held across her chest for balance as she climbed.

There were no lights upstairs, away from Frenzi's staging area, and Bolan hesitated on the edge of darkness, probing with his combat senses for a trace of hostile movement, coming up with nothing. There could be an ambush waiting anywhere along the gallery, he knew, and Bolan had no flash to guide them. He could not have used a light in any case, alerting any gunners who might be out along the upper gallery; they would be traveling in darkness all the way, until they reached his destination at the other end.

"On me," he told the lady, moving out. Claudia looped the fingers of her free hand through his belt in back and kept up that way, carrying her AK-47 underneath one arm. The darkness around them was alive with scuttling rodent sounds, and Bolan heard the lady gasp on one occasion, when they blundered through a dangling spiderweb. He had to give her credit, though; she kept her mouth shut through it all and matched his pace without complaint.

When they had covered about a hundred yards, Bolan paused. There was a light ahead, and for a moment he believed that it might be the other stairway, leading back to Frenzi's bivouac and the communications room. Another instant, though, and Bolan knew that he had been mistaken, for the light was growing closer, moving to the rhythm of a human stride.

A flashlight. And that meant gunners, running a precautionary sweep along the upper galleries. Frenzi would have soldiers posted on the exits now, while others ran the upper levels of the catacombs in search of Bolan and the woman. He had hoped to reach his destination without further contact, saving the advantage of surprise, but he was left no alternative. The gunners, closing in on him now, would have to die, and if the sounds of war were audible to Frenzi on the lower gallery, so be it. The advantage of surprise meant nothing if he never lived to use it, and he was prepared to buck the odds on this one, all the way.

He edged Claudia back against the wall and down into a crouch. No way of counting heads behind the lantern, and he would be forced to go on instinct, estimating targets from a knowledge of the tunnel's width and Frenzi's normal mode of operation. With the lady's staged abduction, with the Trevi Fountain bombing—even when removing Bolan to the kitchen for interrogation—Carlo had relied on three-man teams. It might be nothing, mere coincidence, but then again...

He sighted down the barrel of his captured AK-47, concentrating on the lantern, making little practice sweeps to either side while there was time, before the light was close enough to pick him out. It would require precision timing, and it might be all for nothing if the team was larger than he had anticipated. If there was a fourth man, say, and he was bringing up the rear, he would have time to sight on Bolan's muzzle-flash and fire before the Executioner was aware of him. Bolan could be dead before he recognized his last mistake. But he was playing the percentages, and if they failed him, he would play the rest of it by ear. Like always.

Another yard now, and his finger was already tightening around the rifle's trigger. Light swept over Bolan, passed him by before the hunter could make sense of what he saw, was doubling back when Bolan opened fire. He stitched a 3-round burst above the lantern, sweeping to his right, immediately ripping off another three and tracking left again, to punch three tumblers through the darkness there. He waited, half expecting lethal fire to find him, but a moment passed, then two, without response. He moved in swiftly, guided by the upturned lantern, retrieving it and using it to scan the tiny battlefield.

Three up, three down. The first two gunners had been laid out almost side by side, tight groupings in their chest already leaking crimson. On the left, his target had been moving, trying to escape, and Bolan's burst had ripped his flank, eviscerating him. All three were dead. He helped himself to bandoliers of ammunition for the AK-47, slinging two across his shoulder, and was moving on before Claudia had a chance to focus on the dead.

He used the fallen gunner's lantern now, and they were making better speed. No sign of any other gun crews, but if they were on their way, the light would make them hesitate a moment. Long enough, perhaps, for Bolan to eliminate another threat and clear their path to the communications room.

The light ahead of him now was certainly the staircase, and Bolan ditched the lantern, navigating by the sparse illumination from below. When they had reached the bottom of the staircase—*if* they reached it—they would be within a dozen yards of Frenzi's radio. With any luck, there might be time to call the other strike teams off, abort the demolition plan and flash a message in the clear to someone, anyone, above them on the street. If he was able to connect with a police dispatcher, even a patrol car, Bolan would be satisfied. If not...

Then he would do his best with what he had. And having pulled the plug on Frenzi's master plan, it wouldn't matter in the long run what became of Bolan. If he only had an opportunity to capture Carlo in his sights before they cut him down, it would be worth the price.

He hit the upper landing in a combat crouch, his captured rifle braced against one hip and ready to spit flame at any sign of opposition. Nothing. He heard running footsteps receding into the distance, off to his right, gravel voices shouting orders. He didn't wait for a group of terrorists to spot them, rapidly descending, instead, to the lower level with the lady on his heels.

He glanced around the corner, scanning both directions, and picked up soldiers huddled in a group about thirty yards beyond his destination. They were arguing among themselves, and Bolan wondered if the spat would hold their attention long enough for him to reach the radio. If not, if someone noticed him, he would be forced to take out as many of them as he could with the initial burst, delay their counterstroke until he had a chance to reach the other demolition squads.

"We're going now," he told Claudia. "Normal pace. You stay behind me, out of sight as much as possible. There are some gunners in the tunnel. If they spot us, use your weapon."

Bolan had to give the lady points for poise. She didn't flinch at mention of the soldiers, simply nodded when he told her she might have to kill them where they stood. She might be trembling inside, for all he knew, but she was hiding it well.

He moved, and she was in his shadow, clinging to the wall and hanging back a pace, allowing Bolan to remain between herself and the assembled gunmen. They had halved the distance to their destination when a khaki soldier glanced in their direction, froze and shouted the alarm to his companions.

"Hit it!" Bolan growled, already holding down the trigger of his captured weapon, tracking left to right and back again across the killing ground. Beside him, Claudia had already opened fire, her AK-47 stuttering in counterpoint to Bolan's, ripping bloody holes in Frenzi's finest. Half went down with the initial bursts of automatic fire, the others scrambling in search of cover as the Executioner and the woman ducked into the communications room.

The operator sat and stared at them with bulging eyes, his earphones down around his neck. He wore a sidearm but displayed no tendency toward martyrdom, and Bolan took the pistol from him, slipped in his belt before returning to command the doorway.

"Get on the air to Frenzi's other stations," he instructed the radioman. "Have the others abort, no matter what it takes. Make sure you touch bases with three command posts. You're dead if you try to warn them."

Claudia Perrini prodded at the operator's ample belly with her rifle, making sure he understood the price of failure to obey. The guy was desperate to please, already dialing up the necessary frequencies, and Bolan left him to it under Claudia's watchful eye. Outside, the hostile guns were taking potshots at him, angling from awkward stations farther up the gallery, and Bolan let them have a ragged burst to make it clear that he was still in business. If they had nerve enough to rush him and absorb the casualties, they could take him out at any time, but he was counting on a certain reticence among his adversaries. They were soldiers of the dollar sign, this crew, and therefore lacked the kamikaze-style commitment of a die-hard terrorist fanatic. Few, if any, would be volunteering for a suicide attack, and Bolan saw a gleam of hope in their decision to survive.

It gave him time, and time was all he needed now to call off Frenzi's other strike teams, flash a warning message to police—or someone—on the surface. That accomplished, Bolan would be ready to evacuate...and therein lay the rub.

He would be ready, sure. But he would have no place to go.

CLAUDIA LISTENED CLOSELY as their captive finished speaking, ordering his contacts on the other end to lay their weapons down, evacuate the tunnels. No, they must not detonate the hidden charges under any circumstances; it was Frenzi's order that the city should be spared. The price of disobedience was death.

She had already listened to the message twice, with variations, braced to kill the man at any inkling of a hidden meaning, a suggestive nuance in his words. But he was terrified, and he had followed orders to the letter. It was finished.

"Done," she told Bolan, covering her hostage even now that he was finished with his task. The "mercenary" fired a short burst through the doorway, ducked a lone incoming round and wriggled back to crouch against the wall.

"One more to go," he said. "Our boy should have a frequency for the police. I want him on it with a warning, listing the potential targets." He was ready to repeat them for her, but Claudia shook her head.

"I know them, from your note."

"Okay. Let's have him run it twice, for safety's sake. If no one's reading that, we're wasting time. Get on it, and we'll shake this dive."

"Where can we go?"

He pointed toward the ceiling. "Topside."

Claudia nodded toward the doorway and the gallery beyond. "I think they may not let us pass," she said.

"Let's worry that one when the time comes. First things first."

There was another burst from Bolan's rifle as he kept the enemy at bay. Claudia gave the terrorist his orders, ground the muzzle of her weapon in his ribs when he appeared to hesitate. She watched him change the frequency on his transmitter, listened as he rattled off the message twice, without a hitch. She had no way of telling whether anyone had heard the warning, but that part of it was clearly outside her control.

"All done," she told Belasko, and the big American surprised her with a smile.

"Okay, then, time to go. It wouldn't hurt if we could come up with a smoke screen."

Claudia scanned the cubicle, its stone walls lined with maps and radio equipment, crates and boxes. From the corner of her eye, she saw their captive flicking anxious looks toward one crate in particular. He had begun to fidget, pudgy fingers trembling on his knees like fat, expectant spiders.

Even so, his final gambit almost took Claudia by surprise. Almost. The gunner's movement was so swift, so unexpected from a man his size, a man so frightened, that she nearly let him get away with it. But she had killed at least half a dozen men within the space of twenty minutes, and her tension shaved the customary lag time by a crucial fraction. She was firing even as her pigeon left his chair, her first rounds slamming through the radio transmitter, raining sparks, before the second burst went in on target. Claudia saw the gunner stumble, sprawl, his outstretched hands connecting with the crate that he had died to reach, dragging it down with him to the floor. The lid sprang open, spilling hand grenades around her feet.

Before she could react, Bolan was beside her, scooping up the lethal eggs, attaching several to the bandoliers he wore across his shoulders, clipping others to his belt. Shouldering his rifle, he had a grenade in either hand, already working on the pins as he retreated toward the open doorway.

"Ready when I move," he cautioned. "We won't have any time to spare."

He threw the first grenade without attempting to select a target, lobbing it around the corner, blind. The blast was deafening, despite the walls of stone that partly shielded the woman from its impact, and she felt the shock wave in her feet, the very air around her. She was terribly afraid that he would bring the tunnel down around them, but the big

American seemed unconcerned. Or was he merely desperate? As Claudia watched, he stepped across the threshold, hurled another grenade after the first and stitched a burst of automatic fire across the tunnel's width.

"Come on!" he shouted, moving before she had an opportunity to answer. She was after him and gaining when the second charge exploded in the tunnel at her back, its head, the force of its concussion, lending speed and urgency to Claudia's pace.

Ahead of her, the big mercenary was firing, but she dared not use her weapon now for fear of hitting him. Behind her, there were cries of anguish in the swirling dust and smoke, sufficient evidence that the pursuit had been derailed. Stray shots rang out as blind, disoriented gunners fought a running war with shadows in the gallery.

Claudia risked a glance over her shoulder, froze as she beheld a solitary figure stalking through the smoke and dust. She knew instinctively that it was Carlo Frenzi seeking his revenge on Mike Belasko. On her. She could see the bulky weapon in his hands and knew that he would kill them both on sight for ruining his master plan.

If she permitted it.

The lady raised her weapon, sighting roughly down the barrel, trusting in the rifle's automatic fire to make up for deficiencies in marksmanship. She squeezed the trigger, held it down, prepared to fight the recoil—and was stunned by the metallic snapping of the hammer as it fell upon an empty chamber.

He had seen them now, the bastard, and Claudia just had time to scream, to warn Belasko, as the chunky weapon bucked in Frenzi's grasp. For just the fraction of a heartbeat, she wondered what it was, and then the world fell in around her with a roar, and she was falling, falling, into darkness.

THE RUBBLE COVERED Bolan like a leaden blanket, pinning arms and legs immobile. For a moment, he believed he might be paralyzed, but then his probing fingers recognized the silky touch of marble, and he knew that something—an explosion—had collapsed a portion of the tunnel wall. The marble tombstones, artifacts and all, had been disgorged on impact, littering the gallery and bringing Bolan down beneath their weight.

By slow degrees, he tensed each arm and leg to check for fractures, finding only sprains and bruises. As he caught his breath, the soldier found that he was not, in fact, immobilized. One arm—his right—was absolutely free, and the debris that pinned his aching legs was not as heavy as he had at first supposed. With effort, he could wriggle free, but Bolan wondered if he had the time.

The blast had not resulted from a booby trap, he knew that much. Claudia's warning cry, the dull report of a grenade launcher microseconds prior to detonation, told the warrior all he had to know. Someone had brought them down with an explosive charge, and Bolan estimated that the hunter would be closing swiftly, anxious to confirm the kill. That left him moments, seconds, to prepare himself for combat or for death.

No sound from Claudia, and he put the lady out of mind. If she was still alive, if she was in a position to assist him, he would have to let her call the play. For now, the best defense was silence, immobility, to lull the gunner's senses, bring him into striking distance.

The soldier cracked his eyelids, blinking back a veil of dust, and started as he found a human skull regarding him with bland disinterest from a foot away. The desiccated face was eyeless, grinning at the Executioner through shriveled lips, a wisp of brittle hair above one staring socket. Bolan let his fingers do the walking, searching for the AK-47, coming up with only rubble, jagged rocks and shards of ancient bone. He could not find the rifle, and he dared not thrash around in search of it. His ears were ringing from the blast, but he could make out footsteps now, the sound of boot heels crunching over shattered stone.

His fingers closed around a broken femur, gripped it like a dagger with the jagged tip extending six or seven inches from his fist. It was a meager weapon, in the face of military hardware, but it was the best available to Bolan at the moment. Petrified by centuries of burial, the relic was as tough and rigid as obsidian, its broken edges razor-sharp. And it would have to do.

The soldier waited, knowing he might never have an opportunity to use his weapon, working gingerly to free his left arm from beneath a pile of dirt and rubble. It was coming, gingerly, when Bolan heard the hunter pause, no more than twenty feet away. He felt the hostile eyes upon him, braced himself for the destructive impact of a round that never came.

Instead, the gunman sidled closer, finally standing over Bolan, nudging at the prostrate soldier with a boot. When there was no reaction, he stepped back a pace and dealt a kick to Bolan's rib cage, sending ragged jolts of pain through every part of Bolan's body. Grimacing, his face averted from the gunner, Bolan held his breath, refused to move or make the slightest sound, no matter what might happen next.

Another jolting kick, and then he heard the gunner cursing softly to himself. The guy was clearly disappointed with an easy kill, expecting something better for his efforts. Bolan's lungs were burning now, the colored flecks produced by oxygen starvation dancing across the inside of his eyelids. Soon his vision would begin to swim, his consciousness to fade, and survival instinct would short-circuit self-control. It was impossible to suffocate yourself by sheer willpower, but...

The gunner seized him by the shoulder, tried to roll him over, cursing when the rubble held him down. Bolan felt the marble slab dragged clear, an angry boot heel kicking dirt and stone away from his left arm. The hunter knelt beside him, laying down his weapon in a momentary lapse, intent on seeing Bolan's face to verify the kill.

He let the gunner turn him over, going with it, aching lungs on fire, and at the final moment he exploded, gasping, bringing one arm up around the hunter's neck to lock him in a last embrace. His face was inches from the bulging eyes of Carlo Frenzi when he rammed the jagged femur in beneath his adversary's sternum, twisting, reaming, putting all his weight behind the thrust. Hot blood erupted onto Bolan's wrist, his chest, and in a moment he could smell the reek as Frenzi's bowels let go. The terrorist was struggling, like a game fish on the hook, but there was nowhere he could go, no possibility of extrication. Brief resistance, as the jagged bone ripped through the pericardium, a lung, and then the soldier was awash in Frenzi's final fluids, steaming in it as the enemy went limp and lifeless in his grasp.

He let the flaccid body slip away and scrambled to his feet. Behind him in the darkness, something stirred, emitting sluggish sounds of pain. The soldier spun to face another adversary, empty fingers prepared to lock around a throat before the bastards cut him down.

Claudia Perrini sat up, groggy in the wreckage of the gallery, one hand pressed tight against her bloody forehead. Bolan helped the lady to her feet and wasted precious seconds checking out the superficial wound.

"We're out of time," he told her, and a rising chorus from the lower tunnel emphasized his point. "Let's move."

They moved, with Claudia leaning on him for support and Bolan homing on the nearest of the exit ladders that would take them to the street.

To daylight.

Home.

EPILOGUE

"I still do not profess to understand your role in this affair," the chief inspector said.

"It doesn't matter," Bolan answered.

"I have spoken at some length with a Signor Brognola, of the Justice Department."

"Ah."

"He has assured me that your part in all of this was strictly unofficial."

"That's the rumor."

"As an unofficial operative on Italian soil, you are immediately subject to arrest."

The soldier didn't bother looking startled. It would be a waste of energy, and he would need whatever little still remained if Luciano should produce a pair of handcuffs.

They were standing on the Spanish Steps, alone. The Fiat parked below contained a solitary occupant, but Bolan couldn't make out the lady's features from where he stood.

He didn't have to. They were emblazoned on his memory forever.

Luciano cleared his throat and looked away, across the twinkling lights of the Eternal City. "As an unofficial operative, you are subject to arrest," he said again. "But as the unofficial savior of my only child, I pronounce you free to go."

The soldier let himself relax. "She did her share. The lady's not half bad."

"So I suspect. Unfortunately, the publicity..."

"Can only help her in the business," Bolan finished for him. "Film star proves herself a heroine, stops terrorists from dynamiting Roman landmarks."

"But Claudia..."

"Saved my bacon when the chips were down. Nobody living is prepared to tell you any different."

"I understand."

"I hope so."

He shook the chief inspector's hand, had turned to leave when Luciano called him back. "Signor... it cannot be Belasko, can it?"

"No."

"I see. In any case, you have my thanks, the thanks of Rome."

"You're welcome, both of you."

He left the lawman standing in the shadows, put that place behind him. Other battlefields were waiting, calling Bolan, and he could not keep them waiting any longer. It was over, for the moment, here in Rome. With luck, the ancient city would survive another thousand years and never need an Executioner. But just in case...

He thought of Trevi Fountain, silent now, and dropped a coin into the placid waters of his memory. If Rome should ever need him, Bolan would return and give the savages another taste of cleansing fire.

For now, the lesson was complete, his pupils either dead or occupying cages at the Palace of Justice. Bolan wished them all the luck that they deserved, and mentally consigned their souls to hell.

If they got out somehow, someday, and turned their hands to terrorism again, the warrior would be waiting for them.

And in the meantime, there were other new accounts requiring his attention.

The Reaper passed from dappled shadows into outer darkness and was gone. His work was elsewhere. He was carrying the fire.

BULLETS OF PALESTINE

Howard Kaplan

A Kaplan novel is ''an edge-of-the-chair,
throat-grabbing page-turner! Accurate and terrifying.''
—Gerald Green, writer, NBC's *Holocaust*

His name is Abu Nidal. A breakaway Palestinian known as the
''terrorists' terrorist.'' An Israeli and a Palestinian join forces,
despite the hatreds of their heritage, to eliminate this man. Will
they ensnare Abu Nidal—or trap each other in a bloodbath of
betrayal?

4 FREE BOOKS
1 FREE GIFT
NO RISK
NO OBLIGATION
NO KIDDING